THE
BUTTERFLY
CLUB

THE
SHIP
OF
DOOM

Also by M.A. Bennett
Series for older readers:

S.T.A.G.S.

THE SHIP OF DOOM

R.M.S. TITANIC

M.A. BENNETT

WELBECK
FLAME

First published in 2022 by Welbeck Flame
An imprint of Welbeck Children's Limited,
part of Welbeck Publishing Group.
Based in London and Sydney.
www.welbeckpublishing.com

ISBN: 978 1 80130 004 9

Printed and bound by CPI Group (UK)

10 9 8 7 6 5 4 3 2 1

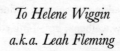

To Helene Wiggin
a.k.a. Leah Fleming

who launched me on this voyage

Dear Reader,

Thank you very much for taking the Time to read this book about Time. And because you are smart enough to read books, you will be smart enough to know that Time works backwards as well as forwards…

2021, England, London
Bennett .A.M

?Time change *you* will How .journey special very a for Aidan and Konstantin, Luna join to ready get – Thursday every meets Club Butterfly The … Effect Butterfly the called phenomenon a in ,to travelled they place the altered did they everything that found children the imagined I Then .future the from artefacts steal to Time through journey a on children the sent Club Butterfly the that imagined I. Observatory Royal the at week a once secret in met and ,Club Butterfly the called society a formed had adults clever very some that discovered who, Aidan and Konstantin, Luna called, children Victorian three imagined I .it along forwards and backwards travel could you timeline the of side either feet your placing of instead ,if happen would what wondered I Then .another

in was foot one and, timezone one in was foot one that so,
line the of side either foot one with, does everyone as just,
stood I .measured is world the in Time the all that line
this from is it and Observatory Royal the of courtyard the
through runs Meridian the called line brass big A .line
a but, concept a nor ,thing a not is Time out turns it
As .lived Time where was, told was I ,This .Observatory
Royal the called place a was hill green biggest the of top
the At .green … well ,Very .from come I'd countryside
the like more was Greenwich and ,hills green to used was
and ,England of north the in up grew I .meant that what
understood I that itself Greenwich to went I until wasn't
it but ,before Meantime Greenwich words the heard I'd
?world the of rest the for clocks the set and ,Time of
home the be city one could How .too lived Time where
was lived now I where city the that heard I London to
moved first I When

LONDON

15 JANUARY 1894

15 JANUARY 1894
10 a.m.

Luna thought that an afternoon at her aunt's butterfly club would be the most deathly boring thing in the world.

She had only been living with her aunt for a month and was already sick of butterflies. Aunt Grace collected them, and they were all over the house, skewered with little pins to little cards, their bright wings spread, never to fly again. Colourful, pathetic and very, very dead.

Sometimes she would look at their names, written underneath in neat calligraphy – Rajah Brooke's Birdwing, the Duke of Burgundy, the Great Purple Emperor. They seemed such romantic titles to end in such a sad fate. They should be fluttering around in a meadow somewhere, not imprisoned in this tall, dark house.

2

Luna sometimes thought of herself as one of them. She had everything she wanted: enough to eat and drink, a nice room of her own and all the pretty gowns she wanted, in bright colours just like the butterflies. But she was pinned up in the tall, dark house too. The house, in a very smart part of Kensington (which was a very smart part of London), somehow seemed taller and skinnier than any in the row. In fact, it looked as stretched as she did.

The smart and skinny house did have a good-sized garden, but Luna was discouraged from playing in it, in case she was 'seen'. It was never explained to her whose gaze she was supposed to be avoiding. She was encouraged to stay indoors and read, but Aunt Grace's books weren't the sort of books with pictures or conversations. They were all books with titles like: *On the Applications of Non-Euclidean Geometry to the Theory of Quadratic Forms.* And who wants to read a book called *that*?

The truth was that Luna Goodhart would have read all the books in the library, however boring they were, if one of them could have told her what had happened to Papa. He'd disappeared very suddenly, with no explanation. Aunt Grace, looking enough like Papa for Luna to trust her at once, had not exactly explained when she'd turned up that Thursday at Luna's house to take her niece home to live with her. 'Your father's on another plane,' she'd said briskly, holding out her gloved hand, and would not say more, no matter how many times Luna asked. Soon, Luna stopped asking, in case she was told what she feared to be the truth.

That 'on another plane' was what grown-ups said when somebody was dead.

It had always been just Luna and Papa, in the little house in Greenwich Park, in the shadow of the Royal Observatory. Papa had given Luna everything, including her strange name, and now he was gone. Luna would spend many moments each day trying to remember the details of his face, the trick of his speech, so terrified was she of forgetting him even a little bit. Sometimes, Luna would sing her father's favourite song in an attempt to feel closer to him. It was called *Yesterday* and he used to sing it all the time. Sang it, hummed it, whistled it. Luna didn't know where her father had heard the song – probably at the music hall – but she had never heard anyone else sing it, so it seemed peculiarly his. Now Papa had disappeared, she certainly longed for yesterday. He'd gone without notice, gone without even a note. In the past, even when he'd had to go to his tailor or his attorney, he'd left little notes for her, always signed in the same way.

Yours until the end of time, Papa x

So Luna didn't want to be rude to Aunt Grace when she called that it was time to leave for an afternoon at the Butterfly Club, because Papa's sister was all the family Luna had left. But she *definitely* didn't want to go. Luna's one day of freedom was every Thursday, regular as clockwork, when her aunt was out all afternoon and evening at her butterfly club.

Luna went into the hallway. Aunt Grace was putting on her gloves, and, in doing so, covering up one of the most interesting things about her.

For Aunt Grace had a tattoo on her left wrist. The mark was so small and discreet that at first Luna had thought it a birthmark or a bruise. But it was neither. Luna had had the opportunity to see the thing properly at dinner, when Aunt Grace had passed the salt. It was a beautifully inked tattoo of a butterfly, but not a butterfly like the ones that hung on the walls of the house. It was a clockwork butterfly made up of little cogs and spindles and wheels, like the things that you'd find in the belly of a timepiece.

Aunt Grace turned to adjust her hat in the looking-glass, tucking in a stray lock of auburn hair. Auburn was that kind of red that you couldn't really call ginger but was much darker, the colour of port wine. Aunt Grace was beautiful, what with the auburn hair and everything, but she had jade-green eyes of the same shade as one of the butterflies on the wall, the one called the Green Hairstreak, and they made her look slightly scary. Because of the eyes it was much easier to talk to her when she wasn't looking directly at you. So while her aunt was looking in the looking-glass Luna took her chance and said, '*Must* I come to the Butterfly Club, Aunt? I'm sure I will be fine with Cook and Mabel.'

Aunt Grace turned and fixed the Green-Hairstreak eyes on Luna. 'Luna Goodhart, I promised your father I would help you pass the time, and that is a promise I intend to keep. Now, come along.'

And she held out a gloved hand. The hand reminded Luna of the day she'd collected Luna from the Greenwich Park house, the day that Father hadn't come home. Then, as now, the leather of her aunt's glove was cold, and the bones inside hard as pistons, almost as if Aunt Grace was part-machine. For the first time, Luna had a dark fantasy that the marking on her aunt's left wrist, which she could see at that moment peeping from the glove, was not a tattoo at all but a butterfly-shaped tear in the skin to reveal the machinery beneath.

The thought was nonsensical, but at the same time so frightening that Luna bit her tongue, and came along at once.

15 JANUARY 1894
11.50 a.m.

When Luna saw the Greenwich Observatory high on its green hill, she felt like she was seeing an old friend. The house she'd shared with Papa had not been far from here, and as Aunt Grace briskly helped her out of the hansom cab right by the entrance, she suddenly missed her father very badly.

Of course, Luna had never been inside the observatory, because such an honour was reserved for the most eminent scientists of the age. Aunt Grace, however, crossed the threshold as if it was her own, leading Luna by the hand through the iron gates and across the paved courtyard. A great brass line, like a single railway track, divided the pavings. She was so curious that she forgot to be frightened of her aunt.

'What's that?'

Aunt Grace actually stopped. 'That,' she said, 'is the Prime Meridian. A geographical reference line that passes through this very spot, which gives us Greenwich Mean Time. This is the place from which all of our clocks are set. You are at the very home of time.'

A doorman let them through the entrance with no more than a touch of his hat. Clearly Aunt Grace was known here. She led Luna along passageways and down stairs and through doorways to the secret heart of the observatory, all the time following the brass line of the Meridian. Eventually the line stopped dead at a blank wall, at the foot of a grandfather clock, tall as Aunt Grace with a pendulum swinging in its belly. Luna looked up at Aunt Grace – it was, quite literally, the end of the line. But Aunt Grace reached up to open the casement, and she altered the gilded hands of the clock until they read 4.45 exactly.

As soon as she did so, the whole body of the clock swung outwards.

It was a door.

Aunt Grace stepped through the clock door into the dark, and Luna found herself in a room that was so dimly lit that at first it was hard to make out what was in it. But as the clock, which had closed behind them, chimed noon with a silvery song, Aunt Grace said, 'Welcome to the Butterfly Room.'

Gradually Luna's eyes adjusted and she could see that the room was twelve-sided in shape, and each wall had a floor-to-ceiling shutter that was tightly closed. And around the walls, just like at the house in Kensington, there were hundreds and thousands of butterflies in a myriad of colours and shapes and sizes, all pinned to cards and carefully captioned. Luna looked at the nearest ones to her head, with their velvety wings and splayed antennae. In Aunt Grace's house she didn't really like them, but here they made her feel strangely at home. She even recognised an old acquaintance, a Blue Morpho butterfly, as big as a handspan, just like the one in Aunt Grace's study, with wings the exact azure-blue as the dress Luna was wearing.

Then she noticed that around the lamplit edges of the room stood many distinguished-looking figures, perhaps forty or fifty in all. There was a mixture of ladies and gentlemen, all in smart evening dress like Aunt Grace, the men in top hats which looked like black stovepipes, the women in bonnets. They were all having hushed but important-sounding conversations, and didn't bother to stop when Luna and Aunt Grace came in. But Luna did notice one or two of them looking at her in an interested way – all kindly but curious, as if she was some sort of new species. Perhaps that could be explained by the fact that there was only one other child in the room, a handsome blonde boy, about the same height as Luna, standing with a handsome blonde man.

Aunt Grace nodded at the company, but headed straight to greet the blonde man, who clicked his heels smartly together, bowed his head sharply and kissed her butterfly wrist. From that moment, they forgot Luna and the boy, and just talked over their heads. Luna didn't understand a word, as they were speaking in a foreign language, but she did learn one thing from the conversation. The blonde man waved his hands about as he talked, and she could see, on his left wrist, a butterfly tattoo.

'Is that your mother?'

Luna could understand why the blonde boy had asked that. She and Aunt Grace shared the Goodhart auburn hair and green eyes.

'My aunt. She's a scientist. Is that your father?'

'Yes.' The boy's golden hair fell in his eyes, and he had a habit of raking it back with a pale hand.

'Is he a scientist too?'

'A doctor.'

'A physician?' asked Luna.

'Yes. But also a great inventor. Dr Tanius Kass.' The boy said his father's name with a touching pride, as if Luna should have heard of him. 'He's from Prussia. That is, we both are.' That explained the boy's slight accent. Luna wasn't too sure exactly where Prussia was – she knew it was an empire somewhere in eastern Europe, and vaguely thought it was perhaps made up of bits of Germany and bits of Russia. What she did know from the front of Papa's newspaper was that they always seemed to be fighting, either for themselves or for others.

'My name's Konstantin,' said the Prussian boy.

'I'm Luna.' Luna studied her new acquaintance. He looked ... she searched for the word ... expensive, in his well-cut silver-grey suit of clothes and his starched white Eton collars and silken cravat. But he seemed very down to earth, and not superior at all, and he smiled a crooked half-smile. Encouraged by his friendliness she said, 'Did you know that your father has a clockwork butterfly tattooed on his wrist?'

'Yes,' said Konstantin. 'I have been asking about it for years.'

'What did he say?'

'That he would explain it to me on my thirteenth birthday.'

'When's that?'

'Today.'

'Happy birthday.'

'Thank you.'

Luna looked at the boy with the respect due from someone who was only twelve to someone who was thirteen. 'Did you get anything nice?'

His answer was a strange one. 'This is the first birthday I have had standing up on my own two feet,' he said in his precise English. 'I have never travelled. I have never even been to school. I have spent most of my life on my sick-bed, with only books for company. My brothers call me "Konstantly-ill".'

'What was wrong with you?'

'My heart. Some disease with a long name. A long word of the heart.'

Luna studied the boy. Because she was so tall, he was almost exactly her height. 'You look well now,' she said comfortingly.

'I had an operation. A very clever surgeon. My father says I have a clockwork heart now.'

Luna smiled at what was clearly a joke. 'So what *did* you get for your birthday? Besides the clockwork heart, I mean?'

He smiled his half-smile again. 'Now I am well, I asked for an adventure.'

'And did you get one?'

He looked about him. 'I think this might be it.'

Luna felt a thrill travel up her spine. 'You may be right,' she said. 'How about this as a starting point? My aunt has the same tattoo as your father.'

Konstantin turned wide grey eyes on her. '*Really?*' He thought for a moment. 'Then I would be willing to wager that everyone else in this room has one too.'

Luna leant forward and looked left and right around the room. Sure enough, every left wrist that was exposed showed the same mark of the clockwork butterfly.

Aunt Grace turned to her. 'Stop fidgeting, child.'

'Who are these people, Aunt? Are they all scientists?'

'Some, not all. Some are authors, like Mr H.G. Wells over there. Explorers, like Miss Mary Kingsley beyond him. Artists, like Mr Burne-Jones to your left. They are the finest minds of our age. A league of extraordinary ladies and gentlemen.' Somehow, when Aunt Grace said this, she managed not to sound big-headed, just matter-of-fact.

'Like the Royal Society?' Luna thought this was an intelligent thing to say. The Royal Society, she knew, was a collection of the cleverest minds in the country.

'Not at *all* like the Royal Society,' sniffed Aunt Grace disapprovingly. 'They do not admit women, much to their detriment.'

Luna was not entirely sure what detriment meant, but *was* sure it was a bad thing just from the way Aunt Grace said it. Slightly crushed, she asked, 'So are all these ladies and gentlemen interested in butterflies?'

Aunt Grace turned and gave her a very direct look with those green eyes. 'No. None of them are. Not even me.'

Luna thought of all the butterflies at home, and looked around the room at all the winged creatures flattened against the walls. 'Then why…?'

'It's a cover,' Aunt Grace said, 'a blind. A respectable pursuit for ladies and gentlemen in order to mask our true business.'

'And what is your true business?'

'Progress,' she said grandly. 'You've heard of the Kodak box camera? The gramophone? The electric lightbulb? We brought them all to the world's attention, and many other wonders besides.'

'So you – the Butterfly Club – invented all these things?'

'No. We borrowed them.'

'Where from?'

'From the future.'

Luna frowned a little, thinking for a moment that she had misheard. 'I'm sorry, Aunt, but I simply don't know what you mean.'

'Those things would not be in our day-to-day lives, in eighteen hundred and ninety four, were it not for the Butterfly Club,' Aunt Grace explained. 'They belonged in the future; we found them, and brought them back.'

'But ... but that's impossible!'

'As Mr Conan Doyle over there will tell you,' said Aunt Grace, pointing to a serious gentleman with an impressive moustache, 'when you have eliminated the impossible, whatever remains, however improbable, must be the truth.'

Luna goggled at the gentleman. If the inventor of the great detective Sherlock Holmes could believe in all of this, it couldn't be an elaborate joke, could it?

Aunt Grace's face was deadly serious. 'I must tell you that time travel is perfectly possible.'

'But how?'

'All in good time.'

Luna looked at Aunt Grace sharply. She didn't *seem* like she was making a joke – she wasn't that type. 'So you are stealing from the future?'

Aunt Grace turned on her. 'Luna! What an ugly word. We are merely *borrowing* – bringing these treasures back in time to bring progress forward. They would have come anyway. We just make them come sooner.'

'So why are you called the Butterfly Club? And why do you all have butterfly tattoos on your wrists?'

She gave a rare smile. 'Ah, you noticed that, did you? It is because of the Butterfly Effect, a scientific phenomenon discovered by our founder. His research is the reason this club exists.'

'What's the Butterfly Effect?'

Aunt Grace shot a look towards the grandfather-clock-which-was-also-a-door. It obviously had two faces, because it looked just the same on this side of the wall as it did on the other. Except for one thing. On this side, its hands showed what was presumably the true time, which was one minute to noon. 'I think,' said Aunt Grace, 'we will let our founder speak for himself.' She turned to Konstantin's father. 'Doctor Kass?' she said sweetly. 'It is time.'

The doctor picked up a little table from the shadows and placed it in the centre of the floor. Luna noticed that the table had twelve sides, just like the room, and that there was something on it covered in a dark cloth. The doctor removed the cloth with a flourish to reveal a little clockwork contraption, which seemed to be in the shape of a bird. A hush settled over the edges of the room as the members seated themselves and fell quiet. 'I now call this meeting of the Butterfly Club to order,' said Aunt Grace into the silence.

The doctor wound a brass key at the contraption's back. There was a whirring noise and the bird began to animate. As it cocked its little head to one side, bright ruby red eyes shining, clockwork wings fluttering and resettling, for all the world as if it lived, Aunt Grace addressed the bird in a commanding voice. 'Chronos,' she said. 'Show us the professor.'

Even more remarkably, the clockwork bird opened its little brass beak and spoke. 'Initiating primary communication,' it said in a tiny, tinny metallic voice. Then it opened its beak wider and a broad beam of light shone forth, as tall as a lamp-post. Luna watched with her mouth open, something young Victorian ladies weren't really supposed to do. But she couldn't be blamed for this, as the beam of light resolved itself into arms and legs and a head, and a ghost appeared in the middle of the room.

15 JANUARY 1894
12.10 p.m.

Of course, Luna only thought the figure was a ghost for a moment.

In the next instant, the scientific mind Aunt Grace insisted Luna possessed had rationalised that what she was seeing was an optical illusion. Luna could see the ladies and gentlemen on the other side of the room through his ghostly flesh. The apparition was a man, and an odd-looking man at that.

He was tall and wore no hat on his head. He was balding and had a slightly bulbous head, as if his brain was so big that it had expanded his skull and there was now not quite enough hair to cover it. But it was his garments that were the strangest things about him. He wore a suit of clothes in a loud check, with a white shirt with long collars, and a thin, striped cravat tied in a neat knot and hanging down flat, not with the silken flourish of the more substantial gentlemen in the room. He wore no waistcoat or pocket watch, and there were no kid gloves on his hands, nor cane by his side. Really, he looked most peculiar. And he sounded most peculiar too, because the illusion spoke.

'Hi, folks. Right on time.' Here the apparition did an odd thing. He checked his left wrist, and Luna almost expected to see a butterfly tattoo, but instead his white cuff retracted to reveal a tiny little clock, like the face of a pocket-watch, strapped to his wrist by a band of thin leather. 'What can I do you for?'

Luna didn't understand this question, but she did understand what it meant when Aunt Grace held out her butterfly hand to her. Although there was no glove on it, the Hand had to be obeyed. Luna shuffled forward reluctantly into the middle of the room and stood by her aunt.

The ghost turned his eyes on Luna. He could obviously see her – it was very unsettling. But then he smiled. 'Who's this?'

'This is Luna, Professor,' said Aunt Grace. 'My niece.'

'Well, hello, little lady.'

Dr Kass then brought the blonde boy forward, steering

him by his shoulders. 'And this is Konstantin, *mein lieber Sohn,* my dear son.'

'Hello, sport,' said the apparition. 'How ya doing?'

It was clear that Konstantin didn't exactly know what to say to this either, so he remained silent.

Luckily Aunt Grace took over. 'Professor. Will you explain to Luna, and young Konstantin here, who you are?'

'Sure. My name is Edward Norton Lorenz, and I'm a professor of mathematics and meteorology.'

'Will you explain to them where you are?' said Aunt Grace.

'I'm in my study at Massachusetts Institute of Technology, where I'm currently employed.'

'And now, Professor,' said Aunt Grace, clearly and distinctly, 'will you explain to them *when* you are?'

'Sure. It's currently January fifteenth, 1969.'

Luna looked at Konstantin, and Konstantin looked back at her. This must be some sort of practical joke, surely? But then she looked around at all the members of the Butterfly Club. They were serious people, with serious expressions. They didn't look like a pack of jokers. In fact, she noticed the author Conan Doyle scribbling away in his pocketbook, writing down everything the professor said.

Aunt Grace spoke to the apparition. 'Professor. Could you explain a little about your work?'

'Certainly,' said the ghost. 'Some years ago I began to study chaos theory, in an attempt to forecast extraordinary weather events. I asked the question, "Does the flap of a butterfly's wings in Brazil set a tornado in Texas?" and discovered that something as small as the beat of a butterfly's wing could indeed have far-reaching effects on the rest of time. Ever since I first discovered I could talk to you good folks, I've been using my calculations to help you … well … time travel.'

Luna's mouth, already gaping, dropped all the way open at this.

'I won't bore you kids with the math, but the golden rule is this. You may only travel *forward*, not back. If you travel back in time you will trigger what I've come to call the Butterfly Effect – you could, by making tiny changes, significantly alter your own world, or even wipe out your own existence.'

'So no Tudors or Romans then?' said Luna. The whole thing was so unbelievable she had to treat it as a joke.

'I'm afraid not, honey. You can't even go back to your version of yesterday.'

This, of course, made Luna think of Papa.

'But the future,' said the professor, 'between where you are in 1894, and where I am in 1969, that is your ballpark. Sorry! I mean to say, that's the hunting ground for your time treasures.' He shook a warning finger at them. 'But even future travel is not without its problems. You won't change your own past, but you could alter the future. You can't change huge events. But remember, small changes can have big consequences. *That's* the Butterfly Effect.'

Now Konstantin spoke up. 'But ... Professor. Aren't you travelling back in time at this very moment?'

'Shake me by the hand, young fella.'

Konstantin stepped forward to shake hands, but the boy's fingers passed right through the man's as if the professor was indeed a spectre.

'What you are seeing is a manifestation of me – a hologram,' said the professor. 'I'm not really there. I'm still in my own time.'

'Professor,' said Aunt Grace. 'Our time is short. I would like you to tell these children about our conversation last week.'

'Well, ma'am, you told me that your Queen Victoria has announced an Empire-wide scientific contest to find a method of communication through the ether.'

'That's correct,' agreed Aunt Grace. 'The Gabriel

Communication Medal. It is worth one thousand gold sovereigns to the person or persons who can invent a way to speak across continents – to send and receive messages without wires.'

'And I said that "through the ether" sounds an awful lot like radio waves, and in that case you can't do better than find a fella called Marconi.'

'Guglielmo Marconi,' put in Dr Kass.

'That's it,' said the professor. 'Guglielmo Marconi. An Italian physicist. He really started cooking with gas around 1912.' The professor chuckled. 'Sorry. Keep forgetting. Mustn't use modern slang. When I said "cooking with gas", I merely meant that's when Marconi had gotten his wireless radio to a competent standard – it was used for maritime communication. I suggested putting 1912 into the old dial. Eighteen years from where you are now.'

'Can I ask a question?' Konstantin piped up.

'Of course, *lieber Sohn*,' said his father.

'Well, my question is: if this is all true, why not go as far as you can, to 1969, and get the most advanced device you can find there?'

Dr Tanius Kass did not quite meet his son's eyes. It was Aunt Grace who explained, 'Because our inventions have to be plausible. If our finds are too advanced our activities would arouse suspicion. We are careful not to go too far into the future.'

'And there is another point to make,' Dr Kass added. 'If we go too far ahead, then we might not have the raw materials, or the manufacturing skill in our own time to create or maintain such machines. Eighteen years is about right.'

'Yes, indeed,' agreed Aunt Grace. 'Professor, when we first discussed this, where did you tell us to go in eighteen years' time?'

'I said to try Southampton on the south coast of England. Huge port for huge ships. By then Marconi's wirelesses were standard in the ships on the White Star Line, so you'll be able to find one in what was called the Marconi Room. That'll get you your Gabriel Medal all right. Any one of those big ocean liners will do. Any ship except for—'

The professor's image stuttered and froze.

Dr Kass knelt down to examine the clockwork bird. 'Regrettably there was a transmission interruption of the phantasmagorical holographic manifestation,' it said in its flat little metallic voice, and the final words got slower and lower and sort of stretched until they finally stopped.

The doctor explained. 'Chronos only works for about

two minutes at a time. His mechanism is clockwork, and he runs down quickly.'

'Can't you just wind him up again?' Konstantin asked his father.

'*Nein, lieber Sohn*,' said the doctor. 'Not for a while. He partly runs on magnets, and their polarity has to be restored before he can work again. He takes a few hours to recharge.'

'No matter,' said Aunt Grace to the room at large. 'We have it from the professor's lips twice now. 1912. Southampton. England. Those are the settings.'

'The settings?' repeated Luna. 'The settings for what?'

'Is Mr Herbert George Wells here?' said Aunt Grace, ignoring Luna's question and peering into the shadows. 'Mr Wells, be good enough to bring the contraption.'

For the first time Luna noticed that the brass meridian line, which ran as wide as a handspan right through the centre of the room, disappeared into the folds of a dark-red velvet curtain cordoning off the far end of the room. Mr H.G. Wells walked the line to the red velvet curtain, and drew it back to reveal another extraordinary sight.

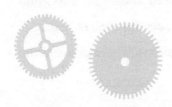

15 JANUARY 1894
12.15 p.m.

It was a machine, made of brass and polished wood and bone-white ivory, set upon four wheels. It had two lamps at the front, and four little doors, and rails around the sides. Inside there was room enough for four souls, on comfortable bench-like seats upholstered in red velvet and set with gilded studs, like something you'd find in a drawing room. At the front of the train was a raised seat for the driver, set before a console with levers and labels and lights, and a trio of ivory dials.

It looked a little like the new trains on the Metropolitan Underground railway, but about a quarter of a carriage long. The train rolled to the very centre of the great twelve-sided room, slowly and smoothly, crackling with forks of lightning as blue as the Morpho butterfly, the wheels rolling either side of the meridian as if the copper line was a track.

As soon as the train stopped, Luna discovered that the person who had been driving the contraption was almost as incredible as the machine itself. A boy, probably not much older than Luna, got out of the cab to stand before them. He was broad and strong, and he had blacker-than-black hair and bluer-than-blue eyes. But it was not so much his colouring that marked him out as his outfit.

He had a cap on his head, and above the peak was a pair of brass-and-glass goggles. He wore shirtsleeves and a waistcoat like a labourer, and brown breeches tucked into boots that were more buckle than shoe-leather. His buttons were cogs, and his belt a bicycle chain. He looked as if his clothes had been cobbled together using bits and pieces from his profession – little bits of iron found along the railways.

Luna's eyes widened. The boy looked dangerous and adventurous and very capable. In fact, he couldn't have looked more different to Konstantin, with his delicate pallor and his well-tailored frock coat. But while Konstantin did look like he fitted in with this company, and this setting, this railway boy was earthy and tanned from a life obviously lived outdoors – he didn't look like he felt at home in a room at all.

Luna was so fascinated by the newcomer that she hardly noticed that there was another, older fellow, dressed very like him, pushing the strange machine from behind. He had a weather-beaten complexion but the same piercing blue eyes as the boy.

Aunt Grace introduced the machine first. 'This,' she said, 'is the Time Train.'

Just from the way she said it, you could tell she was giving both words Capital Letters. She introduced the man next. 'This is Mr Michael O'Connell. He is a navigational engineer.'

Luna knew all about 'navvies'. They were the engineers, often from Ireland, who had the expert skill and knowledge to build the railways that now spanned the Empire like a vast iron spider.

'And this is Aidan,' Aunt Grace went on, indicating the driver boy, 'who is following in his father's profession. Aidan knows everything there is to know about the Time Train, for he helped our Mr H.G. Wells construct it. Didn't you, young man?'

Aidan grinned an enormous grin. If Konstantin had half a smile, Aidan had the rest of it, and then some. The boy touched the goggles on his cap in deference to Aunt

Grace. 'To be sure, missus. What I don't know about the Time Train isn't worth knowing.'

'She's a complex machine, to be sure, but an easy old girl to operate,' said Mr O'Connell.

'Yes indeed,' agreed the boy, who seemed the more talkative of the two. 'To go forward in time you settle yourself on her saddle and push this lever with the ivory handle forward.' Luna noticed that, just like his father, he referred to the Time Train as *she*, just as people spoke about ships and pianos. Aidan pointed to the different bits of the contraption as he spoke. 'You must set these dials for date, time and place, and the mechanism is powered by quartz crystals at the rear.'

'Will it work?' asked Luna doubtfully.

'It will work,' said Aidan, brimming with confidence. 'It *has* worked.'

'Our members have been using this machine for some time,' said Mr Wells kindly. 'There's really no need to worry.'

Luna wondered why it was she and Konstantin who had to have their minds set at rest, and why the Butterfly Club were taking such pains to explain their plans to a pair of mere children. She asked her aunt directly. 'Why are you telling *us* all this?'

Aunt Grace exchanged a look with Dr Kass, then turned to her niece.

'Because, dear Luna,' she said, '*you* will be making the journey to 1912.'

15 JANUARY 1894
12.30 p.m.

'Alone?' Luna was in shock. Aunt Grace had spoken as if the matter was already settled.

'Not alone,' said Dr Kass. 'Konstantin will go with you.'

'And Aidan,' said Aunt Grace, 'as your engineer.'

The tall train boy nodded and grinned, as if this was the most normal proposal in the world. He was clearly the only one of the three who knew anything about this plan.

Dr Kass put his hand on his son's shoulder. 'You asked for an adventure for your birthday, Konstantin. This is it. Chronos will go with you,' he went on. 'You may ask him if you have further questions. I have loaded as much knowledge into him as I can. Every member of the Butterfly Club has spoken to him at length, and he has recorded the vocabulary and digested the specialisms of every one of us. You may ask him anything.'

'And he has another even more important function,' said Aunt Grace. 'Through Chronos you may speak with Professor Lorenz. He will appear to you, and give you aid, just as he did today.'

'How?' asked Konstantin.

'You may easily remember Chronos's properties,' said Dr Kass. 'Turn his key anti-clockwise – *backwards* in time, as it were – to ask Chronos anything we have already recorded into his mechanism in our time of 1894. Turn the key clockwise – *forward* in time – to send a message to the professor in 1969 that you need to speak to him. But remember,' said the doctor, 'Chronos may only speak for about two minutes at a time, either to you or to the professor. Then he runs down. And you cannot wind him up again straightaway – he needs a few hours to reset his polarity. Look. He lives here.'

Dr Kass took the clockwork bird over to the brass contraption. He opened two small doors in the face of the round clock on the dashboard of the Time Train and fitted the little bird inside. Then Luna understood – Chronos was a bird who lived in a clock. Of course! He was a cuckoo. What else?

'Do we go now? Tonight?' Konstantin asked. He

sounded excited, and there was a flush along his pale cheekbones.

'Yes,' said his father.

'Is it dangerous?'

'Not, we think, for you,' said Aunt Grace. 'Children may go about unmarked and unchallenged. That is why we want you to go. We think you may be able to… borrow… the wireless radio.' This made a certain dark sense to Luna. Victorian children were largely ignored – and it seemed that children in the future were too.

'Think of it,' said Aunt Grace, clapping her hands over the three young people before her. 'What an adventure! You will be the first time-travelling children in the *world*.'

Luna looked to her left and right, to the boys who were to be her travelling companions. She plucked her aunt's sleeve and drew her to one side, speaking in an undertone. 'Aunt. In the time I have lived with you, you have barely let me out of the house. You cannot think it… suitable… that I should travel like this – anywhere, let alone through time – unchaperoned in the company of two boys.'

'Oh, but there *will* be another girl with you,' said Aunt Grace. 'Nadia will be there all the time.'

'Who is Nadia?'

Aunt Grace nodded towards Aidan, now seated in the

driver's saddle and checking the settings. 'Ask him. *He* knows.'

But Luna had made up her mind. Whether or not some mysterious girl was going to meet them in 1912, she was not about to take part in this experiment. She knew that it was common practice in mining to send a canary down a coal mine, and if the canary died that meant there were poisonous gases present and that the miners shouldn't risk it. Her father had always encouraged her to speak her mind – she did so now. 'I won't go,' she said. 'I won't be a canary in the coal mine.'

'Oh, I think you will,' said Aunt Grace harshly. Her voice was flint, her green eyes jade. 'You see, your father was the one who didn't come back. *He* was the canary.'

Luna let out a little gasp, and took a pace backward. Papa? *That's* where he had gone?

Aunt Grace must have seen her niece's expression, for she softened her voice, and spoke more kindly than she ever had. 'I'm giving you the chance to follow him, Luna. To find him. I told you he was on another plane, and I spoke the truth. He's out there somewhere. You may be able to bring back more than the wireless radio.'

'*Oh!*' If Luna had been just a little younger she would have stamped her foot. It was too bad. Aunt Grace had her pinned down, as surely as a butterfly on a card.

The grandfather clock seemed to tick louder and louder, intruding on Luna's indecision.

'Come on, *Fräulein*. It'll be fun,' called Konstantin confidently. He was already in the Time Train, having boarded while Luna and her aunt were having their low-voiced conference.

'The train works. I promise you,' said Aidan, holding out his hand.

Luna looked at the grubby fingers with disdain. Her fear and anger made her ungracious. 'I can get up myself, thank you.'

The Irish boy merely hooted with amusement, making her even crosser. 'Oh ho, too hoity-toity for help, are we, Duchess?'

Luna studiously ignored him. She put one buttoned boot on the running board of the Time Train, torn by indecision. She could stay in the present, where it was safe, and face her aunt. Or she could travel to the future, face its dangers, and seek her father.

'Tick tock,' said Aunt Grace warningly.

Luna took hold of the brass rail and lifted her other boot off the ground. She was on board the Time Train.

'Good for you, Duchess.' Aidan, sitting before the

controls, set the ivory dials. The little white tiles were etched with ink-black numbers and letters, just like the word games Luna and her father used to play in the evenings. Aidan turned the tumblers until they read **SOUTHAMPTON 1912**. He hesitated over the third one. 'Time of year?'

'Spring tides, surely,' said Konstantin. 'That's when most of the sailings go, I think.'

'Tenth of April'll do,' said Aidan. 'Me ma's birthday. Day or night?'

'Day,' said Konstantin eagerly. 'We will be better able to move around undetected in a crowd.'

'From your mouth to God's ear,' said Aidan and set the fourth dial for noon.

His brown hand released the ivory lever and eased it forward. The dials began to spin. Luna's stomach lurched as the wheels turned and the train began to move across the vast room, using the meridian as a track, faster and faster, towards the grandfather clock concealing the door. As they gathered speed and the blue lightning danced about the train, every single butterfly on the walls detached from its card and began to fly about the room in a whirling, rainbow twister. The Time Train shot across the vast room until there was nowhere else to go.

They were going to crash into the clock.

There was a blinding flash.

And an ear-splitting bang.

SOUTHAMPTON
ENGLAND

10 APRIL 1912

10 APRIL 1912
Noon

There was a choking, chemical smell, a warmth and a humming sound.

Luna, feeling heavy and sick, looked at the others. Even the ox-strong Aidan looked as if he'd been punched. Konstantin, naturally pale, now looked green. He hauled himself to his feet with the aid of the brass rails. Holding his finger to his lips, he poked his head outside the window of the Time Train. '*Gott in Himmel*,' he said, shocked into his native language. 'Look.'

Luna and Konstantin joined him at the window.

There were boxes and crates piled high as far as the eye could see. At the corners of the huge room were iron staircases and vast galley doors.

'This doesn't look like Southampton docks,' said Luna,

not that she had a very clear idea of what docks looked like.

'You're wrong there, Duchess. It could be a warehouse, like they have on the wharves in Limehouse,' said Aidan, 'for things that are ready to be loaded on to ships.'

'Let's explore,' said Konstantin keenly.

'I'll just put the old girl to bed.' Aidan unfolded one of those enormous waxy green lengths of cloth called tarpaulin. Luna and Konstantin helped him cover up the Time Train completely. In the dark corner it looked almost invisible.

They walked among all the crates and boxes and trunks to one of the metal doors, which opened on to an iron stairway painted white. As they climbed the steps, there was the sound of a low, booming note, which made Luna jump. It was so incredibly loud that she felt it in her very ribs.

'Don't get your bloomers in a twist, Duch,' said Aidan, in an annoyingly calm fashion. 'That's a ship's horn. We're definitely in the right place.'

But as they emerged into the daylight, dazzling after the dim of the inside, they found themselves on a wooden deck. There was a deafening cheer, as if the three of them were being greeted as conquering heroes. But the cheer was not for them. They were greeted by a wall of backs, a dense crowd staring at something and waving. There were men, women and children, and every man had his hat in his hand and was brandishing it above his head. Some of the gentlemen actually threw their hats into the air.

'Come on,' said Aidan, and the three time-thieves forced their way through the crowd.

'I don't care what you say,' said Luna stubbornly, as they were squashed and elbowed as they pushed forward. 'This doesn't look like Southampton docks.'

'No,' said Konstantin, as they found themselves squashed up against a white railing. '*That* does.'

He pointed to a sunlit coastal town in the distance.

There was a silver stretch of water between them and land.

It was Aidan who stated, numbly, what they already knew.

'We're onboard ship,' he said. '*This* ship, to be exact.' Aidan pointed to a lifebelt tethered to the railings, which had a name painted on it.

The name of the ship was printed all the way round the life belt so it was rather like trying to read a word written on a wheel. Luna spelled it out. 'RMS *Titanic*.'

'I suppose the RMS *Titanic* is as good as any other ship.'

'Yes, and look.' Konstantin pointed to a monogram printed on the lifebelt. It featured a little red flag with a white star on it, fluttering above three scrolls that said: WHITE STAR LINE. 'This device says the White Star Line. The professor said any passenger ship of the White Star Line will have a Marconi Room and a wireless radio.'

'So, what now?' asked Aidan.

'I suppose we wait a bit,' said Konstantin, 'until all these crowds disperse. And then we'll go on a radio hunt.'

Luna looked at the hundreds – no, thousands – of people lining the dock, waving goodbye to their loved ones. The noise and the crush were making her feel dizzy and disorientated. In order to calm herself she picked out one family on the shore to concentrate her attention on. They were running along to try to keep pace with the departing boat, just as you might do on a train platform. There was a woman carrying a child in her arms, and a little girl running alongside her. The little girl was wearing a butterfly-bright dress, the rust-scarlet of a Red Admiral. At the very end of the dock the girl stopped and waved frantically. 'Papa, Papa!' she shouted, looking almost straight at Luna.

Luna was struck by the little girl's longing. She looked at the man just beside her, who was waving frantically back. Luna got a lump in her throat. She suddenly missed Papa very much, right in her middle, under her heart. Their parting might have been just like this, had Papa only bothered to say goodbye.

The man waved his hat so hard that it flew from his hand and landed at Luna's feet, she picked it up and handed it back with a smile. He looked at her with his sad eyes and his mouth lifted in a ghost of a smile just for one second. He nodded and said, 'Thank you, *Signorina*,' in an accent foreign to her. Then his eyes returned to the little family on the dock again, as if drawn by an irresistible longing.

'Ah, there you are, *Fräulein* Luna.' Konstantin appeared at her side. 'We lost sight of you.'

'Sweet Jesus, Duch, would you ever stay in one place?' exclaimed Aidan. 'You frightened us half to death, disappearing like a will-o'-the-wisp.'

Luna smiled sweetly at Konstantin and glowered at Aidan. 'Well, now we're all together,' she said, 'let's explore the good ship *Titanic*.'

10 APRIL 1912
12.30 p.m.

*T*itanic was a marvel – more like a floating city than a ship, and exploring her was certainly an adventure.

Luna soon noticed that the boys made the decisions, they decided where they should go and what they should do. Since the mysterious Nadia, the fellow girl traveller she was promised, had not yet turned up, she was outnumbered. Konstantin was very polite, Aidan wasn't, but both attitudes, strangely, added up to the same thing – that girls weren't much good.

But because she wasn't required to lead but only follow, and she wasn't required to talk but could only look and listen, Luna quietly noticed things. She noticed that while they were free to run about on parts of the upper decks, anywhere that might house the wireless radio was closed to them. In reality they had only seen a fraction of the enormous ship. Every time they tried to investigate further, either on the lower or upper decks, they were halted by one of the numerous stewards in White Star uniforms, who always stopped them with white-gloved hands and the question, 'Where's your ticket, young sir? Young miss?' Then they'd be sent on their way, sometimes with a friendly smile, sometimes with what Aidan called a 'clip round the ear'.

As the sun dipped down on the first day they enjoyed the spectacle of landing in Cherbourg, with the coast of France bathed a beautiful rosy gold. There they leant over the white railings and watched the Cherbourg passengers embark. A man in a blue serge suit seemed to have the most luggage with him – trunks and hatboxes and strongboxes and other wealthy trappings.

'I wonder who he is, ' said Luna.

'Someone rich,' said Aidan. 'That's all you need to know about that.'

It was really fascinating watching all these people from 1912 and how they differed from the people of their own time.

'They are not *that* different, the 1912 clothes. I mean,' Konstantin said, 'I thought they'd be wearing silver.'

'Why silver?' asked Luna.

'I don't know,' said Konstantin. 'Silver just seems to be... future-y.'

'The men wear bowler hats instead of top hats,' observed Luna, remembering the bowler she'd handed back to the father on deck. 'Everyone seems to wear them now, even the gentlemen. At home it's just cab drivers and grooms.'

'The lower orders, eh Duch?' said Aidan.

'And the women's dresses are shorter,' giggled Luna, ignoring him. 'There's a *scandalous* amount of ankle on display. Not at *all* respectable.'

'And their hats are huge,' grinned Aidan. 'They look like they are about to take off like hot-air balloons.'

There was one more stop before the open sea, at a port that Aidan pronounced to be Queenstown in Ireland. 'I could have got on here if I'd known,' he remarked. 'This is where I'm from.' There, they watched more passengers embark, although these passengers did not seem quite as rich as the ones who'd got on at Cherbourg. They were ragged and threadbare, and seemed to be carrying all their worldly possessions with them. In exchange for the passengers getting on, sacks of mail were carried off. There was great excitement when word went round the

47

ship that a man had actually posted himself off the ship at Queenstown, hidden in one of the mail sacks. Apparently the man had just wanted free passage to Ireland.

'Mad, quite mad,' pronounced Konstantin, watching the kerfuffle on the shore. 'He'll probably regret that decision for the rest of his life.'

'Too right,' Aidan agreed. 'Who'd want to miss an adventure like this?'

But just as the children stared at the passengers, some of the passengers were beginning to stare back.

'We're attracting a bit too much attention,' said Aidan. 'Let's go back to the Time Train and bed down for the night.'

10 APRIL 1912
8 p.m.

Once they were safely back in the Time Train, tucked under the tarpaulin with only the faint glow of the quartz crystal bars as a nightlight, there was nothing for it but to go to sleep. And of course, the children found that impossible. For one thing, there was not much in the way of room in the Time Train, and although the benches made comfortable seats they made poor beds. There were no bedclothes, so they had to sleep fully dressed, which is a horribly uncomfortable and restricting thing to do. But of course the biggest obstacle to sleep was wondering just what the morning would bring. It was somewhat nerve-wracking to be not just in a new place, but a new time.

So they half-sat, half-lay, listening to the thrumming of the engines and talking sleepily.

'What's that sound?' asked Luna. There was the faintest little regular *tick, tick*, like the sound of a watch.

'That's me,' said Konstantin. 'It is my heart.'

Luna propped herself up on her elbow. 'I thought it was a joke. When you talked about your clockwork heart.'

'I thought so too, when my father first told me,' he said. 'But he was deadly serious.'

'What are you talking about?' asked Aidan from the driver's seat.

Konstantin said, 'I told *Fräulein* Luna at the observatory. I was bedridden until very recently. I was very ill – there was something wrong with my heart. My father brought a surgeon to my sick-bed, and the surgeon put me to sleep and operated on me. When I woke up, I got better. It took a long time – I had to learn to move, then to stand, then to walk. My muscles had wasted, you see – it doesn't matter how many exercises you try to do in bed, they don't really work. But all I know is that before the operation, I couldn't do anything. Now I can do anything that everyone else can do.' He sat up straighter. 'But the other thing that changed was that when I went to sleep my heart did that thumping thing – *lub-dub, lub-dub*. And since I woke up – it ticks. *Tick-tock, tick-tock.*'

The three of them fell silent and listened. It was true.

Konstantin's chest ticked, just like a watch. 'Can it *really* be clockwork?' asked Luna, fascinated. 'Surely your father *was* making a joke.'

'Well, but *something* happened to me,' said Konstantin. 'Look.' He began to unbutton his shirt.

Luna felt uncomfortable with the situation – as an unchaperoned young lady in the company of two boys it wouldn't have been considered 'proper' for her to look at Konstantin's chest. But of course she was burning to see whatever was there, so she found a compromise by covering her own eyes and peeping through her fingers. Konstantin had a livid scar running right down his chest, in the middle of his ribs. Its red puckered edges, raised up like a mountain-ridge of scars, made a stark contrast to the pallor of his skin.

'So now you know what the sound is. Does it trouble you?'

'Not I,' said Aidan. 'I've got six sisters and back in Ireland we all shared a bed. It was noisier than Dublin station with seven women under the covers.'

'And I have four brothers,' said Konstantin. 'All soldiers. So you were in a houseful of women and I was in a houseful of men.'

'What about you, Duch?' asked Aidan.

'There's just me,' Luna said. 'No brothers or sisters.' She was learning that being alone was perhaps overrated.

They were companionably silent for a moment, all listening to the music of Konstantin's heart.

'I believe it,' said Aidan, out of nowhere. 'That there will be mechanical hearts. In the future, I mean. Not now.'

'Really?' said Luna doubtfully.

'Of course,' he said. 'Machines are wonders. They can be as big as the turbines that drive this ship – big as a blue whale, I reckon. Or they can be as small as the insides of a pocket watch. Those cogs are no bigger than a flea's hobnails.' He yawned, making no attempt to cover his mouth. 'One day they'll put a watch in a man's chest all right, to keep his heart ticking along.'

'But we are in the future now,' said Luna, finding it, as she said this, incredible. 'Do you mean there will be such wonders in 1912?'

'No. Not yet,' murmured Aidan drowsily.

'Then when?' asked Konstantin, his voice thick with sleep.

'Oh,' said Aidan breezily, 'say, 1969. The professor's time. When they have rockets to the moon and moving pictures and silver suits.'

Eventually of course, they did sleep, dreaming of

moon-rockets and suits of silver, all supremely confident that tomorrow they would find the radio, and take the Time Train back home.

RMS *TITANIC*

14 APRIL 1912

14 APRIL 1912
7.15 a.m.

The Butterfly Club's plan worked almost too well. As children, even oddly dressed ones, Luna, Konstantin and Aidan were largely ignored aboard the RMS *Titanic*. They managed to steal enough food to keep their stomachs from rumbling, spent hours at the prow of the ship dangling their feet over the ocean below, and slept in the Time Train at night. They were in danger of enjoying themselves and, far from finding the radio, they'd been on the good ship *Titanic* for three days with not so much as a sniff of it.

They needed a new plan, and Luna thought she had one. So instead of 'good morning' she said, as soon as Aidan and Konstantin stirred, 'Here's what we do. Today, instead of sticking together, we take one class each, and try to infiltrate the workings of the ship – behind the scenes, as it were. If we only have to search one deck each for the radio room, we'll find the radio so much faster.'

'I'll take Third and the lower decks,' said Aidan quickly. 'That's where the engine rooms will be. I'm dying to see how this ship works.'

'Then it's you and I to First or Second, *Fräulein*,' said Konstantin to Luna. 'What do you think?'

'Well, you're quite hoity-toity, Duch,' grinned Aidan. 'I would say you're made for First Class. Konstantin should go to Second, where the officers are. One of them is bound to know about the wireless radio.'

'That is true,' said Konstantin. Then he frowned. 'The trouble is that we are children. No one is going to let us in anywhere.'

'Speak for yourself,' said Aidan. 'I've been doing a full day's work for three years.' He scoffed. 'Children indeed. Childhood's a luxury for the quality folk, not for those who toil.'

'How old are you, anyway?' asked Luna, genuinely interested.

'No idea, Duch. Birthdays are for the quality too.'

'You are taller than us,' observed Konstantin. 'And

stronger. But in your manner, and way of talking – well, I reckon you are about our age.'

Aidan shrugged. 'Just goes to show, don't it?' He looked at them, clear-eyed. 'You're seen differently according to the role you play.'

'If you're suggesting—' began Luna hotly.

'Wait,' interrupted Konstantin, holding up a pale hand. 'He's right. *You're seen differently according to the role you play*. We have to find ways to really infiltrate the ship. We have to be more… well… *grown-up* about this.'

'What do you mean?' asked Luna.

'I mean,' said Konstantin, 'that there's no reason why we couldn't have jobs, *all* of us, on board *Titanic*.'

Luna nodded. 'Yes, that's true. And big ships have laundry rooms.'

'So what?' said Aidan.

'Laundry rooms,' said Luna slowly, 'have clothes in them.' She looked up at the others, green eyes blazing. 'If we're playing roles, we need the right costumes. So Aidan finds some work clothes for the engine rooms. I find a modern 1912 dress worthy of First Class.'

'And what about Konstantin?' asked Aidan.

'Since I'm heading to the officers' quarters,' said Konstantin, grey eyes shining too, 'I'm going to need an actual uniform. I've always wanted to wear one – why should my brothers have all the buttons and boots?'

14 APRIL 1912
8 a.m.

It took them no time at all to find the laundry – they only had to follow their noses to the smell of the starch and carbolic soap and quicklime. They peeped round the corner to see an enormous room full of brass vats and laundry maids and racks of drying clothes – there was a phenomenal amount of washing three days into a voyage with a ship the size of the *Titanic*.

They leant back against the wall in the iron passageway, trying to make themselves as unnoticeable as possible.

'What do we do now?' hissed Luna.

'I think I will just walk in there and ask,' said Konstantin. 'Sometimes the simplest solutions are the best. It is all about the confidence.'

And before the other two could stop him, Konstantin

had walked around the corner into the laundry room, and disappeared into a cloud of steam.

'He's so brave,' said Luna, a little enviously.

Aidan sucked in his cheeks. 'Well, as my da says, there's two towns called Brave and Foolhardy,' he said. 'The trick is not to cross the border from the one to the other.'

But Konstantin's method worked. In less than a minute he'd emerged with three outfits over his arm.

'But that's stealing,' protested Luna.

'That's what we are here to do. We're time-thieves,' said Konstantin simply.

'I suppose so,' she admitted.

'And we're not taking them off the ship,' said Konstantin. 'Are we?'

Back in the hold, he handed them the outfits and Luna dived under the tarpaulin to change in the privacy of the Time Train. To her great surprise, Aidan climbed in with her.

'What are you doing?' she asked.

'Getting changed,' he said, already unbuttoning his cog-buttons.

'But… but…' she said, 'you can't watch a young lady getting changed! It's… it's not *gentlemanly*.'

Aidan stopped mid-unbutton, and his cheeks reddened.

'*Sorry*, I'm sure,' he muttered. 'Hand to God, I didn't mean anything by it. Six sisters, you know.'

'That's all right,' said Luna, as kindly as she could. 'But you must have had separate dressing rooms, surely.'

Aidan's laugh was more of a snort. 'You don't know anything, Duch. Seven kids and me ma and da. Two rooms we had in the entire house – one up, one down. We all changed together. There was a tin bath before the fire and we all took turns.'

'Didn't you even turn your back?' asked Luna. She was beginning to appreciate how lucky her childhood had been.

'Barely room to do that either,' he quipped. He grinned and raked his black hair out of his blue eyes. 'I'll wait, will I?' And he climbed out of the train.

Left alone, Luna began to change. By the light of the glowing crystal bars she examined what Konstantin had stolen. He had chosen well. The costume was a tailor-made suit in the subdued brown colour of a Dingy Skipper butterfly. It was made for a lady, and a tall lady at that, and the whole thing was made out of soft worsted wool – no bad thing, thought Luna, now they were sailing into colder waters. In fact, the suit was much more comfortable than her own restrictive Victorian clothes, and actually fitted her better than they ever had. She had to keep on her own button-boots, but there was nothing to be done about that. Finally Luna twisted her mass of auburn hair up into a bun and emerged from under the tarpaulin to show the two boys.

'Is it all right?'

Aidan grinned his lopsided grin. 'You look simply ripping,' he said.

She turned to Konstantin impatiently. 'Konstantin, is it all right?'

'Yes,' he said, matter-of-factly. 'You look like a secretary.'

This wasn't hugely complimentary, but it was better than *ripping*. She concluded that, much as she liked Aidan, the rough Irish boy had no manners at all. And it got worse.

'Thing is,' said Aidan, 'whatever you're dressed in, you'll still have that hair and those eyes. That's your trouble, Duch.'

Luna blushed. It was certainly an education being a stowaway with two boys – she wished, not for the first time, that there was another girl along with them on the adventure.

And then she remembered. 'Aidan,' she said suddenly. 'Who's Nadia?'

His reaction was extraordinary. He started, as if he'd seen a phantom, and the colour drained from his tanned face until he was almost as pale as Konstantin. 'N–Nadia?' he stuttered. 'I don't know any Nadia. What an odd name!' He gave a little laugh, which sounded entirely false. 'How should *I* know someone called Nadia?'

'I don't know,' said Luna, watching him closely. 'My aunt said I wouldn't be the only girl because there would be someone on this ship called Nadia. And that *you* knew who she was.'

'*Me?*' Aidan brayed like a donkey. 'I haven't a clue.' And he did that thing when someone looks you in the eye so hard when they are speaking that you are absolutely convinced that they are telling a lie. 'Anyway, my turn now.' He pushed past her into the belly of the Time Train, and pulled the tarpaulin closed after him.

Luna looked at Konstantin, but he was oblivious. Obviously he hadn't seen anything amiss. Really, what with Aidan calling her *ripping*, and then making personal comments about her hair and eyes, she wished the mysterious Nadia would turn up as soon as possible, and bring a little female gentility to the trip.

Aidan, when he emerged, didn't look much different. His trousers were made of supple suede; he wore a pale shirt made of that rough cotton called cambric, with the sleeves rolled up halfway up his strong brown arms. The trousers were a little loose, so he'd kept his old belt, which was a bicycle chain from their own time. There was a red neckerchief knotted about his neck and he kept on his own hobnail boots. He left his jacket and cap with the goggles in the Time Train, tucked under the seat with Luna's dress.

'Now me,' said Konstantin, and soon emerged, looking completely different.

He was wearing a midnight-blue coat with eight gilt buttons down the front and a single gold stripe around the cuff. He wore a peaked hat in the same midnight blue, with a badge of the White Star Line on the front, also in gold. Under the coat he wore a white shirt with a dark-blue tie, and dark-blue trousers. Luna felt very shy of this new Konstantin. He looked handsome, authoritarian and at least five years older.

They all looked at each other anew, getting used to the 1912 clothes. 'Ready?' Aidan asked.

'As we'll ever be,' said Luna. 'We all meet here tonight. And if anyone is in danger before that,' she said, 'come back here and hide out until the others arrive.'

'Wait,' said Konstantin. He dived back into the Time Train, retrieved a book from the pocket of his Norfolk jacket, and tucked it into his military coat. He tapped the pocket and smiled. 'You're never alone with a book,' he said. '*Now* I'm ready.'

They went as far as the galley stairs together. 'Let's go separately from here, so we're not connected to each other now that we are "grown-ups",' suggested Aidan.

Luna felt very strange saying goodbye to the boys. They had been strangers three days ago, and now she thought of them as family. Konstantin had all those brothers, and Aidan all those sisters, but she'd never had any siblings – until now. But that wasn't the sort of thing you could just come out and say, so she just settled for, 'Who will go first?'

'Me,' said Konstantin fearlessly.

'Aren't you ever scared?' asked Luna, who was.

Konstantin smiled a little sadly. 'When you've been in bed all your life, and you hear all your aunts, and your brothers, and your doctors whispering about how you're going to die, you get used to fear. Fear was my bedfellow, under the covers with me. Now I'm up and about, I feel like I've left it behind, somewhere in the bedclothes.' He stood up very straight. 'That's why I wasn't afraid when I first boarded the Time Train. I'm not afraid now. And I feel like I'll never be afraid again.'

Konstantin, taking his leave with a smart salute, opened

the door to the level on which they stood – the Second Class deck. It was there they had watched Southampton dock disappear on the launch day. Aidan, in the blink of a blue eye, clattered down the galley stairs to the lower decks. And last of all Luna raised her chin, and headed up and up, to somewhere she had never been – the heady heights of First Class.

14 APRIL 1912
9.30 a.m.

Of the three time-thieves, Aidan was the only one to feel a sensation of relief at being alone. He liked both of his time-travelling companions enormously, but he would have to be careful. He'd nearly, *so* nearly slipped up that morning.

So far he had kept his secret as close to his chest as Konstantin kept his clockwork heart. On the railways with Da he hadn't had to worry – Da already knew who Aidan was and no one else would ever guess. On the railways all that mattered was that you could do the work. Machines were straightforward, uncomplicated things compared to people. Humans were the ones who were all cogs and trickiness. Luna had already been asking some awkward questions. At least today he would be safe. Among the pistons and turbines that were the valves of *Titanic*'s great iron heart, he would be with his own kind: engineers.

But as it turned out Aidan found himself not in the engine room, but in the stokehold. And the reason he knew he was in the stokehold was that it was hotter than hell. A man, black with soot, with anxious eyes shining out of his grimy face, collared him as soon as he got through the door. 'You a stoker?'

Aidan took less than a second to think. 'Yes.'

'Come on then, we need all hands. The fire's still in and now it's threatening to get out of control. Hurry.'

'What fire?'

'Where've you been, boy? The one that's been burning since Southampton, and for ten days before that.'

Aidan was astonished. 'We set sail with a fire in the hold?'

'Yes.'

'*Why?*'

'Cost too much to cancel the voyage,' the man yelled. 'The *Olympic* is out of commission, so the White Star Line needed at least *one* of their ships on the seas. That's enough jawing. Come on.'

There were rows upon rows of black iron stoke-holes, burning mouths open like greedy hogs. The heat was unbearable. At each fire-hole a burly man, stripped to the waist, was shovelling coal into the furnaces. Aidan knew, of course, the mechanics behind this – he had seen firemen on trains all his life, shovelling coal to make steam to power the engines. But he'd never seen anything approaching this scale. This was like a thousand trains all at once, and he imagined the head of steam that was needed to drive the *Titanic*'s enormous turbines, and turn her vast propellers.

But there was one other crucial difference between this process and all the others he had seen before. In all other settings the coal had been stacked, black and patient, waiting to be ignited in the heart of the furnace.

Not here.

Here, the enormous stack of coal was already on fire, glowing like a hoard of dragon treasure, not blazing but smoking ominously.

'The coal stacks have been burning for a fortnight,' said the stoker. 'We've decided the only thing to do is shovel it into the furnaces.'

'All of it?' Aidan gaped at the black-and-amber mass.

'It's the only way. There's seven thousand tonnes of coal on board, stacked three decks high. If it all catches fire, this whole ship's in trouble. So if you're done talking, get yourself a shovel and *help*.'

There was nothing else for it. Aidan grabbed one of a pile of shovels resting against the wall, and set to work.

He was younger and slighter than the men, although he was as tall as some. He might as well not have bothered stealing his clothes because each layer came off in very short order – first the jacket, then the kerchief and cap. Aidan did make sure to keep his shirt on, and consequently he was dripping with sweat in no time at all.

After even a few moments the heat became unbearable, wedged as he was between the smouldering coal and the belching furnaces. A foreman called a break every three minutes for the men to go to an airhole and gasp some clean cool air. Then it was back into the inferno once more. Aidan wanted more than anything in the world to give up, to run away and curl up in the cool of the Time Train and wait for the others. But he would not give up, he wouldn't. If he gave up that meant he wasn't as good as these men, and he had to prove that he was. The man who had told him to get to work had disappeared, so he kept his eyes on the stoker next to him, a tall, broad fellow with an eye patch, and did what he did, matching his every action. When Eye Patch dug, he dug. When Eye Patch threw his shovelful into the stokehole, he did likewise. He and his unwitting companion worked shoulder to shoulder, desperate to make a fire break in the glowing mountain.

Even though Aidan was used to hard work this was the toughest labour he had ever known. He was gasping for breath as the heat baked his lungs. The horrible searing air didn't feel like it could sustain life. He was soon as black as pitch from head to foot and the soot stung his eyes.

He thought it would never end.

He thought he would go mad.

14 APRIL 1912
11 a.m.

Luna spent her morning exploring the spit-shine deck, breathing the cool, clean air of First Class.

The fine spring weather had brought the passengers out like bees from a hive, and the promenade resembled a high street. Suddenly, being tall for twelve had a value – Luna felt as if she could mingle undetected. She did feel very alone, though, and wished that she had some of Konstantin's bravado, or Aidan's happy-go-lucky calm.

She remembered something her father had said once, about whistling in the dark to make him feel brave. Well, she couldn't whistle, because it wasn't considered lady-like, but she began to hum, as if she didn't have a care in the world. She hummed Papa's special song, *Yesterday*, as it always made her feel closer to him. But for once, the charm didn't really work.

And then, like a lighthouse in a foggy sea, she saw a familiar face.

There was the man with the drooping mouth and the sad brown eyes that she had seen on the first day, when the *Titanic* had launched from Southampton. The man who had been saying goodbye to his family and had almost committed the greatest sin a man could commit – to cry.

She had to stop herself greeting him like an old acquaintance – and yet he did feel oddly like a friend. She stuck close to him. Following where the man went seemed to give her a purpose, a direction. She followed him to the smart cafés, to the deckchairs, even to a little church. She didn't really know what else to do.

When the sun was at its highest Luna caught a heavenly smell drifting from the upper reaches of the ship. Her rumbling stomach told her what it was.

Luncheon.

She was sure the stewards would only admit those with First Class tickets, or those who were known to the staff after four days at sea. She fell in beside the man she'd been following, in the polite crush with all the other exclusive people heading into the great atrium. If she could only engage in conversation with him as they were walking through the doors, she might just get past the stewards who were watching everyone come in.

As they jostled together in the doorway she took a desperate chance and said, 'Do you remember me, sir?' She knew, as soon as she had uttered the words, that it was hopeless. With the suit and the piled-up hair, she could have been a different person.

He looked at her closely. 'Southampton dock, the day *Titanic* launched. You handed me my hat.'

She nodded, flooded with relief. 'I did.'

'Then I owe you a debt of gratitude.' He studied her again with those sad brown eyes she remembered so well. 'You look somewhat different, if I may say so.'

'I thought you would not know me again.'

'You may have changed your clothes, *Signorina*,' he said gallantly, 'but until you can change the hue of your hair and the colour of your eyes, you will be known wherever you walk.'

Luna hated to admit when Aidan was right, but he had been correct about her colouring. The Goodhart auburn hair and green eyes were obviously noticeable. As if to prove the point at that very moment, the steward at the door stopped them with a raised white-gloved hand, and Luna knew the game was up.

But the steward actually bowed his head to the little man at her side as if he was royalty. '*Signor* Marconi, how delightful to see you again. For luncheon? Directly up the grand staircase, sir. *Bon appetit.*' He nodded in a friendly manner at Luna. 'Sir. Miss. Enjoy your meal.'

Luna did not even have time to register relief that she'd been allowed through the doors. She walked as if in a dream, head spinning.

Signor Marconi.

The Time Train had done its work. It had placed the time-thieves in the very place in the universe where there was not just a wireless radio, but its inventor, Guglielmo Marconi.

14 APRIL 1912
11.30 a.m.

Konstantin made his way to the boat deck, the upper deck where the lifeboats were held. Here, he knew he would find other people in uniform.

He took a deep breath and his clockwork heart quickened. He was at last experiencing what his brothers had felt during their adventures at sea and on the battlefield.

They'd told him their stories, eyes shining, as they sat, still uniformed and booted at the foot of his sickbed, just back from this campaign or that. They were brim-full of tales of heroism and bravery, and he'd drunk in every detail as thirstily as he'd drunk his medicine, and it probably did him more good.

Konstantin had had to make do with the tin soldiers

they'd brought him, their coats crudely painted Prussian blue, and he would march them over the terrain of his bedspread, from Knee Mountain down Shin Ridge to Foot Valley. Konstantin had longed for so many years to be a hero, like his brothers; on a passenger voyage such as this, he was only sorry that there would be little opportunity for him to be one.

Konstantin found himself on E deck, by a corridor that was so long it actually had its own street sign, saying: **SCOTLAND ROAD**. Scotland Road was actually a long iron corridor, painted white, with hand rails all the way along. He hung around for a bit, trying to blend in, until eventually an officer opened a door off the corridor and entered a room and Konstantin followed.

He found himself in a pleasant, airy lounge with couches and desks and lamps. There were several portholes to the outside that were firmly shut against the cold, so the place had a cosy feel. Konstantin glanced around the room. This must be some sort of place of recreation for officers. One man sat at a desk, writing case open in front of him, scribbling a letter, perhaps to a loved one. Another man in a corner chair plucked out a tune on a banjo. A third sat at a desk with an album of stamps, sticking in an addition to his collection. The room had a very Sunday feeling –

things were calm, and even a little dull, and not at all the action and industry that Konstantin had expected to find. Stamp collections and banjos! What would his brothers say?

Luckily Konstantin also had something to do. He got out the book he always carried with him. Not the same book all the time of course, just the one he was reading at that moment. Since books had been Konstantin's only friends for his entire childhood, when he finally got out of bed, he found he couldn't entirely leave them behind. So he drew his latest out of his pocket now and began to read. Naturally, he couldn't concentrate at all, even though the book he was reading, *The Wreck of the Titan*, was a rather good one, about a huge ship that hit an iceberg and sank. He read a whole chapter before realising he hadn't taken in a word, and had to begin again, because in fact, he wasn't really reading at all but thinking about how he could begin a conversation with one of the officers.

In the end, he didn't have to worry.

'Done!' said the young man with the stamp album, as he thumped the last stamp into place with the side of his fist and sat back. 'I say. D'you want to see?'

Konstantin closed his book and tucked it into his inside breast pocket. 'May I?'

''Course. I'm jolly proud of my collection. There aren't any other philatelists on board so you'll have to do.' But he said it in a friendly way.

'Any other... *whats?*' asked Konstantin.

'Philatelists. Stamp collectors. Good job, because I've got a few rare stamps here and no mistake. I'd have to have eyes in the back of my head, make sure no one swiped 'em.'

The young officer had only one pair of dark eyes, in the front of his head where they belonged, a shock of dark curly hair and an open, pleasant face. Konstantin leant over him as invited and looked at the album with the stamps stuck in regimented rows, their perforated edges neatly trimmed. There were all colours and types, some with pictures, such as the flowers of foreign lands, some featuring those strange disembodied heads you often see on stamps. Among them Konstantin recognised the familiar profile of Queen Victoria.

The young officer saw him looking. 'That's a Penny Black from 1840. Quite rare. Should be worth a pretty penny one day, if you'll pardon the pun. And this one,' he pointed to a red version of the same stamp, 'that's a Penny Red from 1841. They changed the colour to red because you couldn't see the black franking stamp against the black. And this,' he tapped his finger on a green-coloured stamp with a man's head on it, 'this is my pride and joy. That's a Downey Head green halfpenny from 1911.'

The date left Konstantin reeling. It was pretty odd to be shown a stamp from a date that hadn't happened yet. 'And who is that gentleman?' he asked.

The young officer tore his eyes away from his prized collection and goggled at Konstantin. 'Are you the village idiot? That's the King of England. His Majesty King George V.'

'But I thought…' stammered Konstantin, 'Victoria…'

'That was his granny. Queen Victoria died in 1901, God rest her soul.'

That was a shock. It was ridiculous to mourn for Her Majesty – they had never met – but it was still a jolt to hear that her long and illustrious reign was over. The monarch who had founded the very prize that the Butterfly Club were hoping to win, the Gabriel Medal for Communication, was now laid low in the grave.

'The old queen was succeeded by her son Edward VII,' the officer went on. 'Then *he* died, and *his* son George came to the throne in 1910. Where've you been?'

'Well, Prussia mostly,' said Konstantin with perfect truth.

'Ah, that's where the accent's from.' The young officer studied him properly for the first time. 'I haven't seen you before.'

Konstantin shrugged. 'Big ship, isn't it?'

'I'll say,' said the young man, seemingly satisfied. 'Biggest I've ever served on. Is Prussia where you saw your service?'

'I beg your pardon?' said Konstantin.

'Your officer's stripe. You've got one on your arm, which makes you a fifth officer like me. You've seen a lot of action for one so young.'

'Er… yes,' said Konstantin, cursing the uniform he'd chosen to steal. Then he had a moment of inspiration. His brothers' military record could become his. 'I served in the Prussian army.'

'Impressive,' said the young man. 'What's your name?'

Konstantin was caught off guard and couldn't think of a lie quickly enough. 'Konstantin Kass.'

'That sounds like a mouthful of broken glass. I'll just call you Stan, if that's all right.'

'Perfectly.' Konstantin quite liked his new name.

'Mine's a bit easier. I'm Harold. Harold Lowe.'

The two shook hands, which was what gentlemen did.

'I say,' said Harold Lowe. 'I'm starving. Let's go and

82

strap on the old nosebag.'

'I beg your pardon?'

'Get some scran. Some grub. Lunch.'

14 APRIL 1912
12.59 p.m.

As Luna walked into the First Class lounge with Signor Marconi, she forced herself to concentrate. She had no idea that the inventor of radio communication would actually be *on board* the *Titanic*, but now she'd found him she had to stick to him like glue, for surely the father of the wireless would know where it was on the ship. Perhaps it was in his very own cabin.

The crowd ahead began to ease as they moved up the grand staircase to the dining rooms. The stairway was breathtaking, a wooden wonder such as you might see in a great country house, carved in two twin curves meeting together on a grand landing. Luna could barely find the coordination to put one foot in front of the other, and she wasn't alone in this. A lady just in front of them, in a yellow gown the colour of an Eastern Tiger Swallowtail butterfly, stumbled on the landing and the gentleman beside her put out his hand to save her. The clock on the landing, chiming one as they passed, brought Luna back to the Butterfly Club and their mission, so she climbed the stairs determinedly, keeping pace with Marconi.

'Will you be joining your family for luncheon, *Signorina*?' asked the little man.

'Alas, no,' she said. She didn't need to play-act her sadness; she felt very alone. 'My mother is dead. And my father' – her voice did that thing that your voice does when you are going to cry, that kind of wobble that means you can't trust it any more – 'my father is on a long voyage too, far away.'

Marconi tactfully handed her a handkerchief. As she lifted it to her eyes she could see that it had the initials GM stitched into the corner in a discreet monogram. She dabbed her wet eyes and handed it back but he said, 'Keep it.' The brown eyes were kind. 'I can assure you he feels your parting as keenly as you do. I can tell you from my own heart there is no greater burden than leaving your family to travel on business.'

They had now passed into a grand dining room, all decked out in a timbered Tudor style. Large round tables were laid with snowy-white tablecloths and groaning with crystal glasses and silver cutlery and fragrant flower arrangements. Marconi strode to the grandest table of all, and found a place with his name written on a little card. There were some very expensive-looking people already sitting at the table, but there were still empty chairs, including one beside his.

'Well,' he said, 'here we must part company. This place is for the stenographer I was promised, and I expect you must go and find your own chair.'

Luna didn't know what a stenographer was but before she could ask, a steward in his smart White Star Line uniform came and spoke in Marconi's ear. Luna, pretending not to listen, looked away, but was actually listening very hard. She heard the steward say 'stenographer', 'very sorry', and 'oversight', and then 'very sorry' again.

Signor Marconi shook his head. 'This would never have happened on the *Lusitania*,' he said crossly as the steward vanished.

'What's the *Lusitania*?'

'*Lusitania* is the flagship of the Cunard Line, a rival shipping company. It left for New York three days before *Titanic*. I *knew* I should have taken it. *An oversight*, he says. *No stenographer on board*, he says. There is a ballroom, a gymnasium and an electric elevator, but a man cannot conduct his business. To be without even a secretary! *Mamma mia!*'

At that moment, Konstantin's comment came back to Luna.

You look like a secretary.

'*I* am a secretary,' she blurted.

'You *are?*'

Luna had never felt less sure. And the doubt made her reply almost a shout. 'Yes!'

Marconi narrowed his eyes. 'You seem very young,' he said thoughtfully. 'But that is not necessarily a fault in this case. Yes. Yes, I think you'll do very well. I expect you have had a good education?'

'The best,' she said. 'The one that only a fond father could give.'

She'd aimed well. She had seen him crumble on Southampton docks when he'd waved to his own daughter. His brown eyes softened just as they had then and he nodded.

'Then, Miss…'

'Goodhart. Luna Goodhart.' It occurred to her too late, as it had to Konstantin, that perhaps she should have given a false name.

'Luna,' he said, smiling a little. 'You know that *luna* means "moon" in Italian?'

'Yes,' she said. 'My father always loved space and the planets.'

'Then, Luna Goodhart, I should be happy to hire your services for the duration of the trip. If you have no other engagements?'

'None,' she said, and shook the hand he held out to her.

'Then, as my new secretary,' he said, 'this place is yours.'

He held the chair out for her, and Luna sat in it, heart thudding.

'I have a great deal to do before I reach New York,' said Marconi, settling himself beside her. 'Work of an urgent nature. I need to file a patent for a new radio, Signorina Goodhart, and with your help, I will.'

'A patent?'

'I must register my invention with a special bureau in America called the Patent Office. Before someone else does. It means it will be written down in history as my invention and all credit and profit comes to me.' He placed his snowy napkin in his lap. 'People think that science is a team sport, a collective endeavour for the betterment of mankind.'

'And it isn't?'

'Not a bit of it. Science is a race. We are all runners on the track, just as at those new-fangled Olympic Games. You only get a gold medal if you get there first.'

There was only one empty place at the table now – the expensive people were waiting for the guest of honour.

At that moment a man walked up to the table. He wore a snow-white uniform, and had a snow-white beard to match. His forearms were ringed with gilded stripes and his chest was covered in glittering medals. He stood in the remaining place, took his hat off to reveal a head of silver hair, and laid it on the table. Everyone at the table stood.

It was then that Luna realised she hadn't just made it to First Class.

She had a seat at the Captain's Table.

14 APRIL 1912
1.10 p.m.

The word 'lunch' made Konstantin's stomach rumble. He followed his new friend Officer Lowe down the corridor to the officers' mess hall – the dining room. Here he had a perfectly nice, if dull, lunch of meat, fish and potatoes, and managed to pocket an apple or two to take back to the Time Train.

Just as they had finished their main course, a fresh-faced messenger boy, even younger than Konstantin, ran into the room. 'Officer Lowe. Message for the Bridge.'

He gave Lowe a flimsy piece of paper, thin as a banknote. Lowe read it without much concern.

'What's the excitement?' asked Konstantin. 'And why would someone send a message to a bridge?'

Lowe smiled and clapped him on the shoulder. 'You

are a comedian and no mistake; you should be at the music hall. As if you didn't know that the Bridge is the commanding station of the ship, with that stripe on your arm! Oh, well…' Harold Lowe sighed and pushed himself out of the chair using his shoulders, like you do when you don't really want to get up. 'Captain won't be on the Bridge though, he'll be at lunch.' The young officer placed his hat on his head, with the badge dead-centre, and twitched his tie into place. 'Got to look smart for the captain – he likes a bit of spit and polish. Can you cover for me? I'll be back in a bit.' He looked regretfully at his place. 'Jolly annoying really. It's jam roly-poly on Sundays and of course that's the day I have to take an ice warning to the captain.'

'An *ice* warning?' Konstantin clutched *The Wreck of the Titan* in his breast pocket, feeling its corners beneath the heavy felt. 'An ice warning sounds serious.'

'Not really. We've had one already today and it's only lunchtime. The cap doesn't set much store by these new-fangled wirelesses. He's crossed the Atlantic more times than a shuttle in a loom, without radio comms. He mostly just ignores 'em.'

Konstantin frowned a little. 'Is that safe?'

'Captain's had fifty years at sea. I've had five. So do I trust him? Yes.'

Konstantin felt relief in his chest, just underneath the book. What a mercy there was nothing to worry about! But his own mission came to mind and he thought he might be able to get some information from this cheery young officer. 'Who gives the ice warnings?'

'Sometimes the fellows from the Watch, but if they see an iceberg, that's not ideal because that means we're right on top of it. This one,' he waved the paper in his hand, 'came from another ship which is further ahead than us. They send messages to us if they see ice. This one, see, is from a ship called the *Baltic*. Look – it says at the top – Marconigram. That means the Marconi Room received the message.'

Konstantin's ears pricked up. 'Marconi Room?'

'Yes. They've got the latest wireless radio in there. Get messages for the passengers mostly. And sometimes safety warnings like this one.'

Konstantin nodded, trying to seem only mildly interested. 'Have you been in there?' he asked casually.

'Not I. It's about as big as a latrine. There are two operators and they're the only ones who can fit in there, I should think.'

'Do you know where it is?'

'Not a clue. The ops always send runners with the

messages. Look here, I've got to get going or I'll catch it from my superiors. Will you hold the fort or not? I need to take this upstairs.' He waved the piece of paper again.

'Of course. What do I need to do?'

'Get hold of some binoculars and take them to the boys on the Watch. If there is ice out there tonight, it would be as well to know where it is with as much notice as possible.'

Konstantin knew what binoculars were. He had been to the opera in Vienna with his father, when he was first able to go out of the house. He'd been given a pair of opera glasses, two tiny brass telescopes mounted side by side in order to better see the stage, and binoculars were just like that. 'Binoculars,' he said, trying to sound knowledgeable. 'Right. Who has them?'

'Ask Chief Officer Wilde. He should have the key to the cabinet where they are kept.'

'Chief Officer Wilde,' Konstantin repeated. 'Got it.'

Lowe hurried out of the dining room, leaving Konstantin alone at the table. But Konstantin no longer felt like he didn't belong. He had a Mission. And to fortify himself for the perils ahead, he felt it was only wise to eat Harold Lowe's jam roly-poly.

14 APRIL 1912
1.15 p.m.

All the diners at the captain's table, including Luna, stood and clapped for their guest of honour. The captain nodded at the company, raised his glass and said, 'May God bless *Titanic* on her maiden voyage. Her first and my last.'

All the diners raised their glasses and repeated the toast. Whatever was in the glasses was bubbly – it tickled Luna's nose and tasted a bit like medicine.

The captain sat down, and as everyone took their places the lady to the captain's right leant as close to him as her enormous hat would allow. 'It that really true, Captain Smith? Is this your last voyage?'

The captain smiled a little sadly. 'Yes, this is my last voyage before retirement. I'm sixty-two years of age, madam. I've spent most of those years at sea, and have only seven days westward to New York remaining.'

'That lady is Mrs Edith Rosenbaum Russell,' said Mr Marconi helpfully, out of the side of his mouth. 'A journalist of some note.'

Luna studied the lady. She seemed to be happy to ask questions, and state her opinions, even in the company of the captain of the ship.

'Moreover,' said the captain, 'in all of those years I never saw a wreck and never have been wrecked, nor was I ever in any predicament that threatened to end in disaster of any sort.'

'How disappointing,' joked the lady gently. 'I speak as a writer, of course. Disaster is my meat and drink.'

Everyone laughed, and Luna felt a creeping admiration for Mrs Russell. Not only was she talkative, she was funny too.

'Then you and I are opposites, madam,' said the captain. 'I desire nothing less. You see, I am not very good material for one of your stories.'

'And that,' said the gentleman to the captain's left, 'is why we asked Captain Edward Smith to helm the *Titanic*. He is a celebrity in himself – "the millionaire's captain", they call him. There is no better man for the task.'

'That is Mr Bruce Ismay,' said Signor Marconi in Luna's ear. 'He is the owner of the White Star Line. *Titanic* is his ship.'

Luna looked at the man, with his smooth dark hair and impressive black moustaches, and imagined being as rich as that.

'And yet, chance played her part in my being here,' said Captain Smith. 'I was to take the helm of *Titanic*'s sister ship, the *Olympic* – but she had a collision, bringing forward the sail date of *Titanic*. So here I am.'

'Well, the *Olympic*'s loss is *Titanic*'s gain,' said a gentleman in a blue serge suit gallantly. 'We hope you will enjoy this little lunch we have thrown in your honour, Captain.' The man spoke a little like the phantom professor, with an American twang.

The captain inclined his head. 'I hope so too,' he joked. 'I cancelled a lifeboat drill to be here.'

As everyone else laughed at what must be a joke, Luna swallowed nervously. She was not at all sure that *she* would enjoy the meal. She did her best with each fanciful dish that was placed in front of her but fear had robbed her of her appetite, so she ate a little and listened a lot.

The talk was all of the ship.

'Comfort,' declared Mr Ismay. 'Comfort is our watchword on the *Titanic*. Here at the White Star we have built a floating palace with cabins fit for the richest people in the world.'

Everyone laughed – Luna supposed that was a rich-person joke so she laughed too.

'But *Titanic* has room for those less fortunate too,' said Mr Ismay. 'There are 709 passengers in Third Class Steerage with a one-way ticket. They are all hoping for a better life in America.'

Luna listened with interest. Why would anyone want to go to America? How could it be a better life? Was Britain not the greatest nation in the world? That was what the Butterfly Club seemed to claim. And if that was the case, surely everyone wanted to stay there?

'Of course Third Class passengers aren't allowed to mix with First Class passengers for… ahem… health reasons.' Mr Ismay lowered his voice. 'Third Class passengers are thoroughly checked for lice before boarding.'

Luna thought of Aidan. Of course, that grin of his was insolent, and his manners were non-existent, but she would never dream of calling him pest-ridden.

'You must have a deal of lifeboats for all those passengers, Mr Ismay,' said Mrs Edith Russell, the journalist.

'Sufficient, sufficient,' said Mr Ismay breezily. 'We

have twenty lifeboats – enough for fifty-two per cent of the passengers.'

Mrs Russell frowned a little. 'Is that enough?'

'My dear Mrs Russell. We don't even need *one*. The ship is unsinkable.'

'Oh?' That lady's eyebrows rose so far they were almost lost in her hat, as if she sensed a story. 'How so, Mr Ismay?'

He looked left and right comically. 'Madam, I suppose you are not working as a secret spy for the Cunard Line?' Everyone laughed again, and Mr Ismay lowered his voice once more, and all the guests at table, including Luna, leant in. 'In the very bowels of this ship, where our engineers toil, there is hidden a great secret of engineering which our rivals at Cunard would shed blood to know. So I will say no more than this: on my honour – and I hold my honour as dear as my life – this ship *cannot sink*.' He sat back in his chair, his voice returning to its normal volume. 'So the number of lifeboats is immaterial. Their purpose is merely to ferry passengers to a rescue vessel, in the unlikely event that our power fails.' He took a self-satisfied sip of his wine. 'Think not of shipwrecks – think only that you are making history. You are travelling on the largest man-made moving object on earth. And the fastest ocean liner in the world too.'

Now Marconi addressed the company for the first time. 'I thought the *Lusitania* was the fastest,' he said drily.

Mr Bruce Ismay looked put out for perhaps a second, then his manners varnished his face with a polite expression. 'Perhaps the *Lusitania* has had the edge in terms of speed in the past,' he said. 'But we are confident that the *Titanic*'s maiden crossing to New York will be the fastest in history. *Lusitania* may have three days' start. But we are closing the gap by the hour.' He spoke to the table at large. 'But the *Titanic* has so much more to recommend it. Our radio communications for example.' He nodded in Luna's direction. 'You'd know about that, Signor Marconi. Think of it, ladies. Mr Marconi's systems can gather messages from the ether from all over the world, all collected in a tiny Marconi Room no bigger than a broom cupboard.'

'It has no need to be bigger,' said Signor Marconi. 'Eventually such technology will fit in the palm of a man's hand.'

The diners laughed at such a ridiculous notion. Luna would have done so herself a few days ago. But after having talked to Aidan she was not so sure that such ideas were as ridiculous as they sounded.

'Of course, my wirelesses have an important safety

function too,' put in Signor Marconi.

'Well,' said Ismay, 'happily that won't be needed.'

Just as he said this a young officer, with dark curls and a pleasant face, came to stand at Captain Smith's shoulder until he was noticed. When the captain turned his head, the officer sprang forward and presented him with a piece of white paper, as flimsy as a banknote. The captain read the message, his forehead gathering into a frown.

'Any instruction, Captain?' said the officer.

'Not at this time.'

The officer, looking slightly surprised, hovered for an instant.

'I *said*,' said the captain, with a certain emphasis, 'that will be *all*, Officer Lowe.'

The officer stood up very straight and saluted. 'Aye aye, sir,' he said, and melted away.

'Speaking of messages,' said Mrs Edith Russell in a prying way. 'Not bad news I hope?' She seemed to want to be in everyone's business, but Luna imagined that was just the attitude you needed to be a reporter.

The captain looked up and his face cleared, as if a storm cloud had passed. 'No no, not at all,' he said, and smiled. 'Nothing of consequence. Merely a message from another ship.' He passed the note to Mr Ismay, who read it and glanced at the captain. Then the owner of the *Titanic* gave a tiny shake of his head, crumpled the piece of paper and put it in his pocket.

Luna barely noticed this little pantomime. She was busy thinking about the crucial bit of information that she had just learned. The radio clearly wasn't in Marconi's cabin, but had its own dedicated room 'no bigger than a broom cupboard'.

Marconi spoke again. 'Well,' he said, 'so long as you get me to New York in time to file my patent, my newest radio will broadcast your ship's supremacy to the four corners of the globe.'

Mr Ismay's eyes seemed to light up at this. 'If it's speed you want, I'll show you what *Titanic* can do. We have more capacity in the engines, do we not, Captain?'

'A little,' said Captain Smith somewhat cautiously. 'But we are entering the icefields of the North Atlantic so we must have a care.'

'Ever the cautious seafarer,' laughed Ismay. 'But you must allow me to overrule you just this once. Let us move to full power and see what *Titanic* can do. We'll get you to New York in no time, Mr Marconi.' Ismay took another sip of his wine. 'Mark my words, *Titanic* will be remembered long after the *Lusitania* is forgot.' He put down his glass and addressed the whole table. '*Titanic* is more than a ship. *Titanic* is an *idea. Titanic* is a *feeling*. Britannia rules the waves – always has and always will.'

At this moving little speech the diners actually burst into spontaneous applause – all except Signor Marconi, who rose from the table.

'Miss Luna. May I ask you to join me in my cabin? We must begin our work.' He thanked his hosts very graciously, and paid his respects to the captain and Mr Ismay – but as Luna got up and followed him from the dining room she got the distinct impression that Guglielmo Marconi did not agree with Mr Ismay's patriotic speech one little bit.

14 APRIL 1912
1.30 p.m.

After four hours at the fireholes, the freezing wind on the lower deck was the loveliest thing Aidan had ever known.

At the end of the morning shift, the stoker with the eye patch had tapped him on the shoulder and led him away from the hellish fireholes into the fresh air.

Aidan tilted his face into the weak spring sun and drank the frigid air right down into his burning lungs. He looked across at his companion. He made an unlikely friend, but, to be honest, Aidan would have followed the Devil himself if he'd shown him the way out of that hellhole. Oddly, the first thing the man with the eye patch did was to light up a cigarette as he leant on the white railings. He offered the pack to Aidan. 'Want one?'

Aidan couldn't imagine anything worse. Lots of navvies smoked, even boys his age, but he couldn't imagine anything he wanted less, right at that moment, than more fire in his burning lungs. The man tucked the pack away. 'You did well in there, considering. Your first day on the Black Gang. No need to explain why we're called that.' He held out a hand that was black with coal. 'Arthur John Priest,' he said.

Aidan shook the grimy hand with his own grimy hand. 'Aidan O'Connell. And thanks.'

Aidan studied his new companion. Arthur John Priest was broad and tall, with a blunted face – his nose looked as if it had been broken at least once, his forehead was bony and his jaw heavy. But the most notable thing about him was his eye patch. Aidan was far too used to eye patches to comment – many navvies he'd known had lost an eye to a rogue spark flying out of an engine, and most couldn't afford to get a glass eye fitted by the barber surgeons who charged a fortune for such things. Some navvies actually fitted a penny coin in the socket, and most peculiar it was, having Queen Victoria's copper head staring at you in place of an eye. But some wore a patch instead, like his new friend who stood beside him, smoking contentedly, seemingly not much inclined to talk. Aidan felt himself staring and turned to lean on the white railing, already covered in frost. He looked down at the churning pewter water behind the propellers. It looked blessedly cold.

'I could just jump in,' he said, breaking the silence.

'Believe me,' said the man, 'sometimes that happens.'

'It does?' said Aidan in surprise. He'd been joking.

'They call it the Fire Insanity. The chaps can't bear it any more and break down. The heat, you see – it cooks your brain. Some fellows run up here screaming and just jump in.'

Aidan could well believe it, after what he'd experienced. He'd only had to do one shift, but he imagined doing that day and night, for the whole of the ten-day voyage. It was unthinkable.

He shook his head. 'Why do they do it?'

'Why do you do it?' said the man bluntly. 'Why do I? Wages. Money. The Working Class can't sit up there smoking cigars like the *quality*.'

He jabbed his thumb upwards, indicating the passengers way above them in First Class. Aidan sensed the way he said *quality* meant just the opposite.

He thought about this. He'd seen the term 'Working Class' on banners on miners' marches, or on political posters, and heard his father say it to his mates in the pub after a hard day. He'd never thought much about the Working Class before, except for the fact that he was part of it. But the term had never meant more to him than now, after the hardest four hours of his life. For the first time, he began to resent the men on the upper decks with their cigars.

'Some of the boys are working their passage to get to America. Start again. So they don't have to shovel coal in the arse of a ship for every day of their lives.' He threw his cigarette into the sea. 'The ones that don't end up in the ocean, that is.'

Aidan watched the glowing cigarette fall and thought of the men that jumped in. 'How do they get rescued? The ones that jump, I mean?'

The man laughed, a humourless sound. 'They don't. Turn a ship around for a working man? Not worth the inconvenience.' He picked a strand of tobacco from between yellow teeth. 'No, if you jump in that water it would be the last thing you ever did. You'd freeze to death in about five minutes, anyway. We're getting into the icefields now.' He turned his back on the water. 'That's why it would be madness to speed up, but Mr Ismay just sent word that that's exactly what we are to do.'

Aidan frowned. 'Who is Mr Ismay?'

'You *are* wet behind the ears and no mistake,' said his companion. 'Mr Bruce Ismay, the owner of the White Star Line. Probably had one too many brandies at lunch, and now he wants *Titanic* to speed up so she can beat the *Lusitania* to New York. He wants the headlines.'

'Headlines?'

'In the newspapers. We've had "*Titanic*: Unsinkable". We've had "*Titanic*: Biggest Man-made Object On Earth".'

Aidan thought that something in the way he said the words sort of sounded like he was using capitals, the kind of black-letter characters that shouted from the newsstands.

'Now he wants "*Titanic*: Fastest Ship In The World".'

'Why?'

'It's all about the chinks.' The stoker rubbed his filthy finger tips together. 'The money. And the pride too. I'll bet you sixpence that one of the hoity-toity passengers told Ismay they were in a hurry to get to New York, and he made a promise he can't keep. The curse of this nation, pride. Britannia rules the waves.' He spat precisely into the ocean.

Aidan watched the oyster of spit become one with the waves. 'Is she really unsinkable? *Titanic*, I mean?'

'So they say.'

Aidan looked back along the bow at the massive bulk of

the ship. It was indeed a floating city. Sure, it looked sturdy enough, invincible even. But still, 'unsinkable' was quite a claim to make. 'How come?'

Arthur John Priest shoved himself away from the railing and jerked his head in invitation. 'Come on, let's get back to work. But if you do as good a job as you did this morning, after the next shift I'll show you *Titanic*'s Big Secret.'

14 APRIL 1912
1.30 p.m.

Konstantin thought that finding a pair of binoculars was not exactly like finding the Holy Grail or a fearsome dragon, which was the kind of mission that faced the heroes of his books. It did, however, give him the opportunity to pretty much go anywhere on the boat deck that he pleased, and if anyone asked him what the Devil he thought he was doing – which they did, quite often – he could just say, with perfect truth, that he was looking for Chief Officer Wilde and the key to the binoculars.

Eventually he tracked down Wilde to the Bridge, which, as Lowe had told him, was the navigational heart of the ship. The Bridge housed the ship's wheel and all of the other instruments: compasses and binnacles and charts and lots of other exciting things Konstantin didn't really have time to take in. He expected to see the captain at the wheel, like you did in books, but it seemed to be staffed by junior navigators, with a tall officer supervising.

'I'm Officer Wilde,' said the tall man in answer to Konstantin's enquiry. 'What can I do for you, Officer…?'

'Stan,' said Konstantin quickly. 'They call me Stan.'

'Well, what is it, Stan? Spit it out, lad.'

'If you please, sir,' said Konstantin, who had no idea how to speak to high-ranking naval officers, and just settled for speaking as he would to a priest or a school master, 'Officer Lowe asks you to kindly surrender the key to the binocular cabinet, so as I can give a pair to the Watch.'

'Ah,' said Wilde, rubbing the side of his long nose with his index finger. 'Now, I'm afraid, young fellow, there's a slight problem with that.' He steered Konstantin towards the door. 'Take a walk with me, son.'

They stepped out on to the freezing deck and Wilde began to walk briskly, with his hands clasped behind his back. Konstantin sensed that whatever the issue was, Officer Wilde didn't want the navigators to know about it.

'The fact is, the key to the binocular cabinet is in the possession of an officer called David Blair.'

'And where is Officer Blair, sir?'

'Well, not to put too fine a point on it, he's in Southampton.'

Konstantin stopped walking. 'He is?'

'Yes.' Officer Wilde stopped too, and pulled up the collar of his greatcoat against the cold. 'You see, Blair *was* to be the Chief Officer on the *Titanic*. I was Chief Officer of the *Olympic*, *Titanic*'s sister ship, but *Olympic* had an… an accident, and it was decided that I, as the more experienced officer, should take Blair's place on the *Titanic* for her maiden voyage. So we swapped.' He didn't say this boastfully, just in a matter-of-fact way.

'So did Blair take the key deliberately?' breathed Konstantin. 'As a sort of… revenge?'

It was possible that Konstantin had read too many spy books, because Wilde looked a little shocked.

'Good God, no, boy! A man who would deliberately deprive his own ship of binoculars would be a monster. No, it was an oversight. I just didn't want the men in the Bridge to know there'd been a foul-up, however small. Confidence in the voyage is key, you see. No, David Blair is a good man, one of the best. And he deserves our pity rather than our censure.'

'Pity?' said Konstantin. 'Why?'

Officer Wilde looked at him very directly. 'Because, my

111

lad, he is the unluckiest blighter in the Empire. He missed the *Titanic*.' He clapped Konstantin on the shoulder. 'You and I, lad, we're the lucky ones.'

Konstantin suddenly felt a sense of pride in his clockwork heart. He suddenly wanted to do his pretend job as well as he possibly could. He didn't want anything to happen to this ship. 'So we *don't* have binoculars?' he clarified.

'We have binoculars all right. But we don't have the key to the cabinet. So we can't get to them. No matter. I'll just have to buy some in New York.'

'If you'll forgive me, sir, this cabinet… Could it not be forced open?'

'I should think not. Otherwise, the security on this ship would leave a great deal to be desired. And you look too well-bred to be a pick lock to me.' The officer smiled. 'Besides, I think such an action would be a little excessive. Such a small thing as a missing pair of binoculars cannot trouble the progress of a vast ship like *Titanic*.'

Something about this speech, about small things having big consequences, seemed familiar to Konstantin. Then he remembered – Professor Lorenz and his Butterfly Effect. He got a sudden shiver; not of cold, but of foreboding. 'But sir, Officer Lowe just received an ice warning from the Marconi Room. He's taken it up to the captain.'

'Well, they come in all the time. I'm sure our Watch can see an iceberg by daylight.'

Konstantin had an idea. 'Perhaps, if there are no binoculars, I should inform the Marconi Room? If you could just remind me where that is?'

'Never mind the Marconi Room, boy,' said Wilde. 'Hop up to the crow's nest and inform the Watch of the ice warning, just in case.'

'And… if you'd be so kind… sir, could you just tell me please where I might find the crow's nest?'

'Good gracious boy, haven't you been on shipboard before?' Officer Wilde sighed and turned Konstantin around by the shoulders. He pointed way over Konstantin's head, impossibly high above the deck, where, fixed to the top of the mast, was an enclosed white platform that looked no bigger than a good-sized beer barrel. 'Up *there*.'

14 APRIL 1912
2 p.m.

Konstantin found a small door at the foot of the mast and entered to find an iron ladder inside. Climbing for what seemed like an age, he emerged into the dazzling sunshine at the top of the world. The only thing above him was a searing blue sky slashed with the ropes and cables of the mast. Two men in White Star uniforms but huddled in mufflers and gloves regarded him with curiosity.

Feebly catching his breath, he gasped, 'Are you the Watch?' to the taller of the two.

'At your service, sir,' said the first man. 'I'm Frederick Fleet and he's Reginald Lee. Are you the officer with the key for the binocular cabinet?' he asked in his turn.

'No, I'm afraid not. I have a message from Chief Officer Wilde. The key stayed in Southampton with David

Blair, the man he replaced.'

'Ah,' said Frederick, and sucked at his teeth. He slapped a metal cabinet that was fixed to the mast with the flat of his hand. 'They'll just have to stay in there then.'

'Is that where they're kept?' asked Konstantin.

'So near and yet so far, eh?' said Reginald poetically. 'No matter. We can see pretty well with the naked eye. It's what we're trained to do. We just scan the horizon and see what's what.'

It was then that Konstantin made the mistake of looking out to sea. The view, so bright and vivid, even this late in the afternoon, was suddenly too big – from this height the horizon seemed to curve and surround him, the colours of the sunset weighing him down.

'Bit of a silencer, isn't it?' said Frederick.

Konstantin felt sick and his vison began to blur – he felt he would fall, not just to this tiny platform, but all the way down to the deck.

'Steady,' said Frederick, laying a firm hand on his arm. 'It takes us all that way the first time. Trick is, don't try to take it all in. Break it into bits. Look at details.'

Konstantin took his advice. He didn't look at the deck, which made him feel sick, but instead fixed his eyes on a pied gull, who bent his wings and dipped towards the waves. Below him, through the green-blue translucent water, he saw a shoal of shifting silver fishes, and below them, the enormous dark bruise of a whale.

Konstantin started to smile.

'Ah yes, you get me now,' said Frederick, smiling too. 'Now you see the wonder of it.'

Konstantin looked at the young man with gratitude. 'So you'll be all right without the binoculars?'

'Have to be, won't we?' said Frederick. 'Weather doesn't help though. It's very calm, which is a bit of a worry.'

'Why is that a problem?' asked Konstantin. He would have thought a calm sea would be a gift.

'You don't really look for the bergs themselves but the waves breaking at the base,' explained Reginald. 'Flat calms mean you can't see any waves.'

Konstantin must have looked worried, because Frederick said comfortingly, 'Don't worry. Reggie and I have been at this a while. All's well. You get down now sir, before you fall down.'

Konstantin took himself off down the ladder again and as his feet hit the planks of the boat deck he felt absurdly grateful, not just because he was on firm ground but because there were good men like Frederick and Reginald watching the horizon every second of every day to keep the passengers safe. Konstantin had learned some things of interest but he was no nearer finding the radio. He could only hope that Aidan and Luna were doing a little better.

14 APRIL 1912
3 p.m.

Working as Signor Marconi's stenographer made that afternoon one of the most demanding of Luna's short life.

She didn't have time to think of how Aidan and Konstantin were getting on, about the Butterfly Club, or the radio. She even forgot about Papa for the first time since he'd gone.

She sat in Marconi's study, part of a suite of rooms that made up his First Class cabin. It was like being in the nicest living room you could imagine, with chandeliers, and overstuffed armchairs, and walnut panelling, but Luna didn't even have a moment to appreciate the loveliness of the room. Her world had shrunk down to the small mahogany table and the black machine under her hands.

It looked a little like a typewriter, but the lettered keys were spread out and skinny like a spider's legs.

'This is a stenograph,' said Signor Marconi. 'It is a small portable typing machine with different keys for each hand. The left hand types the beginning of a word, and the right hand the end.' He seated himself in the chair opposite. 'I will speak slowly at first and you simply enter what I say. It is just like dictation, and I imagine in your secretarial apprenticeship you have become well used to that?'

She ducked her head, somehow thinking that a nod was better than a lie.

'The words are transferred to this ream of paper.' He indicated a roll at the back of the machine.

Luna looked at the arrangement of letters on the keys, the consonants on the left, vowels on the right. She had a moment of panic, as if she had never seen letters before.

Marconi leant forward in his chair. 'Now, *cara mia*, my dear. These are *secrets* that I tell here. Industrial secrets. And that is why, while I am sure there are other secretaries aboard, competent men much older than you, I think you will suit very well. For, to tell you the truth, there are those who would seek to take my intellectual property away from me.' Luna must have looked confused because he explained. 'Steal my ideas.'

Luna swallowed. Marconi could hardly have chosen worse than to employ her, unless he'd picked Konstantin or Aidan, if he didn't want someone to steal his ideas. Of all the passengers on the *Titanic* there were only three people planning to do exactly that, and she was one of them.

'Now,' he said, 'are you ready?'

She took a deep breath, as if she was about to dive off the side of the ship. 'Yes.'

In the course of the afternoon, she learned more about the science behind the wireless radio than she ever thought there was to know, and if possible, understood less than before. As she typed down Marconi's words she could have been writing in a new language – a language of condensers and dischargers and tuning lamps and wires and switches and aerial pillars and magnetic keys and variable coupling jiggers and dynamo flexes. A whole world opened up to her that she'd never conceived of – a way to communicate across oceans, across continents.

In the middle of the afternoon – since *Titanic* was, after all, a British ship – tea arrived, and Luna felt able to start a conversation. '*Signor* Marconi?'

'My dear?'

'Is this radio I'm writing about like the radios in the Marconi Room on this ship?'

'No. This is the next stage. This is a "timed spark" radio, which will be able to generate continuous radio waves, instead of the stop-start transmissions we have now. One day a person will be able to talk to another person on the other side of the world. But like most developments in the evolution of science, there are others working in the same field. I *must* patent my idea *first*.' He looked at her. 'Speaking of evolution, did you ever hear of Mr Wallace? Mr Alfred Wallace?'

She shook her head. 'No.'

'No,' said Marconi, 'no one has. That is his tragedy.' He looked at her closely. 'How about Mr Darwin. Mr Charles Darwin?'

'Of course!' she said, eager to show her knowledge. *Everyone* had heard of Mr Charles Darwin. 'He went on the Voyage of the Beagle and wrote a book called *On the Origin of Species.*'

'Well, Mr Wallace came up with the idea of the origin of species before Mr Darwin did. His mistake was to publish his theory *after* Darwin. And that's why today we talk about Darwinism and not Wallaceism.' He sniffed.

'I'm not about to make the same mistake.'

'Mr Marconi?'

'*Cara mia*?'

'Who is *your* Alfred Wallace?'

He smiled and the sad eyes lifted. 'An excellent question,' he said. 'A Mr Tesla. Mr Nikola Tesla.'

'And has Mr Tesla had this idea yet? For the timed spark?'

'I don't know. He has so far concerned himself more with the field of electricity, if you'll pardon the pun.'

Luna hadn't noticed a pun, but kept quiet.

'But he may be close. For the moment, I am a little ahead of Mr Tesla in the field of radiographic telecommunication, since there are Marconi Rooms on all of the White Star ships.' He sat back in his chair. 'If we have leisure tomorrow, I will take you to the Marconi Room and show you.'

Luna was so excited by this prospect that she felt it must have shown in her eyes, a flame leaping like when she turned up the gas lamps at home. So she said, as casually as she could, 'If it wouldn't be an inconvenience.'

'Not at all. I am very gratified that you are interested in my work. You remind me very much of Degna.'

'Degna?'

The brown eyes softened again. 'My daughter.'

The girl on the dock in the butterfly-bright dress, the colour of a Red Admiral.

'I can picture her now,' he said fondly. 'We took a lovely little white cottage on the cliffs above Southampton next to the church, with yellow roses growing about the door. When the weather was clement she would sit on the doorstep and play with the toys I made for her. She is always so interested in my work, and always likes to know about the science behind it.'

Luna warmed to him even more, for the love he felt for his daughter.

'Why did your father name you Luna?' He sounded interested.

'My father loves the Royal Observatory. We used to live in Greenwich, where it is situated.' She smiled fondly. 'He has an obsession.'

Marconi smiled too. 'An obsession is no bad thing. It is common to all scientists. And in this case, no one could blame him. The Royal Greenwich Observatory is the home of time. And space. I would love to visit it one day.'

'I hope you shall,' said Luna.

'I too.'

'Perhaps if you ever visit London, *Signor*.' She suddenly

missed home terribly.

'Oh, I have been to London,' said Marconi. 'I was there in the winter of 1894.'

'Really?'

'Yes. I have very fond memories of the visit, because I was doing one of my earliest experiments in radio telegraphy. On January the 15th, 1894, from the Post Office headquarters in Carter Lane, near St Paul's.'

Luna was struck by the coincidence. That was the exact day they had left London. How odd to think that Signor Marconi was beginning his scientific journey the day they had begun their journey to the future. She must have been lost in a daydream of time and space for some moments, because Signor Marconi was obliged to say, 'Shall we continue?'

Day had turned to twilight before Marconi looked out of the porthole and said, '*Mamma mia*, it grows dark already. I must release you to your dinner. Shall we resume tomorrow? Nine o'clock sharp? I will instruct the purser to pay your wages.' He rose. 'Take the papers with you.'

Luna stood too and flexed all of her fingers. They were stiff and tired and her back was aching from sitting so long. She folded the transcript carefully into her jacket pocket and took her leave, promising to return the next day. She'd learned some very useful things, and had so much to tell Konstantin and Aidan. She wondered how they were getting on.

14 APRIL 1912
8.30 p.m.

Aidan stood in the middle of a huge echoing iron room, lit by yellow sodium lamps.

'There.' Arthur John Priest's own voice mocked him eerily as he threw out his arms to show Aidan where they were.

After their second back-breaking shift, Aidan had followed his one-eyed friend through a network of tunnels here, to the very heart of the ship. He was hotter and tireder than he had ever been, but the desire to know the unique secret of the *Titanic* powered him along like an engine.

But when he looked about him he could see nothing in the room except themselves. The room was as big as his whole house in Ireland, and must have been two floors high. It was bounded in iron bars and rivets as big as fists. The fourth wall was missing, and Arthur John Priest pointed upwards with his blackened hand. 'That's the door.' An enormous iron panel, big as a church door, was winched up on tracks and rollers, ready to descend and shut off the room completely.

'There's a lever that closes the chamber. Once the mechanism is activated it can't be stopped. And once the door is closed it can't be opened again.'

Arthur John Priest slapped one of the iron walls with his hand and the room began to ring like a bell, a threatening, low metallic chime echoing round and round them, getting louder and more menacing. Aidan began to feel dizzy. The idea of being trapped in this room, a vast metal coffin, made him sweat.

'There are fifteen of these watertight chambers altogether,' said his companion, 'subdivisions of the hull, along the port and starboard sides of the ship.'

It seemed very strange to Aidan that a ship, even a ship of *Titanic*'s size, should have so many of these huge bare empty iron rooms, with no furniture, or storage, or even passengers.

'What are they meant for?' he asked. 'I mean, what's meant to go *in* them?'

'Nothing,' said Arthur John Priest. 'Nothing at all. That's precisely the point.'

'I don't understand.' Aidan took a few steps into the room and turned all the way around, looking at the bare iron walls.

'Say the *Titanic* has some sort of collision,' said Arthur John Priest, 'and it punches a hole in the hull. The *Titanic* starts taking on water and we all go down. Right?'

Aidan shrugged. 'Right.'

'Wrong. If the *Titanic* starts taking on water, according to which side she's been hit, the captain will order some of these chambers to be closed. They're completely watertight. So because there will be a good few rooms full of fresh air, the ship will still float.' Arthur John Priest walked over to Aidan, his footsteps sounding on the iron floor. 'So that's it. Now you know. That's the hush-hush system the White Star Line don't want the Cunard Line to know, in case they steal the idea. That's why Mr Bruce Fancypants Ismay thinks *Titanic* is unsinkable.'

Aidan caught the odd tone of his voice. 'And you *don't* think so?'

'Only time will tell, won't it?' said the stoker. 'All I know is that this is the big secret that *Titanic* holds in her heart. And we've all got secrets, haven't we, *boy*?'

He peered closely at Aidan as he said this, so closely that Aidan felt that his single eye, eerily black like a shark's due to the dim of the chamber, was peering into his very soul. And then, as if the single eye was not sufficient for the soul-peering, Arthur John Priest raised his hand to his eye patch and peeled it off.

Aidan's mouth dropped open, as he could not quite believe what was behind the patch.

It was a pocket watch, round and perfect, and small enough to fit exactly into the empty eye socket.

Aidan stared, wide-eyed himself. The thing had a brass surround, a casing of bright convex glass, and tiny hands as black and glossy as streaks of ink, showing 4.45 as the hour. The watch was very much like the one he'd had to take apart and put together again before he could join his father out on the railways and follow those tracks wherever they took them. Aidan's mind did that trick that it did whenever he looked at a machine. It could see through the surface layers into the workings behind, and he could picture every cog that made up the watch – pistons as tiny as hatter's pins and cogs the size of a ladybird. He guessed the watch dated from his own time, 1894. It even had the maker's mark, *Ruebens & Son Liverpool*, in tiny fairy writing across the face.

'I wear the patch when I'm working at the stoke-holes but this thing still heats up like a coin in a stove,' said Arthur John Priest. 'Gives me a headache.' He tapped the watch, and it was so odd to hear the dirty fingernail connect with the glass, as if someone was touching the front of their eye.

Aidan continued to stare – he couldn't help himself. The second hand, thin as a hair, seemed to be still, so the time, according to Arthur John Priest's eye, would be 4.45 for ever. Of course it was stopped, how could it work – how would you wind such a thing? Aidan blinked but could not look away. He had seen timepieces a hundred, a thousand times, but never set into a man's *head*. 'Why d'you have a watch in your eye?'

'I'll tell you that if you'll tell me another,' said the stoker. 'Why've you got a Starley skip-link bicycle chain from the 1890s holding up your trousers?'

Aidan was stumped. It should have occurred to him that among his people, the engineers, he would be bound to meet someone else who spoke Machine. He hesitated for a few seconds, searching the workings of his own brain for an answer. 'It was my father's. He… er… loved his old bicycle and when it broke he gave the chain to me.'

'Oh, yes?' Arthur John Priest looked at Aidan again,

this time with the combined gaze of the shark's eye and the watch. Aidan took a step backwards, fear striking his heart like a bell.

Then the stoker broke his gaze and laughed. 'Well, that coal's not going to shovel itself. See you back in Hell, boy.'

Suddenly Aidan was alone in the iron chamber. He stayed rooted to the spot, unable to move even if he wanted to. In spite of the heat of the place he felt icy cold. He never wanted to return to the hellish stoke-holes anyway, but now he knew he could not.

He'd been found out.

Finding his feet at last he hurried back to the Time Train, all the while with the uncomfortable feeling that Arthur John Priest knew *exactly* where he'd come from.

14 APRIL 1912
9 p.m.

As it turned out, Aidan was the first one back at the Time Train.

He didn't have long to wait, but at every moment he thought that a grimy hand would lift the tarpaulin, and a grimy face would peer in at him; a face with a watch for an eye. To his immense relief, the hand that did lift the tarpaulin was pale and clean and belonged to Konstantin, and, a little later, Luna joined them too. He'd never been so pleased to see two people in his life. He could have hugged them both. 'Am I glad to see you!'

The time-thieves huddled together and they all shared their particular version of the 14th of April 1912.

Luna told the boys about church, lunch at the Captain's Table and her new job working for – wonder of wonders – Signor Marconi himself. Konstantin told them about Harold Lowe and his stamps, and the muddle with the binoculars, and the glorious, terrifying view from the crow's nest. Then it was Aidan's turn to recount his adventures in the fiery belly of the ship, with the stokers who were literally powering their way to America.

As close as they were, they all kept something back from their encounters. Luna didn't want to share with Aidan the offhand way Mr Ismay had spoken about Third Class passengers, and the smart ladies in the hats laughing behind their hands about the tests for lice. Konstantin didn't share what Frederick Fleet had said – that something so small as the lack of binoculars might actually put the ship in danger. And Aidan did not speak of his strange acquaintance Arthur John Priest, the man with a watch for an eye, because he felt that if he did that he would have to share the possibility that Arthur John Priest might have guessed his secret.

'There's one thing I don't understand,' said Luna. 'Those stokers trying to get to America. Mr Ismay said that too. That there are 709 Third Class steerage passengers with a one-way ticket.'

'What don't you understand?' asked Aidan quietly.

'Well,' said Luna. 'No offence to you, Konstantin, I'm

sure Prussia's lovely. But surely Britain is the best country in the world? So it follows it must be the best place to live too?' She looked at the boys' astonished faces. 'My point is, why would anyone want to leave Britain? How could anywhere else be a better life?'

'You've got no idea what you're talking about,' said Aidan, shaking his head. 'Did you not hear about our house in Queenstown? Six sisters, all out to work? Dad and me don't go home from one year's end to the next, now. So *hell* yes, I would take the chance to go to America.' He looked at her with a very direct blue gaze. 'I don't expect you to understand. You've never worked a day in your life.'

'I have now,' said Luna, her Goodhart temper rising.

'In a fancy cabin sitting on a fancy chair,' said Aidan. 'That gang of stokers I worked with – the Black Gang, they're called, 'cos they're constantly covered in coal – they work themselves to death, some of them.'

'Well, anyway, your working day did have value,' said Konstantin soothingly to Luna. 'Sounds like you got the closest to achieving our mission.'

Luna could feel her temper subsiding, to be replaced by pride. 'Tomorrow Mr Marconi is going to show me the radio room,' she boasted. 'So this might be our last night aboard.'

Konstantin yawned hugely. 'What time is it?'

Aidan consulted the clock among the dials of the Time Train. They'd talked for longer than he'd imagined.

'Eleven-thirty.'

'Gosh,' said Luna. 'It's late. We'd better get some sleep.'

They tried to settle, not very easily, in their new outfits.

Konstantin wriggled uncomfortably. 'What the Devil am I lying on? Oh yes, my book.' He drew out *The Wreck of the Titan*, and this time he looked more carefully at the cover than he ever had. The great ocean liner, blazing with lights in a night sea, was at a horrid angle, sinking beneath the inky waves.

Luna looked at it too and gave a little laugh. 'At least we know that can't happen to *Titanic*. She's unsinkable.'

'How do you know?' asked Konstantin.

'Because when I was at lunch at the Captain's Table, Mr Bruce Ismay – the owner of the White Star Line – was there. He said that *Titanic* had some secret system that made it unsinkable.'

'I know what it is!' exclaimed Aidan, propping himself up on his elbow. 'There are special compartments all along the ship that can be locked down to keep the water out. I've been in one.'

'How does that help?' asked Luna.

Aidan had to remember that the other two might not know the engineering principles behind the compartments. 'If the chambers are watertight, that means that air is trapped in the belly of the ship and it won't go under. Imagine' – he searched for an example – 'a glass bottle. If you put a cork in the bottle, trapping the air inside, and cast it into the ocean, it will float. If you leave the cork out, the bottle fills with water, and it sinks to the bottom. A ship is the same.'

'Then Mr Ismay was right,' said Luna. '*Titanic* really *is* unsinkable.'

'I suppose so,' said Konstantin uneasily. The thought of the missing binoculars dug into his flesh like the buttons of his greatcoat. He sat up. 'No, I can't sleep in this uniform. Would you mind awfully turning away while I change?'

Luna assumed the question was for her – until the mysterious Nadia turned up, she was the only young lady who was likely to be offended by a young gentleman getting undressed. But Aidan turned at once, covering his eyes. This was very odd, as Luna had had to speak to him before about manners when *she'd* been getting changed. 'Why do you need to turn your back, Aidan?'

'What do you mean?' He would not look at her. 'I wasn't turning my back. I was just trying to get comfortable in this infernal boneshaker.' He gave a little, awkward laugh. It was the second time he'd acted oddly when they'd been changing. He'd had to be practically told to get out of the Time Train when she was disguising herself as a secretary, but now he was too shy to watch a boy take off his coat. Then other odd things connected in her mind like cogs biting together. Aunt Grace had said Aidan knew who Nadia was – *ask him, he knows* – yet he'd acted so strangely when she'd mentioned Nadia's name. And he'd said there were *seven women in a bed* back in Ireland when he only had six sisters…

Luna sat up. 'Aidan?'

She saw the name in her head, like the ivory letter tiles she and Papa used to play word games with. The letters A-I-D-A-N floated in her mind's eye, revolved and rearranged themselves.

N-A-D-I-A

Her eyes flew wide. '*You're* Nadia,' she exclaimed, 'aren't you?'

14 APRIL 1912
11.30 p.m.

'Yes,' said Aidan, breathing out a big sigh that sounded almost like relief. 'I'm Nadia.'

'Wait. Who's Nadia?' asked Konstantin.

'My Aunt Grace told me when we were about to take the Time Train, that I wouldn't be the only girl on this mission. She said there would be another girl with us, a girl called Nadia, and that Aidan knew who she was. She's you, isn't she?'

Aidan nodded.

'So you're…' Konstantin pieced it together. 'You're a *girl*?'

'I was *born* a girl.'

'And no one knows?' asked Luna.

Aidan thought of Arthur John Priest. But he said, 'No.'

'But your parents…' said Konstantin. 'They must know.'

'Of course *they* know. It was my dad's idea.'

'To… disguise yourself?'

'To *be* myself,' said Aidan, his eyes very blue. 'I was always supposed to be Aidan anyway – they had the name all saved up for me – after six girls they were sure the seventh child would be a boy and my da's brother was called Aidan. When I was born they just reversed it and called me Nadia. Da had worked on the railways in Siberia and said it was a girl's name.'

'It is,' said Konstantin. 'In Prussia too.'

'But I was always more Aidan than Nadia,' said Aidan, as if a sluice-gate had been opened and the words were free to pour out. 'I always was getting dirty, getting myself into scrapes. Me ma started dressing me in breeches. Got sick of washing petticoats, she said. I used to mess about with engines and caught my hair in a camshaft once. They had to cut it all off with shears to get me free. Me ma was furious, but then she neatened it up herself and always kept it short after that; she just cut mine the way she cut my da's.' He ran a hand through his short black locks. 'When I was eleven, Da taught me to take his pocket watch apart and put it together again, properly I mean, so it would work. I remember the mess of cogs on our kitchen table, thinking it was impossible. But it wasn't. It's just engineering. He told me what all the parts do – every pin, every cog. Then it made sense. And I did it. When I closed the casement and it started to tick I felt like the king of the world.' He smiled at the memory, suddenly miles away. 'Da said I was ready. He said he would take me to work on the railways, and me ma agreed – I could earn my keep that way, send money home. So I reversed my name and became a navvy, just like my da. Built railways all over the British Isles we have – Cardiff, Edinburgh, London, you name it. Everyone just thought Michael O'Connell had brought his son with him. His son, Aidan.' The flood of words stopped. Everything was out now, out in the open. Aidan sat back, almost as exhausted as he'd been when he'd finished his shift at the stokeholds. But he felt better, much better.

Luna and Konstantin were silent for a moment, taking all this in. Luna was the first to speak. 'So… now you don't have to pretend any more.'

'I'm not pretending,' said Aidan. 'I was before. It's like…' Clearly not used to talking like this, he seemed to search for the right words to illustrate what he wanted to say. 'Have you ever seen a caterpillar turn into a butterfly? They're just grubs, really, crawling around on the ground.

Then they turn into a chrysalis, and then they sort of… burst forth, fully formed, and colourful, and beautiful. They spread their wings, and fly.'

Luna thought of the butterflies in the Butterfly Room at the Greenwich Observatory, whirling around the Time Train in a maelstrom of colour.

'Butterflies are free,' said Aidan passionately. 'They were never meant to be caterpillars. They were just born that way. Aidan is more me than Nadia. Nadia couldn't do what I do. She couldn't live her life alongside machines, building them, tending them, working on the railways with my da. Perhaps one day, but not now.'

Luna tried to express what she was feeling. 'It doesn't matter what you are,' she began.

'It does to me,' put in Aidan.

'What I meant was' – gosh, she seemed to be saying everything wrong – 'whoever you are, you are our *friend*.' And she held out her hand. Aidan took it, and she could see that, at last, she had found the right thing to say. His blue eyes had turned to glass.

'Yes,' said Konstantin. 'Our friend, Aidan.'

He held out his hand too, and put it on theirs, and the three time-thieves sat like that for a moment, locked in a triple handshake.

There was no knowing how long that moment would have gone on, because just then there was a terrible scraping, rending sound, like the tearing of calico, but ten thousand times louder.

14 APRIL 1912
11.40 p.m.

The three of them broke their grasp and sat bolt upright.

'What was that?'

Suddenly everything was forgotten but the sound, that terrible sound of screaming metal. Aidan pulled the tarpaulin to one side and they all peered out of the Time Train. The screaming stopped but the boom and echo lasted for a full minute more, and then subsided into utter, utter silence.

'All quiet now,' breathed Aidan.

'What *was* that?' asked Luna, her eyes wide with fear. 'Shall we investigate?'

'Better had,' said Konstantin. 'Aidan and I will go to our different battle stations, just like this morning, and report back here. *Fräulein* Luna, you stay hidden and guard the Time Train.'

Konstantin shrugged on his greatcoat, but before he had fastened even one of the brass buttons Luna said, 'No.'

They looked at her.

'I'll go.'

'But,' said Konstantin, 'there might be danger. You heard that sound. I…' He looked at Aidan. '*We* would rather you were here, safe.'

Feeling their eyes on her Luna tried to explain, to jumble together the thoughts and feelings she'd been collecting for the last four days, about girls and boys and their place in the world. 'If anything, I might be even more use than you *both* this time. I will be able to find out what there is to know,' Luna went on, 'without being given anything to *do*. If there is an emergency you will, *both* of you, be given a job. Men are creatures of action – they think and do. Women are creatures of observation – they wait and watch. Aidan, you understand me, don't you? That's precisely why you live the life you live.'

'Yes,' he said quietly. 'Yes, I understand you. Meet us back here then, Duch. We'll be waiting for you.'

So once again, Luna climbed the galley stair and emerged on the First Class deck. But this time she was greeted by quite a different sight.

She went to the white railings at the edge of the ship, put her hands on the freezing metal, and just stared and stared.

There was a huge iceberg, so close to the ship she could have reached out and touched it. In the moonlight it seemed to be lit from within, glowing with its own strange blue-white light, a cathedral of ice. Some of the ice had shattered on to the deck with the impact, and her feet crunched on it, like broken glass. Just for a moment she was utterly alone with the iceberg, marvelling in horror, cocooned in an eerie, frigid silence. You could even see through it and to the stars beyond, like looking through the wing of a Glasswing butterfly.

Then all of a sudden somebody was shouting, from far above, somewhere at the top of the mast. For a moment she couldn't make out the words. Then she realised that they were saying – too late, too terribly late, 'Iceberg dead ahead! Iceberg dead ahead!'

Then a bell rang out, clear as Christmas, the peal cleaving through the night.

People began to gather on the deck, in ones and twos,

to point and exclaim. They were not afraid, not yet, more curious. Three boys, in Norfolk jackets and caps, began to play football with a lump of ice on the deck – the thing skittered about, sliding easily, and they shouted with joy. A man in evening dress came to the railing beside Luna, holding a glass in his hand. He stooped, picked up a couple of lumps of iceberg from the deck, and plopped them into his drink. He raised the glass to Luna. 'Jolly useful,' he slurred.

Luna backed away. No one seemed to be taking the iceberg seriously, but she felt it was serious – deadly serious. She would never forget that screeching sound of impact. So she hurried as fast as she could across the icy deck, to report back to the hold.

But when she reached the door in the funnel, there was a paper wrapped around the handle and tied with string. In her urgency to get back to the Time Train and tell the boys what she had learned, she might have ignored it, but for the fact that she saw her own name.

She took the scroll of paper off the handle and unfurled it.

It was a letter.

With shaking hands, Luna held the stiff notepaper to the moonlight. Along the fold of the paper was a large, symmetrical blot. Perhaps the writer had been in a hurry and spilled the ink. But below the fold there were a few lines of scrawled handwriting.

> My dearest Luna,
> If you love me, please ensure that you are nowhere near the Greenwich Observatory at the hour of 4.45 p.m. precisely on Thursday the 15th of February 1894.
> Yours until the end of time,
>
> Papa x

Luna looked closely at the letter, her heart thumping. It was from Papa, no doubt about it. For one thing, the writing was his. For a second, he always signed himself Papa with a little cross which he said represented a kiss. And for a third, he used to sign off every note he ever left for her in the same way.

Yours until the end of time.

So. The letter was from Papa, that was certain. But what did the message mean? How could any other time and place be important, when the *Titanic* had just rammed an iceberg? But she did a quick calculation. The 15th of February 1894 was exactly a month after the meeting of the Butterfly Club, when she, Konstantin and Aidan had taken the Time Train. What was destined to happen at 4.45 p.m. a month later? And had whatever it was already occurred?

And there was a more pressing question. Who had left the note? A vain hope grasped at her heart. Could it be... was it possible? She looked about her. The only person on that part of the deck was a lone officer, walking away from her. She followed the figure, paper in hand.

And then, on the freezing night air, she heard a tune drifting towards her, clear as birdsong. It was just a phrase, from the lips of the dark figure, snatched away by the breeze almost before she heard it. But Luna would know that song anywhere.

Yesterday.

'Papa?'

Agonisingly slowly, the figure turned round. He was dressed in the night-blue uniform of the White Star Line, much like the one that Konstantin had stolen. But it was beautifully, unmistakably him.

14 APRIL 1912
11.50 p.m.

Luna launched herself at her father and held him as if she would never let go.

It was Papa, warm, solid and real. He wrapped his arms round her and greeted her as he always did, by fluttering his eyelashes on her cheek in a tickly butterfly kiss. But after a time – much too short a time for Luna – he stood her away from him, holding her shoulders. 'You look so grown-up, my Luna.'

'I'm in disguise,' she said, rather proudly.

'I too.' He was just the same – the trim beard, the sparkling eyes with the lines gathering at the corners when he smiled, the auburn curls all but covered by the officer's hat. She would have liked to stand there and drink him in, but he seemed in a hurry. He spoke urgently.

'Did you find my letter?'

'Yes – what does it mean?'

'I can't tell you yet. The time isn't right. You just have to trust me. You trust me, don't you, Luna?'

She did. That is – she used to. But when he'd left like that, with no word…

'Of course,' she said. 'It's just…'

'Just?' he asked gently.

Her eyes felt hot and stinging, but she was determined not to cry. 'Why did you go away? Without even one of these?' She waved the letter.

His expression grew serious. 'Believe me. I would *never* have gone away like that if I had any kind of choice,' he said. 'One day I will explain. But now there's no time. The *Titanic* will go down soon – very soon. It's already begun.'

'But she's unsinkable.'

'No,' he said vehemently. 'Not so.'

She'd never known Papa sound so sure about anything. 'How do you know?'

'Because I've seen it happen before.'

Before she could question this extraordinary statement he said, 'Time is running out.

'You have a way off this ship. Take it. Go back to the 15th of January 1894, but remember what my letter said –

don't be at the observatory at four forty-five a month later. *Promise* me, Luna.'

He looked so concerned that she didn't hesitate. 'I promise.'

'Good girl.' He held her cheek for an instant and she felt the cold of the gold wedding ring he always wore. A crowd was gathering on the deck so they were no longer alone, but were jostled every second by passengers flooding to the starboard railing to take a look at the receding iceberg. 'I'll write again soon. Look – you see this inkblot here?' He took the letter from her hand and pointed to the dark stain across the fold.

'Yes. Did you spill the ink?'

'In a sense,' he said. 'This is a Rorschach blot.'

'A what?'

'You make a puddle of ink and then fold the paper to make a pattern.'

'What a funny name,' said Luna. 'I've never heard of such a thing.'

'You wouldn't have,' said her father. 'It hasn't been invented yet. It will be conceived by Hermann Rorschach in 1921.'

Luna looked at Papa, wide-eyed. 'So you – you've travelled to the future? I mean... even more into the future? Is that where you've been?'

'That's *when* I've been,' he corrected gently. 'That and other times. See here,' he held his letter to the moonlight as the crowd streamed past them. 'Rorschach said that different people would see what they want to see in the same inkblot. What do *you* see, Luna?'

She looked closely – the dark blot with the frilled edges looked to her like only one thing. 'A butterfly.'

He smiled, quite like the old Papa. 'Precisely. Now look.' He tore the letter neatly in half across the fold, so the butterfly was split neatly in half, one wing on each piece. 'I'll write to you again, on my half of the paper. Look out for my letter. But always, *always* check the Rorschach blot.' He held the two pieces together in front of her face. 'If the butterfly doesn't match, it's *not from me*.

Do you understand?'

Luna nodded. 'Yes.'

Now they could hardly move for the press of people on the deck. 'I must go,' said Papa. 'But one last thing I'll tell you. *Watch out for the Watch*. Repeat it.'

'Watch out for the Watch,' parroted Luna obediently.

He held her shoulders again and looked her in the eyes. 'That's the most important advice that I can give you about this ship. Now go.'

'What about you?' protested Luna.

'I'll be fine,' he said. 'There's something that yet remains for me to do. *Dear* Luna.' He drew her close again and kissed her forehead.

'Will I see you again?' she said, suddenly unable to bear the thought of another parting.

'Yes, of course,' he murmured into her hair.

'When?'

She knew what he was going to say before he said it.

'Yesterday,' he whispered; and with that, he vanished into the crowd.

14 APRIL 1912
Midnight

Biting her lip, Luna tucked the letter into her bodice, where it sat, scratchily, next to her heart. It had suddenly become her dearest possession. But she didn't allow herself time to think. She had to get back to Konstantin and Aidan and the Time Train, and report what she had seen and heard. She hurried along the freezing, ice-strewn deck, praying that in the growing crowd she could get back to the galley door without being noticed.

It was not to be.

A hand caught at her sleeve.

'Signorina Goodhart! *Grazie Dio!*' It was Signor Marconi, dressed once more in his greatcoat and bowler hat, just as she had first seen him as they left Southampton dock. 'I have been seeking you up and down the ship. I was not sure where your cabin was. You must come with me at *once*. Make haste.'

Luna hesitated, her mind racing. She could not say she had to get back to her friends, for she'd told Signor Marconi she was alone in the world. So when he offered her the crook of his arm she took it and went with him, and he guided her through the crush, making way with his cane. He spoke low as they went, from the side of his mouth, like people do when they are telling you a secret they don't want other people to know. 'I have to tell you, Signorina Goodhart, that I am in possession of some privileged information. I have just now been in the Marconi Room, and it is a fact that the ship will surely sink. I have it from the captain's own lips. He was there and told the operators to go – he said that they had done all they could and that it was every man for himself.'

Luna felt a chill in her stomach – it was just as Papa had said. 'So where are we going?'

'To the boat deck.'

'What's the boat deck?' she asked.

'Where the lifeboats are kept. Signorina, we must get you in a lifeboat *at once*.'

Swiftly, Marconi led Luna through the growing crowd.

More and more people surged on to the boat deck by the second. Somewhere a baby started to cry, and the burble of concerned chatter threatened to boil over into panic. At last they were at the ship's rail, where a young officer was supervising the winching down of the boat. To Luna the creamy-coloured vessel with the number 14 painted on the side seemed enormous, but she could see it was already half-full. A crowd of First Class passengers had abandoned their fine manners and were pushing and shoving to get in.

'Women and children first,' shouted the young officer over the chaos. 'Women and children *only* at this time.'

Marconi began to push and shove with the best of them. He lifted Luna bodily over the railing and she found herself plonked into one of the only remaining seats. She had been thwarted by the very thing that she thought had made her safe – her sex. It had never occurred to her that in the event of a wreck, she would be first in the lifeboats.

She began to panic – but for the exact opposite reason to the other passengers. They would do anything to get in the lifeboat. She would do anything to get out. She needed to find the others. Now she was to be taken away from them, she thought more fondly of her travelling companions than ever – dear Konstantin with his clockwork heart and his soldier's courage. And Aidan with a brain like a machine and that big grin that seemed to hang in the air. She could no more leave them than she could stay herself. She had no thought for the radio now, only them. If she was cast off in the lifeboat, what then? She'd be on the high seas, taking her chances with the other passengers, and how would she ever get home with no Time Train?

She had a sudden thought. 'Signor Marconi. *You* must get in the boat. Take my place.' She reached out her hand over the railing and took his gloved hand in her own.

He forced a sad smile and shook his head. 'I cannot rob you of your reunion with your father. His heart will be so glad of the sight of you.' The smile faded. 'I know how I would smile to see my own daughter again.'

Time had travelled, as it always does, in a circle, and she saw him last as she saw him first, with tears in his eyes. And then, of course, she thought of the daughter he had left behind, waving and waving on the dock.

'Signor Marconi. Please,' she said desperately. 'Take my seat. I'll… I'll be all right.'

Now he shook his head. 'Never in this world. No gentleman would get in.'

'Not even to see Degna again?'

She thought she could see the exact moment his heart

broke. But he raised his chin. 'Signorina Goodhart.' The brown eyes softened. 'Luna. If I did, I could never again look her in the eye. I could never feel glad to see the sky and hear the birdsong, no, nor even be glad of my daughter's fond looks, when girls such as she had perished for want of a place in a lifeboat.'

It was no use. That thing called chivalry, that existed in this time and her own, was in the way. Women and girls must be protected, and that was that.

The boat was almost full, and was rocking perilously. Desperately, Luna scanned the faces of the passengers in the crowd. Then, a miracle – she saw someone she recognised.

It was Konstantin.

15 APRIL 1912
12.20 a.m.

'Stan! Stan! Over here.'

Amid the chaos of the boat deck, Konstantin recognised Harold Lowe, the young officer with the stamp collection. Gratefully he pushed through the passengers to his side, his uniform giving him the authority to part the crowd.

'I need you to pilot this lifeboat,' said Harold. 'Get in.'

'Me?' Konstantin's voice was the squawk of a crow.

'Yes. You have the experience.' He tapped the gold stripe on Konstantin's arm, and Konstantin cursed the stolen uniform. 'Quick, man.'

'What about you?'

'Someone's got to keep the men back,' said Harold. 'They're behaving like savages, trying to get in the boat.'

Konstantin was shocked. What kind of gentleman would take a woman's place in a lifeboat?

'If the men overrun the boat, all the women will drown. Just keep them afloat until a rescue ship comes. And Stan,' Lowe locked eyes with him. 'Goodbye. And good luck.' Then he stood poker-straight and saluted.

Konstantin saluted back, feeling a total fraud. He could feel a lump rising in his throat as he was confronted by true courage for the first time in his life. He knew in that moment that Fifth Officer Harold Lowe had no expectation of getting off *Titanic* alive. The young man could have piloted the boat himself but he had given his own place to Konstantin.

In the face of such sacrifice, Konstantin had no choice but to scramble over the railing into the lifeboat. Only when he'd seated himself in the prow did he recognise Luna. It was all he could do not to cry out with relief, but she had obviously spotted him first and had taken the chance to arrange her features. Following her example, he showed no sign of knowing her. He just gave her a tiny nod and said, in a general way to the boat at large, 'It's all right. Everything's going to be all right.' But he did not believe one slightest little part of it. How could everything be all right if Luna and he were on a lifeboat, Aidan was not, and the Time Train and Chronos were stuck in the watery hold of a sinking ship?

'Stan?' shouted Harold suddenly from the deck. 'Room for one more?'

He was proud to see Luna budge up and make a space – that was very like her. 'Just,' he yelled back.

For a moment he was hopeful that Harold would jump aboard himself, but he might have known the young man had too much honour in him for that. He was giving his arm to a bent figure with a shawl about its head – some old lady who needed rescue. Konstantin stood in the prow to help the lady over the railing, but the hand that gripped his was remarkably strong. It was also blackened with soot and had filthy square nails. A man's hand.

Konstantin dipped his head and looked beneath the shawl, and if his heart hadn't been clockwork it would have stopped from the shock.

The face had blunt features and a broken nose. But that wasn't the most remarkable thing about it. The man who had claimed the last place in the lifeboat had a watch for an eye.

Before Konstantin could open his mouth, another voice, a voice he knew by its Irish accent, shouted the very words he'd been forming in his mind.

'That's not a woman! It's a man!'

Konstantin looked back to the deck to find the speaker.

It was Aidan.

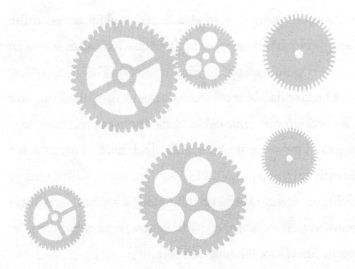

15 APRIL 1912
12.05 a.m.

When Aidan left the others and descended to the lower decks, the hellfires had transformed into a head of steam such as he had never seen – not even in the biggest railway stations in the world. It was as if a thousand locomotives had let off steam at the same time; he could barely see his hand in front of his face. His engineer's brain told him the grim truth. The encroaching seawater had met the furious heat of the furnaces, and filled the lower decks with these blinding white indoor clouds. There was nothing to be done here – the ship was already taking on water. He must just get himself to safety before he ran into Arthur John Priest. But of course, that gentleman was the first person he saw, emerging from the steam like a tuppenny conjurer.

Aidan reversed as quickly as he could, but it was too late. The stoker grabbed a handful of his jacket. '*Titanic*'s going down,' he said urgently.

'But what about the compartments you showed me?'

'They'd be all right if they weren't already breached on the starboard side. If three of them had filled, or even four, we'd have been all right. But five of them are flooded and now the whole ship's unbalanced. And that only means one thing.' The stoker pointed a grimy finger downwards – down to the bottom of the ocean. To Aidan's horror, Arthur John Priest didn't release his grip but began to drag him along. 'We have to get to a lifeboat. Fast. And you're coming with me.'

'Why?'

'Because you're a girl. It will be women and children first. And you're both. Come on.'

So it was true. Somehow, Arthur John Priest knew everything about him.

'Wait,' said Aidan desperately. 'I can't go with you. I have somewhere to be.'

Arthur John Priest stopped abruptly. He turned and shoved Aidan back against the metal galley wall with a clang. He put his face very close to Aidan's, so Aidan could smell his sour tobacco breath. 'You got another way off this ship?'

Aidan opened his eyes very wide and steeled himself not to look away. 'Of course not.'

Arthur John Priest gave him a searching look with his watch eye. Aidan felt himself begin to sweat, as if the watch could see into his soul. He instinctively knew that he couldn't let this man know about the Time Train. Luckily Arthur John Priest let him go and he slumped with relief. 'Come on then,' he said, hauling Aidan with him. 'I know a secret way. They'll have locked the gates from Third Class, to keep them all in.'

'Why?'

'Haven't you listened to a word I've been telling you? To keep the likes of us away from the lifeboats. Third Class'll drown like rats in a trap.' He spat a great gob of spit and it landed on the gantry, glistening wetly. 'Like it or not, I'm your best chance to get off this ship. You do right by me, and I'll do right by you.'

Through a maze of passageways, stinking of oil and coal, and up a dozen metal ladders that clanged under their boots, Aidan and Arthur John Priest emerged on to the chaos of the boat deck. 'Stick with me, girlie,' hissed the stoker viciously. Aidan hated this name almost as much as he hated Arthur John Priest. For him it was a reminder of the person he no longer wanted to be, but he would be willing to bet that Luna too would hate that nasty little label. Then a thought struck him – perhaps *all* nicknames were tiresome. For the first time, he wondered how Luna liked being called 'Duch'.

Arthur John Priest shoved his way through the crowd, dragging Aidan in his wake, and went right up to the young officer in charge of filling the lifeboat. 'This is my daughter. I need to get her into the lifeboat.'

The young officer took one look at Aidan and laughed bitterly. 'Go on with you. That's a boy!'

'She's a girl, I promise you,' Arthur John Priest protested desperately. 'She's just dressed up. She's a bit funny in the head. Thinks she's a boy. That's why I have to go with her – look after her, like.'

'And I'm the Archbishop of Canterbury,' said the officer. 'Stand back there. This boat's about ready to go.'

Arthur John Priest withdrew, and turned on Aidan, shoving him away. 'You're no good to me. Good luck. It's every man for himself, and that doesn't include you.'

Casting desperately around, the stoker saw a young mother feeding her child, covering herself and the babe with a voluminous shawl. He ripped the shawl away from them, leaving mother and baby exposed, and wrapped the thing around himself. Aidan watched him bend nearly double and hobble through the crowd to the front once more, this time with the help of a few decent souls who said things like, 'Mind your step, Mother,' and, 'Make way for this old lady'. He saw the young officer give 'the old lady' an arm into the boat, to be helped on board by another young officer.

The unfairness of it all rose in his throat like tears. It never once occurred to him to reveal the secret of his birth and claim a place in the lifeboat for himself. He thought instead of his ma, and his six sisters, and of what his da would do in his place. His new friend Konstantin thought that honour and chivalry belonged to the rich people, and perhaps he was right. They were the ones who literally made a song and dance about it, with their operas and their parades and their high-and-mighty poetry. They thought everyone working class was like Arthur John Priest, a sly and self-serving knave. And Aidan couldn't let that be true, he just couldn't.

He grabbed the rigging and clambered up to stand on the rail like a ship's figurehead. As clearly as he could, Aidan shouted over the panic and chaos what he knew he needed to say.

'That's not a woman! It's a man!'

15 APRIL 1912
12.25 a.m.

Konstantin had only a second to think. He snatched the shawl away and shouted, 'The boy is right! This is a man!'

Harold Lowe acted at once. He ran to the ship's rail and pointed his forefinger at Arthur John Priest. 'You,' he said icily to the stowaway. 'Get out of the boat.'

Arthur John Priest, still bent over to conceal his full height, began to wheedle. 'Please, sir, I've a disadvantage on account of my eye. I swim in circles. I'll never get out of here alive.'

Harold Lowe, without wavering, said, 'I cannot cast off until you are out of the boat. I will not let such a fellow as you go to sea with these respectable ladies. Now, Get. Out. Of. The. Boat.'

The crowd now took up the cry. 'Get out of the boat! Get out of the boat!' and a hundred hands reached for the stowaway. Konstantin and Luna did their part, and what with them pushing and the passengers pulling, Arthur John Priest was ejected from the boat. Once on deck he pulled himself up to his full height and threw off the hands that held him. He turned on Aidan and spat.

'You and I are daggers drawn now. Girl or no girl.'

'That young man has more courage in his little finger than you have in your whole sorry carcass,' said Harold Lowe. 'Now stand clear there.'

With a filthy parting look for all, Arthur John Priest shoved his way back through the crowd and disappeared.

Luna watched the scene with her heart racing. She did not know, of course, how Aidan was acquainted with the man with a watch for an eye, but at that moment she had no leisure to think about it. Their problem remained the same – she and Konstantin were in a lifeboat, Aidan wasn't, and though the confrontation had served to delay their departure, the lifeboat was now winching downwards along the side of the ship. To add to the nightmarish quality of the scene, the valiant little band on deck began to play a hymn. Through all the screaming and crying, she thought she recognised the tune of *Nearer My God to*

Thee. She swallowed down the sick feeling in her throat. She hoped they weren't about to meet their maker just yet.

Just then a strident voice called, 'Stop! *I* will take the last place.'

Their descent halted with a sickening jerk.

A figure strode through the crowd, one that Luna recognised. He was most inappropriately dressed for a shipwreck, in a black tailcoat and white collars, and a black tie in the shape of a bow.

'Who are you?' asked Harold Lowe bluntly.

'I am Mr Bruce Ismay,' said that gentleman, 'owner of the White Star Line. Stand aside, man.'

Everyone looked from Officer Lowe to Mr Ismay.

To his credit Harold stood for a moment in Mr Ismay's path, unmoving.

'Boy,' said Mr Ismay, getting very close to Harold's face. 'I am the owner of this ship, and many others. Stand aside or I'll have you discharged.'

Lowering his eyes, Harold stood to one side, and Mr Ismay clambered into the ship. He held out his hand to Konstantin for help, clearly expecting his own officer to assist him. But Konstantin did not proffer a hand. He sat firmly in his place and let Mr Ismay shift for himself. Mr Ismay settled himself between a nursing mother and

Luna, sitting bolt upright as if he were in a carriage, his gloved hands folded on the silver top of his cane, looking neither left nor right. At that moment a huge distress flare, like the biggest firework in the world, burst high in the sky over his head in a fiery flower of rose and gold. A further sign, if it were needed, that his ship was in terrible trouble.

Lowe, disgusted, slapped the side of the boat smartly with his hand. 'Anchors away then,' he commanded. But his expression was a picture of contempt.

The boat lurched downwards on its winches, and Luna looked desperately at Aidan, who was reaching out his hand. She remembered when he'd offered the same hand to her in the Greenwich Observatory, to help her board the Time Train, and she'd haughtily rejected it, prompting him to nickname her Duch. Now she didn't hesitate. She threw out her hand in return to clasp his, hard. His blue eyes under the lock of dark hair blazed with determination. 'Hold on, Luna,' he said – the first time he'd used her given name. 'Just hold on.'

The boat lowered and her hand was cruelly torn from his. Could this really be goodbye? 'Hold on,' Aidan called, now to Konstantin, and Konstantin, swallowing, nodded his head. What on earth were they to do?

Now, as they were winched down the side of the ship,

Luna appreciated the sheer size of the thing. It was like being a flea on a dog. Already *Titanic* was at a sickening angle. The water had reached the name badge on the bow, and the pewter-grey ocean seethed angrily below, troubled by the suck of the sinking hull.

Down and down the lifeboat lurched, past First Class, past Second, past Third, the rails and decks of the vast ship passing by their eyes. The great ship gave voice to her agony, groaning eerily as her iron and timbers felt the pull of the encroaching water. The lights flickered, dimmed and then brightened again. Still Luna could hear Aidan, above the chaos of the screaming, panicking passengers, bellowing, 'HOLD on! HOLD on!' The word 'HOLD' was much louder than the word 'on', which all but disappeared in the general hubbub.

She turned to Konstantin, abandoning all pretence that she didn't know him. 'It's a message,' she said. 'Aidan's sending us a message.'

'What do you mean?'

'He's telling us to go to the hold.'

'But how?'

'We are passing every level of the ship. Every deck one by one. When we are low enough, we should get out, and go to the hold and the Time Train.'

'Do you think he'll meet us there?'

'I'm sure of it. That's what he's trying to tell us.'

It was no easy task. It was hard, in the icy night, to get their bearings. What if they went too early, and the hold was barred to them by those gates keeping the Third Class passengers away from the First Class ones? What if they went too late, and they ran out of decks? Luckily the lifeboat was descending quite slowly, with a series of sickening jerks. It would be fairly easy to scramble back on to the ship, but the question was, where?

There was one person aboard who would know.

'Mr Ismay, said Luna, 'when are we at the level of the cargo hold?'

He turned to her, his eyes blank, as if he was still reliving what he had just done.

Luna grabbed one of his gloved hands and gave it a little waggle. 'Mr Ismay, this is important. We need to get to the hold. It's a matter of life and death.'

Still he was silent, his eyes dead.

She tried one last time. 'Mr Ismay, no one knows this ship like you. You could yet save a young lady's life. It is not too late to act with honour.'

Then a small spark kindled in the eyes. 'Here,' he said. Then he stood and gave her his arm, just as Signor

Marconi had done on the boat deck.

With his help Luna clambered back over the rail of the *Titanic*, followed by Konstantin. It was their last opportunity to do so, because after that there was nothing but bare iron and no deck to re-enter the ship.

The lifeboat reached the water with a splash, and Konstantin could see Mr Ismay cast off the ropes. The boat floated out into the icy seas – its little crew safe, at least for now.

'All right,' said Konstantin. 'Let's go.' He took Luna's hand and together they waded through the icy water, so cold they had to catch their breath. In the hold too the water was rising – ropes had frayed and dampened, crates were floating freely, turning in little circles on the flood, and the seawater was approaching the wheels of the Time Train.

But there, at the window, gesturing wildly, was Aidan.

15 APRIL 1912
12.45 a.m.

'Thank the Good Lord you understood what I was saying,' said Aidan. 'I thought if I was more obvious we might get some company down here.'

Luna took his outstretched hand gratefully and scrambled up. 'Do you mean the man with a watch for an eye?'

'I do, yes,' said Aidan grimly.

'Who is he?' asked Konstantin, clambering into the machine.

'No time,' said Aidan, without looking at either of them. 'Sit yourselves down. I'll set the dials.'

Luna and Konstantin, still wet and shivering, settled themselves in the rear of the Time Train, soaking the red velvet seats at once.

'So,' said Aidan as he moved the brass tumblers around. 'Greenwich Observatory, London, 15th of January 1894. What time?'

'Early,' said Luna. 'Noon, when the meeting began.'

'Noon it is,' said Aidan.

At that moment there was a tremendous crash. The hold doors had been breached and the water began to flood in in earnest, filling up the hold. The lights flickered and finally died, leaving only the eerie blue-white light of the crystal columns, which were now positively pulsating with energy.

'Quick,' said Konstantin.

The water was creeping higher, above the wheels of the Time Train.

Luna thought of the other passengers, now in the dark, on a sinking ship. Of the sheer terror and hopelessness of it. She thought of her father holding her tight and kissing her head as he'd used to. He'd seemed confident that he would be all right – he'd seen the sinking before, he said. But what of the others? What of the 709 Third Class passengers? And what about Signor Marconi, that kindly, serious gentleman who'd given her a place in the lifeboat for the price of never seeing his family again?

She lurched forward and reached for the dials, her

chilled fingers just dextrous enough to turn the brass tumblers and line up the little ivory letter tiles.

Aidan grabbed at her wrists. 'What are you *doing*?'

Aidan was much stronger than she, but when he took her wrists like that the famous Goodhart temper rose to the surface and Luna found herself with a strength she didn't know she had. With a desperate effort, she shoved him aside and bought just enough time to enter new directions and the new date. Then, before she could change her mind, she reached for the smooth ivory knob of the brass activation lever and wrenched it backwards as hard as she could. There was a blinding flash, and they were plunged into starlit darkness as the Time Train surged through time once more. This time there was hardly time to register that well-remembered sick and heavy feeling before the machine stopped.

The first voice to be heard was Aidan's as he groggily sat up and registered the settings, spelled out in the little ivory tiles.

'Jesus, Mary and Joseph, Luna Goodhart. What have you *done*?'

RMS *TITANIC*

14 APRIL 1912

14 APRIL 1912
9.45 a.m.

A idan ran his hands through his dark hair until it stood on end, and his blue eyes were blazing. 'My God, Luna, we're back on the day of the sinking! It's the 14th of April 1912! We'll be living yesterday all over again!'

It was hard to believe, but when the time-thieves peeped out of the tarpaulin they could see that the hold was exactly as it had been the morning before. There were no frayed and dampened ropes, no floating crates, no seawater approaching the wheels of the Time Train. They were dressed the same as they had been the previous night, but were now warm and dry. They sat back in the velvet seats and drew the tarpaulin closed again.

There was a dangerous silence, almost as if there had been a quarrel. Luna's wrists still burned where Aidan had grabbed her. She was sure with the shove she had hurt him too. But she had done what she had to do. She lifted her chin defiantly. She was not sorry, but she owed the boys a reason. 'I just felt,' she began, 'that we can't just leave everybody here. I felt that we had to do *something*.' She tried to explain. 'I didn't just meet Signor Marconi, we became friends. He was a good man. He has children too.'

'She's right you know,' Konstantin said. 'We shouldn't have run away. That's not honour. That officer at the lifeboats: Harold Lowe. I'd like to save him. And Reginald and Frederick in the crow's nest. They were nice to me. If I had my time again I would save them all.'

'Look,' said Aidan hotly. 'I'm sure your Officer Lowe is a lovely feller. I'm sure Frederick and Reginald are champion too.' He turned to Luna. 'I'm sorry for your Mr Marconi, I understand that he's a father. But we have fathers too, and ours are back in 1894.'

It was time to tell them. 'Mine's not,' said Luna. 'Mine's here.'

'*What?*' the other two exclaimed together.

'He's here on the ship. I saw him, on deck. Last night.'

'Why didn't you tell us?'

'There wasn't exactly time,' said Luna defensively. 'I'm telling you now. He was there, and I spoke to him.'

'Like Hamlet,' said Konstantin, who saw everything in terms of books. 'He saw his dead father walking the castle battlements at night.'

'Well, except my father didn't die,' said Luna. 'I thought he did. But I know now that he went forward in time and didn't come back. That's how my aunt got me to board the Time Train in the first place.'

'And what did he say?'

Luna recounted the conversation that she would never forget. She put her hand to her bodice and felt, with relief, that the letter her father had left for her was still there. She pulled it out, handing it first to Aidan, who seemed to be the one who would take the most convincing.

Aidan passed it to Konstantin, in an odd, shamefaced way – and Luna, appalled at her tactlessness, realised in that moment that he couldn't read.

'Please ensure that you are nowhere near the Green-wich Observatory at the hour of 4.45 p.m. precisely on Thursday the 15th of February 1894,' read Konstantin. 'That's exactly a month after we left.' He looked up. 'Why not?'

'He didn't say,' said Luna. 'We'd hit the berg by then, and *Titanic* was starting to sink. It was all a bit rushed. He said he'd seen the ship sink before, so he must have survived it somehow, but of course I want to save him this time too.'

'Well,' said Aidan, stubbornly. 'I didn't meet a single person that I felt was worth saving. It's all very well for you with your Captain's Table,' he said to Luna, 'and you with your Officers' Mess,' to Konstantin. 'But the only feller I met was a no-good criminal with a watch for an eye, and if he goes down with the ship it would be nothing but a mercy.'

'Who *was* that man?' asked Luna. 'The one who tried to get in the boat?'

'A stoker in the engine rooms. Name of Arthur John Priest. He… befriended me. But there was something off about him.' Now Aidan confessed what he hadn't told the others the night before. 'He knew… or he seemed to know… that I was…' he found it hard to say it, 'born a girl.'

'How could he possibly know that?' asked Konstantin.

'My aunt knew,' said Luna quietly. 'That's how it was possible for her to hint to me. Might your father have told her?'

Aidan shook his dark head, very definitely. 'No. My father's never told anyone. And that's not all. Arthur John Priest knew I was a time traveller. He spotted this.' Aidan flicked the bicycle chain at his waist. 'He knew it was from the 1890s.'

'Well, but it could just be a very old chain,' reasoned Konstantin. 'It doesn't mean you're from the past.'

'No, I know, but it was just a feeling. I can't explain. And then later, when we all went to investigate the noise, he asked me if I had another way off the ship. He definitely suspects something. Just one more reason to get off this death-trap as soon as possible.' He pointed upwards in the direction of the boat deck. 'This thing has plenty of lifeboats – let the passengers take their chances. I say we set the dials for Greenwich and get the bejesus out of here.'

Luna had been searching her mind for a way to persuade him. The events of yesterday seemed dreamlike, but when Aidan said the word 'lifeboats' one memory became clear. She remembered what Mr Bruce Ismay had said at lunch.

'There are lifeboats, but not nearly enough,' she said bluntly.

'What are you talking about?' he snapped.

'There aren't enough lifeboats.'

'But there *must* be.'

'No. Ismay said at lunch there were enough lifeboats if they were used as ferries to make multiple trips to and from a rescue vessel, not as a sole means of escape. And did you see any other ships last night?'

'Well… no… All I saw was a bleeding great iceberg.'

'Exactly. There are only enough for *half* of the passengers. And which half do you think will get the lifeboats? First and Second Class. Not Third. Not the 700-odd people in steerage. Seven hundred people like *you*, Aidan. They'll all drown, because the White Star Line think they're not worth saving.' It was brutal, but she had to say something to get him to stay. She had overpowered him once, with the element of surprise, but she knew she wouldn't be able to do it again – he was much stronger than she. Aidan hesitated, hands already on the brass dials.

'It's true,' said Konstantin. 'Look how that Ismay fellow just got in the boat himself, with no regard for other people. A general should be the *last* to leave the battlefield, not the first.' He laid his hand on Aidan's shoulder. 'If we go now, and leave them all to it, we're no better. You, Aidan O'Connell, would be just like Mr Bruce Ismay, except for instead of a lifeboat you've got a Time Train.'

That hit home. Aidan took his hands away from the dials. 'You're right,' he whispered. 'The Third Class won't get anywhere near the lifeboats. And if they go in the sea they'll surely die.' Aidan remembered what Arthur John

Priest had said. *If you jump in that water it would be the last thing you ever did.* On that crowded boat deck the night before, Aidan was convinced that in an emergency he would act with more honour than the quality folk. Now was the time to step up. 'What can we do, though?' he said. 'This ship is as big as a city. Remember, I've seen the boiler rooms and the engine rooms. They were created for giants. I felt like a pygmy down there. And the bigger engineering projects are, the harder they fall. The design faults are just as massive. The bulkheads that were designed to make the ship unsinkable were breached by the collision and just flooded. We're only three children — how can we do anything? We're fighting flawed engineering *and* nature.'

The word *nature* gave Luna an idea. 'We can do *little* things. Don't you remember meeting Professor Lorenz when we were at the Greenwich Observatory?

'I'm not likely to forget that.'

'He said that something as small as the beat of a butterfly's wings could create a tornado in Texas. That is his theory of the Butterfly Effect. That's why the whole Butterfly Club was started, that's how it got its name. Tiny, tiny changes can have huge consequences.'

'So what are you saying?' challenged Aidan.

'We've got the chance to live the 14th of April 1912 all

over again, the day the *Titanic* hit an iceberg,' said Luna. 'We have to look at what went wrong. The *little* things. And try to put them right.'

Aidan crossed his arms, unconvinced. 'Like what?'

Luna thought hard. 'Very well. For instance, when I was at lunch, the captain got an ice warning from a junior officer.'

'That's true!' burst out Konstantin. 'I was there in the Officers' Mess when it came down from the Marconi Room. The officer who took the warning to the captain was Harold Lowe.'

'Well,' Luna went on, 'that means that other ships must have seen the iceberg before *Titanic* did. Ones that were further ahead on the same course. But the captain ignored the warning – perhaps because he was at the table with so many important people. Our friend Mr Bruce Ismay, owner of the ship, just put the paper in his pocket, and your Harold Lowe was dismissed. Don't you see?' She appealed to them both. 'It's things like that. Something as small as a warning that was ignored. If Captain Smith could be made to take it seriously, that might have saved the ship.'

'It might *just* work,' admitted Aidan. 'What about you, Konstantin? What happened on your version of the 14th of April that could be changed?'

Konstantin considered. 'So far as the crew is concerned, it would have been the binoculars that were the small thing that could have made the difference. If I could somehow have got them to the Watch, perhaps they would have seen the iceberg earlier, instead of when we were right on top of it, and the captain could have avoided it.'

Then Luna remembered. 'The Watch,' she exclaimed. 'that's what my father said.'

'What do you mean?'

'*Watch out for the Watch*. He said that's the most important thing to know about the ship.'

'There we are then,' said Konstantin, pleased to have a mission. 'I'll take care of that today. So what about you, Aidan? What went wrong below decks?'

'Easy,' said Aidan. 'There was a fire in the hold that wouldn't go out and they shovelled the burning coal into the stokeholds. That meant the ship was travelling at top speed when she hit the iceberg. If I could find a way to slow it down...' He shrugged.

Luna laid a hand on his crossed arms. 'So you'll stay?'

'Yes.' But he still looked sulky.

'I'm sorry I pushed you,' said Luna.

'And I'm sorry I grabbed your wrists.'

'Call it even?'

'Yes.'

Aidan unfurled his arms and he and Luna shook hands like gentlemen. Konstantin laid his hand over the top in a three-way handshake, just as they'd done the night before, the moment the iceberg hit. Luna smiled shyly, Konstantin saluted with his free hand, and Aidan grinned his enormous grin.

They got out of the Time Train, stretched and smoothed down their clothes.

'At least we don't have to steal our outfits again,' said Luna, trying to make the boys see the positives. 'That's a mercy.'

'I wonder why not,' said Konstantin, pleased to still have his uniform.

'I think because they were in the Time Train with us,' said Aidan. 'I think anything in the Time Train stays the same.'

Luna put her hand to her pocket and felt the notes she'd made for Signor Marconi the day before on the stenograph. She had a thought as they walked to the galley stairs through the dry and tidy hold.

'Everyone we met – will we have to get to know them all over again?'

'I think so,' said Aidan. 'They won't know *you*. They can't, can they? They haven't met you yet.'

'All right, soldiers,' said Konstantin, when they were in the iron stairwell. 'Let's go into battle once more.'

'The same battle,' said Luna, 'on the same battlefield.'

'See you back here tonight,' said Aidan, then added, 'again.'

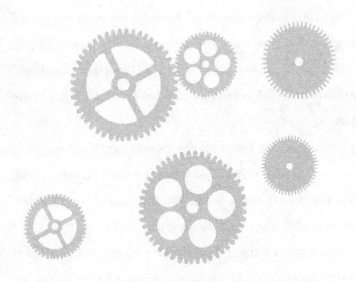

14 APRIL 1912
10 a.m.

Aidan went back down to the engine rooms, to live the 14th of April for the second time. He felt nervous, as if the butterflies from the Butterfly Room were whirling around again, but this time in his stomach. At least, he comforted himself, if he encountered the peculiar man with a watch for an eye again, they would not know each other. That was the good thing about time travel – you could make a fresh start every time you went back. But just to be safe, Aidan removed the bicycle belt holding up his trousers and put it in his pocket. The skip-link must look old-fashioned to the modern 1912 eye. The stolen trousers now felt a bit loose, but it was a price worth paying.

He wandered through the engine rooms and wondered at the huge turbines, positively thrumming with power.

This was what he'd wanted yesterday – an opportunity to explore the massive feat of engineering driving the ship. But today he felt a little overwhelmed. What could he, one little person, do to slow this great ship, speeding through the icy Atlantic waters? How could he save a hull that, in a little over twelve hours, would be ripped apart by an iceberg?

He stood right in the middle of the turbine hall, dwarfed by the massive engines, deafened by the din of the pistons. He closed his eyes and engaged his engineer's brain, and the cacophony went away. He could see the entire ship in his head like a blueprint. From what he'd seen last night the iceberg had hit on the starboard side, ripping a long series of holes in the hull of the ship. Last time he'd lived this day, the stokers had moved all the coal away from the sides of the ship, so there was nothing to dull the impact of the iceberg, nothing to stop the sides of the ship caving in. If the coal had still been there, would the damage have been as bad? He couldn't stop the stokers shovelling the burning coal into the furnaces, and accelerating the ship. But if he could somehow move the cold coal stores so that they were packed against the side of the ship that took the impact, maybe that would stop the iceberg penetrating the hull?

He left the racket of the turbine hall and went to the coal stores. He took up a shovel and stood looking up at the vast black mountain. He climbed as high as he could, boots slipping on a landslide of coal. Then he began to dig.

For the rest of the morning he dug, on the side of that black mountain. Some of the lads joined him and he had a lie ready for them. 'Gaffer asked us to do a bit of redistribution,' he said, 'so the heaps don't collapse.' And because, like most navvies, they understood weights and measures, they were happy to help.

At lunchtime there was strong tea, bread and butter, and thick gobbets of ham that the men just ate with their grimy hands. It was nothing to the fancy food that would be served in First Class, but right at that moment Aidan had never tasted anything better. He was just taking a grateful swallow of tea when, over the rim of his tin mug, he met the single eye of Arthur John Priest.

The stoker wandered over, never taking that eye off Aidan. He smiled to reveal his sooty teeth. 'Hello again, girlie,' he said.

Aidan's mouth dropped open, and the tea fell out of it. How was this possible? He'd travelled back in time – he and Arthur John Priest hadn't met yet. How had the stoker known him again?

'How are you finding it, second time around?' asked the stoker pleasantly, as if they were discussing the weather.

Aidan looked around. Luckily the other men were busy eating or talking or smoking – no one seemed much interested in two stokers talking. 'I don't know what you mean.'

'Yes you do,' said Arthur John Priest. 'You've come back to live the 14th of April again, haven't you? I wonder why? Once wasn't enough for you?'

Aidan abandoned all pretence. 'How did you know?'

'Well,' said Arthur John Priest. 'There's an old saying. Takes one to know one. Fact is you and I, except for the *obvious* differences' – Aidan knew he was referring to his own secret – 'are not that different.'

'God forbid,' Aidan said.

'Oh,' said Arthur John Priest, cocking his lantern head to one side and pouting a grimy lip. 'Don't be like that. I thought you might like to team up. That is, if you're here for the same reason as me.'

'No thanks,' said Aidan shortly.

'Hmm,' said Arthur John Priest. 'I'm beginning to think you're *not* here for the same reason as me. Moving all the coal, that your idea, was it? Reinforce the hull ready for tonight's crash, that's it, eh?'

Aidan said nothing.

'Pity,' said the stoker, finishing his tea. 'Well, no matter. I'd better be getting on. I can't risk you spoiling things for me, if you're going to be like that.'

'Where are you going?' said Aidan in a panic. An Arthur John Priest he could see was terrifying enough, but the thought of the stoker wandering about the ship, getting up to God knows what, was even more unsettling. 'What *is* the reason that you're here?'

The stoker tapped his sooty nose with his sooty finger. 'Never you mind. Your Uncle Arthur has things to do. People to see. Fish to fry. But I'll be seeing you later, don't worry about that.'

He chucked Aidan under the chin and Aidan was sorely tempted to bite the filthy fingers. 'You see, you are my ticket off this ship.'

And with that, Arthur John Priest melted into the crowd of men and out of sight.

14 APRIL 1912
10 a.m.

Emerging from the galley door on to the First Class deck, Luna felt the sun on her face. She remembered the day before, humming *Yesterday* – how could she have known then that she would see her father that very night, singing the very same song? Today she looked out for him among the smart people – somehow knowing that he was here on the ship made her feel less alone. Not that she was really alone – she had Konstantin and Aidan.

Aidan-Nadia.

For the first time in the madness of the last few hours, she had a moment, with the sun on her face, just to be and to think. And what she thought about was Aidan, and what Aidan had told them. She could not think of Aidan as Nadia. She had got to know him as a boy, and as far as she was concerned, that was what he was. She'd never really thought about the roles of men and women in society before boarding *Titanic* but since then she'd thought of little else. She watched the passengers on deck – the women in their enormous hats and furs, chatting as they took the air, and the men in important-looking huddles, wreathed in cigar smoke. The women looked like decorations, the men looked like *doers*, like they *did* something. It was just as she'd thought the night before – that in an emergency, men would be pressed into action, whereas the women had to watch and wait and be bundled into lifeboats.

Today, she didn't waste time. She went straight to find Signor Marconi and followed him as before until he went into lunch. Timing was crucial here – she must be in conversation with him just as they entered the grand doors, so the stewards assumed they were together. As they jostled together in the doorway she said, 'Do you remember me, sir?' just as she had done before.

He looked at her closely, and her heart all but stopped. Everything depended on him recognising her this time. What if he didn't?

'Southampton dock, the day *Titanic* launched. You handed me my hat.'

It was all right. She nodded in relief. 'I did.'

Living the same day over again was a truly strange experience. Luna was beginning to get the hang of it now. She sensed that, as she was the only thing that was different about the day, unless she herself changed her behaviour, nothing else would change. She knew that the steward on the door would bow his head as if Marconi were royalty, and greet him by name and direct them up the stairs. And as if he was an actor picking up a cue, he did exactly that. 'Signor Marconi, how delightful to see you again. For luncheon? Directly up the grand staircase, sir. *Bon appetit*.' He nodded in a friendly way at Luna. 'Sir. Miss. Enjoy your meal.'

As they mounted the grand staircase Luna watched, almost in a dream, as events played out exactly as they had the day before. *Now,* she thought, *the lady in the yellow will trip on the stairs. And now, the gentleman with the fur collar will throw out his arm to steady her. And now, the clock on the landing will chime one o'clock.* And all happened as she predicted. Then they entered the dining room, and Luna waited for Marconi to ask about her family.

'Will you be joining your family for luncheon, signorina?'

'Alas, no,' she said. 'My mother is dead. And my

father—' She stopped. What to say about Papa today? 'My father is at sea.' She didn't feel sad about Papa any more, because she knew he was here, somewhere, on the *Titanic*. But she knew that her emotion about her own father had been one of the things that had drawn Signor Marconi to her in the first place, because she had reminded him of his own daughter. So she dabbed at her eyes and turned away slightly, as if overcome with emotion.

Signor Marconi fumbled in his breast pocket, as she'd known he would, for a handkerchief – but drew his hand out empty. 'That's the oddest thing,' he said. 'I usually have a handkerchief in this pocket. I must beg that you forgive me.' His eyes were kind. 'I can assure you your father felt the parting as keenly you do.'

But while Marconi went on to talk of the wrench of leaving his own family, Luna felt the little bump in her sleeve, just under her cuff. In that mound of fine cloth, silken and monogrammed with the initials GM, the true strangeness of time travel came home to her. Mr Marconi couldn't offer her a handkerchief because he'd already given it to her. At exactly this place and this moment, one day ago. This, she supposed, was Professor Lorenz's Butterfly Effect in action.

They now passed into the grand dining room, and just

as before Marconi strode to the grandest table of all. He found his place card and turned to her, as she knew he would.

'Well, here we must part company. This place is for the stenographer I was promised, and I expect you must go and find your own chair.'

Right on cue, the steward in his smart White Star Line uniform came and spoke in Marconi's ear. Luna knew now that he was telling Marconi that there was no stenographer on board, and that Marconi would then go on to say *this would never have happened on the* Lusitania, the flagship of the rival Cunard Line. She just had to supply her lines as before and then wait for her cue.

'To be without even a secretary! *Mamma mia!*'

This time Luna was ready. 'I am a secretary,' she said smoothly. 'And I am experienced in stenography.'

That was perfectly true; but of course she couldn't say that the experience she'd had was a day's work under Marconi's own strict schooling. All went as before, she was engaged to work for him, and he said, 'Then, as my new stenographer, this place is yours.'

So that was all right.

14 APRIL 1912
1.10 p.m.

While they waited for the captain, Marconi told Luna all about his new radio and science being a race, just as she'd known he would. She thought of Aunt Grace and the Butterfly Club with a pang. The time-thieves had all but abandoned their mission to steal the radio. It seemed so unimportant next to saving the *Titanic*.

The captain duly appeared and everyone stood and clapped as before. He nodded at the company, and gave his toast. 'May God bless *Titanic* on her maiden voyage,' he said. 'Her first and my last.'

Luna shivered – if the time-thieves didn't succeed in their mission, it would be everyone's last voyage.

Now she knew that Mrs Edith Rosenbaum Russell, the journalist, would say, 'Disaster is my meat and drink.'

Again, Luna felt a shiver of foreboding. Before the night was out, Mrs Edith Rosenbaum Russell would have more than enough to write about, unless she and the boys could change the fate of the *Titanic*. Luna listened again to the captain's retort.

'Then you and I are opposites, madam,' said the captain. 'I desire nothing less. I never saw a wreck and never have been wrecked, nor was I ever in any predicament that threatened to end in disaster of any sort. You see, I am not very good material for one of your stories.'

This was awful. With the benefit of hindsight, everything anyone said took on a horrid new significance. If time marched on unchanging, Captain Smith would be very good material for a story, for as long as his memory lived. It was vital that Luna could somehow get the captain to take notice of the ice warning that would be given to him any minute now. Appetite gone, she watched the lunch guests, not a care in the world, drink their champagne and eat their fancy food, arguing the merits of the *Lusitania* and the *Titanic*. Then they discussed the Marconi Room, and all the time Luna, who yesterday had been hanging on every mention of that prized radio, barely listened. She was just willing the officer to come with the ice warning.

'Of course, my wirelesses have an important safety

function too,' said Marconi.

'Well,' said Ismay, 'happily that won't be needed.'

That was it. That was the moment. It was when they'd been talking about safety yesterday that an officer had come with the ice warning. And sure enough, an officer did come to stand at the captain's shoulder, waiting patiently until he was noticed. The officer was handsome and young, but Luna was so used to being the only difference in this repeated day that it took her a few seconds to notice that he was very handsome, and *very* young, and not at all the same officer as the one that had been here yesterday.

In fact, he was Konstantin.

14 APRIL 1912
11.30 a.m.

Konstantin made his way to the boat deck, the upper deck where the lifeboats were held.

His clockwork heart beat steadily. The air was fresh and cold, and he knew that *Titanic* must be heading into the North Atlantic. Yesterday, at this time, he'd thought of his brothers going into battle. Today he was *really* experiencing what his brothers had felt – real jeopardy, real danger. Yesterday, he'd only been playing. Now he knew, because of the heroism – and the cowardice – that he had seen the night before, that the status of 'hero' had to be earned.

He found his way to E deck, to the corridor named Scotland Road. As before, he followed the chap in the uniform and slipped in behind him when he entered the officers' rest room.

There once again was the pleasant airy room with couches and desks and lamps. There was the man sitting at a desk, writing case open in front of him, writing a letter to a loved one, while the other man in the corner chair plucked out a tune on a banjo. Yesterday, this had seemed such a restful scene – today, Konstantin saw it for what it was. The calm before the storm. That man with the writing case could be writing the last letter he would ever write. That man with the banjo, playing a plinky-plonky folk tune, could be playing the last song he would ever play. The thought made him quicken his pace and hurry over to the third man, sitting at a desk with an album of stamps, sticking in the latest acquisition in his collection.

Harold Lowe.

He stood at the young man's shoulder for a moment, before announcing himself. He wasn't looking at the album of stamps but at the back of Harold Lowe's head. He felt ridiculously fond of him, as he might have felt about one of his brothers. He admired, very much, the way Harold had conducted himself at the lifeboats, and what he was feeling now felt a lot like hero worship. He felt very moved by seeing him again, and if he was to save the ship, he would save it for Harold.

Just like Luna, he could not be sure that events would

play out today exactly as they had yesterday. What if Harold never spoke to him? What if he called another officer over to look at his album? Konstantin couldn't take that chance, so he didn't settle in a chair and take out *The Wreck of the Titan* to read. Instead he did something his father always called 'taking the initiative'.

'Good Lord,' he said, leaning in over Harold's shoulder. 'That's a Penny Black. And a Penny Red. And surely that's a Downey Head green halfpenny from 1911.'

Harold Lowe turned around and goggled at Konstantin. 'How the Devil do you know that?'

'Oh, I collect a bit, you know,' said Konstantin casually, and then he had a brainwave. He'd use the word Harold had used yesterday. 'Always nice to meet a fellow philatelist.'

Harold positively beamed. He shook Konstantin's hand until it nearly fell off. 'I'm Harold Lowe. Very glad to make your acquaintance, I'm sure. Most of these chaps wouldn't know what philatelist meant, and would care less. I say – I haven't seen you before.'

Konstantin shrugged. 'Big ship, isn't it?'

'I'll say. Biggest I've ever served on. What's your name?'

'Konstantin Kass.'

'That sounds like a mouthful of broken glass. I'll just

call you Stan, if that's all right.'

'Perfectly.'

'Foreign, are you?'

'Prussian.'

'Well, I'm glad to meet you. I don't know a soul on here. Most of the chaps came from the *Olympic*.'

'Ah,' said Konstantin, recalling what he'd been told the day before by Chief Officer Wilde. '*Titanic*'s sister ship. Had a collision and went back to dock.'

'That's right. A lot of the crew fetched up on here. Including the captain. I say,' said Harold Lowe. 'I'm starving. Let's go and strap on the old nosebag.'

Of course, this time around Konstantin knew this meant lunch. 'Good idea.'

He followed Lowe down the corridor to the officers' mess hall – the dining room. He had the same perfectly nice, if dull, lunch of meat, fish, potatoes and vegetables.

'Not bad grub, is it?' said Harold, sitting back in his chair. 'Not as good as they get in First of course. You should see the menu at the captain's table. Lush.' He stretched contentedly. 'That'll be me one day, if I play my cards right.'

'You'd like to be a captain?'

'Wouldn't I? Sitting up there with his champagne and

his caviar.'

'One day,' said Konstantin encouragingly.

'Yes. Takes time though. Best I've done is tested one of *Titanic*'s lifeboats for the Board of Trade – to check it's sound, you know. I rowed it round Southampton dock. So I've a bit of a way to go.' He took a gulp from his mug of tea. 'Smith's been at sea for more than fifty years.'

Konstantin whistled through his teeth. 'Long time.'

'Hmm,' said Harold. 'Maybe *too* long.'

Konstantin put down his mug of tea. 'What do you mean?' he asked.

Harold hesitated. He looked over his shoulder, like people do when they are trying to check that they are not being overheard. 'Well,' he said, 'there was that incident with the *Olympic*.'

'What incident?'

'That "collision" you mentioned. She bumped a warship, the HMS *Hawke*, so hard that the *Hawke*'s prow sheared right off. The navy blamed the *Olympic*, said that the ship created a suction because of her massive size. And guess who was on the Bridge?'

Konstantin kept quiet, guessing, correctly, that this was one of those questions that you weren't expected to answer.

'Our very own Captain Edward Smith, that's who. They say he saw the *Hawke* coming, but he couldn't avoid it in time.'

Just like the iceberg, thought Konstantin with a shiver. He kept his eyes on the door – any minute now, the messenger boy would come with the ice warning.

'So between you and me,' concluded Harold, 'the captain doesn't exactly have a perfect record when it comes to big ships.'

Right on cue, the messenger boy ran into the room. 'Officer Lowe. Message for the Bridge.'

He gave Lowe the flimsy piece of paper. Lowe read it without much concern.

'What's the excitement?' asked Konstantin, although of course he knew very well.

'Jolly annoying really. It's jam roly-poly on Sundays and *of course* that's the day I have to take an ice warning to the captain.'

It was then that Konstantin had a quite brilliant notion. 'Why don't *I* go?'

Harold looked at him sideways. 'Would you really?'

'Of course.'

'Well,' said the young officer, 'that's awfully kind. He won't be on the Bridge though, he'll be at lunch in the

First Class dining room.' He passed Konstantin the piece of white paper typed with black ink, and then sat back in his chair in delicious anticipation of the jam roll.

Konstantin got to his feet and smartened himself up for the captain, just as he'd seen Harold do the day before. He adjusted the knot of his tie, centred his hat on his head, nodded to his new friend, then made for the door.

'I say,' said Harold.

Konstantin turned.

'Ninety-nine times out of a hundred, they're nothing. But one time out of a hundred, they're something.' Harold lowered his voice again. 'Cap's a bit of a one for ignoring ice warnings – so make sure he actually reads it.'

'Oh, don't worry,' said Konstantin grimly. 'I will.'

14 APRIL 1912
1.15 p.m.

On the way up the grand wooden staircase to the First Class dining room, Konstantin did something highly out of character, which was to read a message that was not meant for him.

The message said it was from the SS *Baltic*. It was headed THE MARCONI INTERNATIONAL MARINE COMMUNICATION COMPANY LTD., and the text read:

Greek steamer *Athenai* reports passing icebergs and large quantities of field ice today in lat. 41 51 N., long. 49 52 W.

Written down like that in black and white, it seemed urgent enough to make Konstantin run up the rest of the stairs.

He thought of the story of the *Olympic* hitting the *Hawke* so hard that the prow sheared right off. Surely the sooner the *Titanic* could change course, the better chance she'd have of avoiding the iceberg that night.

As he entered the grand dining room to the heavenly smells of food and the tinkling of crystal glasses and the clash of silver cutlery, Konstantin soon identified the Captain's Table, partly because he spotted Luna's auburn head, shining out like a garnet in one of his mother's rings. He was not as surprised to see Luna as she was to see him. After all, she had told Aidan and him that she had lunch at the Captain's Table, so he had time to compose his features as he stood at the captain's shoulder, waiting patiently until he was noticed. He saw Luna's green eyes flare as she saw him, and he couldn't help noticing that she looked jolly pretty, with her auburn hair piled up like that. But he tore his eyes away and looked straight ahead, like a military man should, and awaited his captain's signal.

When at last Captain Smith turned his head to look at him, he suddenly felt a qualm. The man looked so noble with his silver hair and beard, and his face was etched with the lines of experience. The white uniform was so pristine, the gilded stripes and medals so well-earned and blindingly bright. He swallowed nervously. Was he,

Konstantin, a mere boy, to challenge this man? But he knew he must. He sprang forward and bent to speak in the captain's ear.

'An ice warning, Captain. It's urgent.'

He handed him the Marconigram, as flimsy as a banknote but worth far more – it had a value of thousands of lives.

The captain glanced at the paper and a frown gathered his forehead. 'That will be all, Officer.'

Konstantin knew he had been dismissed, and that he should go. But he didn't. 'Forgive me, Captain, but I was instructed to convey to you the *seriousness* of the warning.'

'I *said*,' said the captain, with a biting emphasis, 'that will be *all*, Officer.'

Konstantin stood up very straight, as straight as the tin soldier he hoped to be – the one that was cool and stiff and strong. 'If we hit an iceberg, particularly after dark, the ship will go down.'

The captain gave all his attention to his plate. 'In all my years at sea I've never had a collision and I'm not about to start now.'

'Well, that's not entirely true, is it?' said Konstantin pointedly.

'*What?*' The captain turned back to his officer, his

voice dangerously soft.

Loud enough that the whole table could hear, Konstantin said, 'In 1911, just last year, the RMS *Olympic*, the *Titanic*'s sister ship, under *your* command, failed to avoid the HMS *Hawke*, and the *Hawke*'s prow was sheared clean off.' His Germanic accent always emerged when he was in a passion, and it did so now. 'The inquiry ruled that the *Olympic* was at fault. *You* were at fault.'

The captain threw down his napkin and stood. Then, of course, because this was one of those peculiar rules of the time, all the other men at the table stood too, so a circle of millionaires and men of consequence surrounded Konstantin. Every conversation in the vast room stopped, every silver spoon stilled, and every eye turned to him. And then Konstantin felt it – something he'd never felt before, even last night at the lifeboat. Then, there'd been no time to think. Now, in this dreadful silence, under the eye of all these powerful men, and every guest in the dining room, some strange emotion twisted at his stomach. It felt exactly like it was full of butterflies.

The captain broke the dangerous silence. 'You insolent young *puppy*. If this was a naval ship I'd have you whipped. How dare *you*, a junior officer, question my record?' He pointed his forefinger right in Konstantin's face. 'Get back to quarters. If it wasn't the Lord's day I'd have you clapped in irons, but I can and will have you court-martialled in the morning.'

'You won't,' said Konstantin confidently.

'Well,' blustered the captain, 'this is your last day under my command, believe me.'

'Oh, I do,' said Konstantin, looking the captain dead in the eye. The same could be said of anyone in the crew – it was *everyone*'s last day under the captain's command. And all these men, for all their money and power, would be gone by the dawn if they didn't heed his warning. It was like arguing with his tin soldiers; figures that weren't real, or wouldn't be by morning. But he tried one last time. 'Sir,' he said, in a softer voice. 'You have had a long and distinguished career. If you heed this ice warning and change the course of the ship, you will be remembered as a hero. If you don't, you will be remembered all right, but your name will be forever linked with the most infamous shipwreck in history.'

Now every eye was on the captain. His face was almost purple with rage, the livid skin forming a marked contrast with the silver hair and beard. He almost spat five words at Konstantin, biting as bullets. 'Get out of my sight.'

Konstantin saluted smartly to the captain, his grey eyes

cold. But the captain's right hand stayed resolutely at his side. The fingers twitched a little, as if fifty years at sea had instilled them with an instinct that was almost impossible to resist, but resist it he did. He refused to salute his officer.

Konstantin turned on his heel and walked out. Only when he passed the clock on the landing of the grand staircase did his legs begin to shake.

14 APRIL 1912
1.20 p.m.

Luna's heart was singing with admiration for Konstantin. The way he'd held his ground, so dashing in his uniform, and literally stood up to the captain like that, filled her with awe. Now she had to try to be as brave as him.

'What an *extraordinarily* forthright young man,' said Mrs Russell in a prying way.

'An insolent young pup,' said the captain. 'What these boys need is a war. Give them some respect for authority. That one's a born liar into the bargain,' he went on. 'In the matter of the *Olympic* I was guiltless.'

'Well, I sure hope he was lying about the ice,' said Mrs Russell. She seemed to want to be in everyone's business, but today Luna was grateful for her reporter's nosiness.

The captain looked up and his face cleared, as if a storm cloud had passed. 'Of course he was,' he said, forcing a smile. 'Nothing of consequence. Merely a note from the Marconi Room.' And he passed the message to Mr Ismay, who crumpled the piece of paper and put it in his pocket.

Luna felt desperate. They were not going to take any notice of the ice warning. Either of them. History was going to repeat itself. Now Signor Marconi would talk about how anxious he was to get to New York quickly, to file the patent for his new wireless radio, and Mr Bruce Ismay would say, 'Let us move to full power and see what *Titanic* can do. We'll get you to New York in no time, Mr Marconi.'

This was madness. Luna *had* to say something. 'Captain,' she said, trying to sound as confident as Mrs Russell. 'Imagine for a moment that your... insolent young officer is right.' She remembered well the terror of the shipwreck the night before. Indeed, she didn't think she would ever forget it. 'Imagine this ship hits an iceberg, not a small insignificant thing but a berg as big as the ship itself. Imagine the *Titanic* begins to take on water. Imagine the terror of the passengers.' She urged the diners to see what she had seen, trying to make the scene live, just as she had seen it. 'Imagine that the ship begins to sink, and the lights go out, and the screams sound out in total darkness. Imagine the bow sinks into the depths, the stern lifts from the ocean, the ship cleaves in two, and all souls are lost in the icy sea.'

There was a small, shocked silence. All the exalted guests stared at Luna down their noses, as if the salmon lying on their porcelain plates had opened their fishy mouths and learned to speak. Only Mrs Russell smiled at her approvingly.

The silence was broken by Mr Bruce Ismay slowly clapping his hands. 'Brava, my dear,' said the owner of the White Star Line. 'I think you might look forward to a career on the stage. Ladies and gentlemen, we might have discovered the new Ellen Terry.'

Luna didn't know who Ellen Terry was, but she understood the polite laughter. They were indulging her – in their eyes she was just a silly girl.

'However admirable the flights of your imagination, my dear, that would never happen in this case. *Titanic* is the greatest ship in the greatest nation in the world, and will be remembered long after the *Lusitania* is forgot.' He looked around the table, gathering all the admiring glances. '*Titanic* is more than a ship. *Titanic* is an idea.

Titanic is a feeling. Britannia rules the waves – always has and always will.'

Luna felt sick. This arrogance, this Imperial pride, this belief that Britain was exceptional and unstoppable, would sink this ship and cost the lives of all the people on it. Not just the ones sitting around this table, but the people in Third Class who had paid everything they had to get to America. She lost the famous Goodhart temper.

'Well, perhaps Britannia *shouldn't* rule the waves.'

The captain, his colour rising once more, turned horrified eyes on her. 'How *dare* you, young miss! I've given my life to the service of that Empire. What an opinion for a young lady to hold, and worse, to express!'

'Ah, you've glimpsed the future there, Captain,' said Mrs Russell, whom Luna was liking more and more each minute. 'Young women will be heard much more in the coming years, don't you know. We may even have the vote, eh, my dear?' She reached out a hand and squeezed Luna's in a friendly way. Luna smiled politely at what she assumed was a joke.

'If that is the future, madam,' said the captain, 'I am glad that this is my final voyage. It is bad enough to be questioned by a junior officer, but I will certainly not be dictated to by girls, and I have no wish to live in a world where their voices are heard. Who is this insolent child, and why is she at my table?'

'She is my stenographer,' said Signor Marconi evenly, 'and she deserves to be spoken to with civility.' He spoke quietly, but with a certain power. As a man whose business was communication, he certainly knew how to send a message.

Even the captain seemed chastened. 'Well,' he said huffily, 'perhaps you'll control your employee.'

Luna had no appetite for her dessert, so just pushed it round her plate in silence. She looked under her eyelashes at Signor Marconi. Was he angry at her outburst? He had defended her, but would she now lose her job? But after two days' acquaintance she was beginning to learn that the only thing you could be sure of about Signor Marconi was that he was unpredictable. The extraordinary man was looking at her with something like approval.

He leant close and spoke in her ear. 'Chin up,' he said. 'Don't forget I am the father of a daughter, and I applaud you. Shall we go? We have much work to do.'

14 APRIL 1912
2 p.m.

Konstantin did actually go back to his quarters, just as the captain had commanded. He wasn't obeying orders, though. He went back to the Time Train for a very particular reason.

It was apparent that the captain wasn't going to heed the ice warning, either from the Marconi Room or from him. But he might listen to the Watch.

Konstantin had an idea. He was going to get the Watch some binoculars.

He knew there was no point in going to find Officer Wilde, as he'd done yesterday. The officer had been no help, but he had given Konstantin an idea. When Konstantin had suggested forcing the binocular cabinet open, he'd said, *You look too well-bred to be a pick lock.* Well, appearances could be deceptive.

So Konstantin went down the galley stairs, all the way into the hold. He sneaked under the tarpaulin to the Time Train, and in the light of the strange crystal glow turned the hands of the clock on the dashboard to 4.45. Chronos with a mechanical *Cuckoo!* popped out on his brass spring to hang in mid-air, bouncing gently. Konstantin wound the butterfly key clockwise until the ruby eyes lit up and the beak began to work. 'Chronos,' Konstantin said. 'How do you pick a lock?'

The little head cocked to one side. 'Well, that is theoretically dependent on the provenance of the security device.'

'I have not the slightest idea what you just said.'

Konstantin could have sworn that Chronos gave a tiny mechanical sigh. 'What kind of lock is it?'

'Oh.' Konstantin thought about this. 'I don't know. I just saw a little keyhole, such as you might see on a door.'

Chronos blinked. 'That level of information is woefully insufficient. Let me attempt to ascertain the necessary particulars by posing the following interrogative in as simplistic a manner as possible. Ahem.' He gave a little tinny cough. 'What kind of cupboard is it?'

Konstantin tried to remember as accurately as possible,

because the little bird was quite strict. 'It's a strongbox, black, up high in the crow's nest, attached to the mast. Four square, pig iron I think, with a brass lock about as big as a ha'penny coin.'

Chronos nodded approvingly. 'That's better. Secure lockers or cupboards of that nature use a four-lever deadlock. I'm assuming you do not have the key to this lock?

'No. Someone called David Blair has the key. Back in Southampton. The luckiest blighter in the Empire.'

'I have not the pleasure of understanding you.'

'He was—'

'No matter,' interrupted the bird brutally. 'Deadlocks have levers within the lock body which are normally lifted by the key. When something is locked, the levers in turn move a deadbolt out of the lock body and into a "keep", which is the bolt-shaped gap in the corresponding door. Is my language simplistic enough for you?'

Konstantin smiled to himself. 'Yes, thank you.'

'Very well. You need to unlock the deadlock, which means sliding the deadbolt from the keep into the body of the lock. What you need in order to pick a four-lever deadlock are two separate tools. You need a pick, which is a thin straight piece of metal, and a tension wrench, which is a piece of metal bent at ninety degrees. I am not sure where you will find such things on this ship.'

But Konstantin's eyes lit on Chronos's feathers – thin, long, pliable, made of bright brass.

Chronos saw him looking. 'I advise you not to contemplate such an action,' he warned.

'Oh, come on, Chronos,' Konstantin wheedled. 'Just two feathers. I'll give them back.'

'I will assume that you are jesting.'

'My father created you. He can mend you. I'll bring them back, I promise.'

'Dr Kass's skill as an inventor is hardly the point.'

It was odd to think of the bird having a better nature, but Konstantin appealed to it anyway. 'The fate of the ship might depend on your two feathers.'

Chronos was silent for a time and Konstantin thought he might have run down. But at length the bird said grudgingly, 'Very well. Be gentle, though.'

Konstantin eased out two little brass feathers as kindly as he could, smoothed one of them straight and bent the very end of the other one into a ninety-degree angle. He now had a pick and a tension wrench. 'Ready.'

'Now listen carefully. You insert the short end of the tension wrench into the bottom of the keyhole and put tension on the wrench handle *in the direction the lock turns.* Maintain this tension while you're picking.'

'All right.'

'Then poke the pick into the top of the lock and push until you feel one of the pins. Use the end of the pick to lift the pin up and then push the pick in farther until you contact the next pin. You need the tension wrench to stop the pins you've moved falling back. Keep pushing the pin deeper and lifting up the pins until you've lifted all of them. At this point, you should be able to turn the lock with the wrench.'

'I'll try,' said Konstantin, rather wishing he had Aidan with him. He was sure Aidan would understand the workings of a lock with no trouble. 'Anything else?'

'Yes. If the weather is cold, which I'm assuming it is, you may need to breathe on the lock to defrost the mechanism.' Almost before he had finished this useful sentence, Chronos's ruby eyes went dull, his voice slurred to a stop. He had run down.

14 APRIL 1912
3 p.m.

Once again, Luna spent the afternoon of the 14th of April in Marconi's study, among the chandeliers, overstuffed armchairs, and walnut panelling.

And once again her world shrank down to the small mahogany table and the little black machine under her hands. But she found her second afternoon as a stenographer much more difficult than the first, even though she knew how to use the stenograph, because she found it hard to keep her mind on her work. The thought of that cathedral of glittering ice floated constantly into her mind – she knew it was out there, floating malevolently in a dark sea directly on their course, just a few hours away, ready to herald disaster if that course did not change. But how could she make that change? The captain had ignored one ice warning. Might she be able to get Signor Marconi to take notice of another, if only she could get him to his own radio room? Instead of repeating her behaviour from the day before, she was learning how to use her *knowledge* from the day before to make her path easier.

So after what seemed like a long, long time she sat back from the stenograph and flexed all of her fingers. They were stiff and tired and her back was aching from sitting so long. 'Signor Marconi?'

'My dear?'

'You know how Mr Wallace came up with the idea of the origin of species before Mr Darwin did?'

'Yes,' he said. He looked pleased. 'Very clever, my dear Signorina Goodhart. Not many people know about Alfred Wallace.'

Luna did not like to take credit for something he himself had told her, but she did want to ask a question. 'You said at luncheon that science is a race.'

'It is indeed. And the winner takes all.'

'Well, my question is, if... someone... beat you to the idea for your new radio, would you care deeply about that?' she said, her conscience pricking her.

'My radio is my third child,' he said simply. 'If someone – someone like Nikola Tesla – took my idea it would be as if he took my child.' He smiled. 'It is hard to explain. If we have leisure tomorrow, I will take you to the Marconi Room and show you my pride and joy. I will even let you send a Marconigram if you please. Then you may understand better.'

Here it was – her chance.

Luna said, urgently, 'Could you take me today? Tomorrow it will be too late.' Even to her own ears, she sounded desperate. 'I'm sorry. I meant to say, if it's not too much trouble. You see, I would *love* to see the radio. I would *adore* to send a Marconigram.'

'Don't be sorry,' he said. 'I am very gratified that you are interested in my work. You remind me very much of Degna.'

'Is that your daughter?' Of course, Luna knew very well that it was.

The brown eyes softened again. 'Yes.'

'What would you do if your daughter begged you for something?' She looked him full in the face. 'Like I'm begging you now?'

He didn't answer straightaway. He just looked out of the porthole and said, '*Mamma mia*, it grows dark already.' Then he turned back and gave her half a smile. 'We should hurry if I'm to show you the Marconi Room before dinner.'

And he held out his hand.

14 APRIL 1912
4 p.m.

Konstantin climbed back up to the crow's nest, emerging into the dazzling sunshine at the top of the world.

Of course, he had to meet Frederick Fleet and Reginald Lee all over again.

'At your service,' said Reginald. 'Actually, at your service until six p.m.,' he joked. 'And then again from ten 'til midnight.'

Ten 'til midnight. The fateful Watch during which the collision occurred, at 11.40 at night. Konstantin wished he could blurt out what was going to happen and warn these two friendly boys who were not much older than him, but he knew they would never believe him. All he could do was to help the Watch see the iceberg for themselves, and for that, they needed the binoculars.

'Are you the officer with the key for the binocular cabinet?' asked Frederick, just as he had the day before.

'Sort of,' said Konstantin. He knelt down and took out the little brass tools he'd fashioned from Chronos's feathers. He breathed on the lock as he'd been told, and his breath smoked like a dragon's. It was getting colder, and cold meant they were entering the icefields. There was no time to waste.

Konstantin regarded the cabinet. The lock was a little scratched and blurred, as if it had had a little wear and tear since yesterday. But the weather must be harsh this far up the mast at times, and Konstantin thought nothing of this detail.

He fitted the tools into the lock, the pick above, in the round hole, and the tension wrench into the bit below, the part of a lock which looks like a bit like a bell. He tried to recall everything Chronos had said, and held the tension constant with the wrench while trying to push back the levers in turn with the pick. Time after time the tumblers slipped from his hold, and he began to think that Officer Wilde had been right – he wasn't the lock-picking type. And it wasn't ideal to pick his first lock in those conditions, thirty feet above the deck of the biggest ship in the world, in the freezing elements, with even the sturdy steel mast wavering like a reed in the wind. Nor did it help that these two hardened young men of the Watch were regarding him with dubious eyes. They didn't believe he could do it any more than he did.

It was fiddly, and his fingers were clumsy with cold, but on the third try the tumblers clicked and the metal door sprang open. 'Cor, sir,' said Reginald, 'that was quick work!'

'Have you jimmied a lock before?' asked Frederick.

Konstantin jumped up in triumph, suddenly ten feet tall, but his joy was short-lived. As the metal doors shrieked open, complaining of the cold, they revealed a set of hooks where the binoculars would have been, but the cabinet was empty.

'Someone's had 'em away,' said Reginald. 'No matter. We can see pretty well with the naked eye. It's what we're trained to do. And the other fellows of the Watch too.'

The other fellows of the Watch.

Konstantin felt a chill that had nothing to do with the weather. 'Who was up here before you?' he said urgently.

'There was only one of them. Not two. Suppose we must be shorthanded or something.'

Frederick added, 'I never seen him before in my life.

He's not one of the regulars. I remember thinking he was an odd choice for a lookout, though.'

'Very well,' said Konstantin. 'Thank you, men.' He saluted smartly and made for the ladder, but at the last minute a thought struck him and he turned.

'Why was he an odd choice?'

'Beg pardon?' said Frederick.

'The fellow you didn't know. You said he was an odd choice for a lookout. Why?'

'Well.' Frederick looked at Reginald, and then back to Konstantin. 'Not to put too fine a point on it, he only had one eye.'

14 APRIL 1912
7.15 p.m.

As it turned out, Luna had passed the Marconi Room a dozen times, and would never have seen it, even if she had come back to the 14th of April a million times.

It was on the boat deck, through a tiny door between the Bridge and the grand staircase of the First Class quarters.

'Here we are,' said Signor Marconi. 'There are actually three rooms. A small bunk room for the operators to sleep, a "silent room" with soundproofed walls to house the noisy radio equipment, and this, the operator room itself.' When he opened the door Luna had been seeking for so long she could see that Mr Ismay had been right – it was no bigger than a broom cupboard.

One wall was covered with equipment – coils and pipes and wires and cylinders and dials and clocks and charts. If the engine room where Aidan toiled was the pumping heart of the ship, she was now seeing the brain. And at the centre of it all, connected to everything else, sat a small wood and brass cabinet. A mahogany plaque with a little see-saw of brass was connected to it with a wire. Two Marconi operators were working busily at their stations – they did not even look up when the door opened. One of them, wearing a peculiar set of what looked like ear muffs, was busily tapping the little see-saw up and down.

'Excuse us,' said Signor Marconi as they entered, trying not to disturb the activity.

Without turning around, the Marconi operator flapped his hand in an irritated way and said, 'Shut up, I'm on with Cape Race.'

'I'm very glad to hear it,' said Signor Marconi drily, 'since I invented the system.' He turned to Luna. 'Cape Race is the message relay station in Newfoundland.'

'Mr Marconi!' Face scarlet, the operator got to his feet and removed the contraptions that he wore on his ears.

'Miss Goodhart, meet Mr John Phillips, Senior Marconi Operator. And that there – don't get up, young man – is

Mr Bride, his junior.' Mr Bride waved a hand and smiled. He looked about the age of Konstantin and Aidan.

'Do forgive me,' said Mr Phillips in that polite but flustered way adults have when something goes wrong. 'We are in a bit of a state, to be frank.'

'What's wrong?'

'Nothing now,' said the operator. 'We had a terrible time of it yesterday – the spark was down and we were doing maintenance, so now we are playing catch-up with all the telegrams. All the passengers are frantic to send their personal messages, as you know.'

'Indeed,' said Signor Marconi. 'Well, I won't interrupt you – only I promised Miss Goodhart here a tour.'

'Very good, sir.' Mr Phillips sat down and continued his work.

'Those clocks are on New York and Greenwich Mean Time,' said Signor Marconi, pointing to the wall. Luna nodded. She knew a little bit about Greenwich Mean Time herself. 'This chart is the communication chart, which tells us where other ships with Marconi transmitters are in the ocean.' She looked at the chart, an incomprehensible web of lines that resembled nothing so much as a fisherman's net. 'And *this*' – Marconi pointed to the glossy wooden box bristling with brass cylinders and dials – 'this is the wireless radio transmitter.'

Luna stared as a trumpet fanfare seemed to play in her head.

There it was – the ultimate prize. A humble box of wood and brass. This was it – this was what the Butterfly Club wanted to steal. The Gabriel Medal, the money – it was for this. Thanks to her new job, Luna knew a little of the science behind wireless transmission, but frankly it still seemed like a kind of magic. She watched Mr Phillips deftly operate the brass hammer that sent the messages. 'How does it work?'

'Radio transmission has a language all of its own, called Morse code. Mr Phillips is using that language now, and instead of words it uses dots and dashes. These are expressed using only electrical pulses and the pauses between them. A dash is three times the length of a dot.' He turned to the junior operator. 'Have you a Morse chart to hand?'

'Yes sir, somewhere. Here it is.'

Mr Bride produced a sheet which seemed to be just a series of dots and dashes. And then Luna noticed that, mercifully, there was the normal alphabet listed down the side:

INTERNATIONAL MORSE CODE

A ·—	I ··	Q ——·—
B —···	J ·———	R ·—·
C —·—·	K —·—	S ···
D —··	L ·—··	T —
E ·	M ——	U ··—
F ··—·	N —·	V ···—
G ——·	O ———	W ·——
H ····	P ·——·	X —··—
	Y —·——	Z ——··

1 ·————	6 —····
2 ··———	7 ——···
3 ···——	8 ———··
4 ····—	9 ————·
5 ·····	0 —————

'It looks jolly complicated,' she said.

'Some letters are easier than others, miss. The brand-new international distress signal, for example – S.O.S. –

has to be easy to transmit. So it's just three dots, three dashes and three dots.'

'And what does that stand for?'

'Save Our Souls,' said Signor Marconi, and Luna shivered.

'And now if you'll excuse me a moment, I must borrow Mr Phillips. I would just like to check the transmitter in the silent room and be assured that everything is in good order.'

Once they had left the room, Luna gazed at the glossy radio cabinet. If Mr Bride hadn't been there she could have easily disconnected the wires and taken it, just as the Butterfly Club had intended. But she wasn't thinking of what the radio was worth any more, only what it could do. For the first time in their short acquaintance, she fully appreciated Signor Marconi's genius. The radio could receive messages that could save this ship and everyone on it. She looked at the Junior Marconi Operator. He looked very young, and that made her less shy of him.

'Mr Bride,' she said. 'Is someone here in this room all the time?'

'Yes,' he replied. 'The radio is covered twenty-four hours of the day. If it's not busy one of us will get some kip. Today we're both on because of the backlog.' He stretched expansively. 'Ah well. We'll sleep when we're dead, eh?'

Luna couldn't laugh at this, not today, but she just about managed a smile. 'So you wouldn't ever miss anything important? Like… an ice warning, for example?'

'Well, we might at the moment, there are too many bleeding messages – pardon my language, miss. But ice warnings are ten a penny – we've had twenty-one today alone.'

Twenty-one. 'And what happens to them?'

'We have a runner take them to the officers, who then convey them to the captain.'

Just as Konstantin had done. 'And are they heeded?'

'If they're serious, yes. If you'll forgive me, I have to get back to it.'

Luna took the hint. 'Of course.' She kept mouse-quiet and waited for Signor Marconi, listening to the percussion of the tap-tap-tap of the little brass hammer. Her eyes lighted on a stack of telegrams that had been shoved under a paperweight, presumably to deliver later. Idly, she glanced at the top one. It was a creamy-coloured page, and at the head of the paper it said *Marconigram* in important-looking letters. Then she read the message below and her eyes flew wide. It said:

SS *Mesaba* to RMS *Titanic* and All Eastbound
Ships: "Ice report: Saw much heavy pack ice
and a great number of large icebergs, also
field ice.
Weather good, clear."

The SS *Mesaba*. Now *another* ship had sent a warning.
This, by any definition, seemed pretty serious to Luna. Had
it been missed? Had the backlog of passenger messages,
about expensive nothings such as stocks and shares or
upcoming balls and benefits in New York, crowded out
such dire warnings?

If you need something, her father used to say, *go to the top*.
She'd tackled the captain earlier, to no avail. She didn't
bother Mr Bride, who was feverishly tapping Morse code
into the transmitter. Instead, when Signor Marconi came
back, she meekly waited while he took his leave of the
operators and followed him out on to the now-freezing
deck. Then she made her move. She would appeal to the
very man who had invented the wireless system. She told
him quickly and quietly about the ice warning from the SS
Mesaba. 'It said "a great number of large icebergs".'

Marconi considered. 'I expect if they put it to one side,
they thought it of little consequence. They know what

they are doing. *Titanic* is unsinkable.'

This was hopeless. If Signor Marconi wouldn't listen to her, what hope was there? She tried one final argument. 'Signor Marconi, has anything ever gone wrong? With anything you've invented?'

'My dear *Signorina*.' He chuckled. '*Everything* I've ever invented has gone wrong. That's how you get things right. Mistakes are much more valuable than successes.'

'And do things still go wrong? Even now you are successful and have a room bearing your name on all of the White Star ships?'

'Well, yes,' he said. 'All the time. You just witnessed it. The spark gave out in the silent room, and no messages were sent yesterday at all.'

'Well, is there a chance, *just* a chance, however tiny, that Mr Ismay be wrong about his unsinkable ship?'

He hesitated, standing still as an ice sculpture on the freezing deck. 'Very well,' he said with a smile. 'Let us go back. I'll have a runner take the warning to the captain. Will that satisfy you? Since you are now, seemingly, my employer?'

At the door to the Marconi Room a tall man in a White Star uniform was coming out, pushing past them in a tearing hurry. Signor Marconi, a stickler for good manners, turned in his wake to stare disapprovingly, but Luna was too busy thinking about the telegram to notice.

'Mr Phillips,' said Signor Marconi, 'my young companion is most anxious that the ice warning be sent to the Bridge.'

'Way ahead of you sir,' said the elder Marconi operator. 'A runner came for it – he passed you just now in the doorway.'

'Ah,' said Signor Marconi, 'I suppose in that case we must forgive his breach of manners.'

'To be fair, he might not have seen you,' said Mr Phillips. 'Bloke had an eye patch.'

An eye patch.

Luna heard Marconi bid his operators goodnight, as if in a dream, and numbly followed him to the deck. This time she hardly felt the cold. She could only think of what she had heard. If Arthur John Priest had the ice warning in his possession, what were the chances of it ever reaching the captain?

14 APRIL 1912
9.15 p.m.

After hours of back-breaking coal digging, Aidan went on deck to inhale a lungful of blessedly clean air.

He stood in the very place he'd talked with Arthur John Priest the day before, feeling utterly downhearted. He had achieved nothing. He'd worked all day in that black landscape. But it had been no use. There were seven thousand tonnes of coal and he could do no more than a beetle on a dungheap. So now he was here, at the bow of the ship, leaning over the churning water and the whirling propellers, watching the vast ship speed ever faster to its doom.

A voice penetrated his thoughts. 'Cooling off, are we?'

He turned. He'd recognise that voice anywhere, but

Arthur John Priest looked entirely different. He was clean and tidy and dressed head to foot in an immaculate White Star uniform, just like Konstantin. If it wasn't for the eye patch he might not have known him again.

'I visited the laundry and got myself smartened up. You know all about that, don't you? Yes, I needed a uniform to get where I needed to go.'

'And where was that?'

'Oh, here and there,' he said breezily. 'There and here.' He leant on the rail companionably next to Aidan, as if they were friends. Something on a long leather strap fell forward from the neck of his greatcoat and clashed against the railings. Casings of brass and leather glinted in the moonlight, as did the round lenses of luminous glass.

A pair of binoculars.

Arthur John Priest had a pair of binoculars hanging about his neck.

Aidan's mouth dropped open. 'How did you get hold of those?' These must be the very binoculars that Konstantin had intended to give to the Watch in the crow's nest.

'Never you mind. Let's just say I had to *pick* my moment. They are rather swell, don't you think? I might try them out.'

He looped one strap over his head so it hung free from his hand, and held the pair of binoculars so that only his blind eye was looking through them. The lens of the binoculars met the glass of the watch with a sharp click. 'Can't see a blind thing,' he said. He made a little pantomime of lowering the glasses, looking at them, giving them a little shake and then trying to look through them again. This time he held the binoculars to his good eye. 'Ah,' he said, 'that's better.'

Aidan edged closer. He thought that there might, if he was quick, be an opportunity to grab the binoculars. 'What do you see?' he asked.

'Nothing much. Oh. Oh, wait!'

Aidan stopped moving.

'There's… can it be…' said the stoker theatrically, a catch in his voice, 'a bloody great iceberg! Here,' he said, holding out the binoculars to Aidan, right over the sea. 'Take a look.'

Aidan made a grab for the glasses, but before he could reach them, Arthur John Priest, to Aidan's horror, threw them in the sea.

Aidan watched them fall, open-mouthed, just as he had watched the stoker's cigarette pirouette down into the swell the day before. 'What did you *do*?' he shouted above the churn of the waves.

Arthur John Priest smiled his yellow smile. 'Oops,' he said.

Aidan grabbed the rail, knuckles white, eyes closed, in a silent rage. There were so many things he could have said to Arthur John Priest in that moment. He was not short of swear words – he'd learned every curse under the sun on the railways, words that would make Luna blush. But, with a supreme effort, he kept all the terrible words back. He had to be very careful not to antagonise this villain before the fellow could get away.

'Ah, well,' said Arthur John Priest airily. 'I suppose without the binoculars the Watch just won't see the iceberg in time.'

Aidan swallowed – suddenly there seemed to be a lump of ice in his own throat.

'Not to worry,' Arthur John Priest went on happily. 'We still have those plucky fellows in the Marconi Room. You've heard of Mr Marconi, I'm sure? An *I*-talian, and a clever fellow. Well, he's worked out how to get ice warnings from other ships on his fancy wireless radio. So don't worry your pretty little head,' he said confidently. 'They'll get fair warning.'

Aidan said nothing, but he began to edge away again

along the railing. If he could just gain the shadows, he could get away from this dangerous conversation, this dangerous man.

'Unless…'

Aidan stopped moving.

'Unless someone was to see that ice warning, and steal it away, before it got to the proper authorities.' Arthur John Priest brought out a piece of paper, flimsy as a banknote, from his pocket. 'Here, I'll read it to you. It says, "SS *Mesaba* to RMS *Titanic* and All Eastbound Ships: "Ice report: Saw much heavy pack ice and a great number of large icebergs, also field ice. Weather good, clear".'

Aidan's eyes widened. This was the clearest warning yet that there was disaster in their path.

'I thought I'd better… dispose of it. Just in case.' Arthur John Priest held the ice warning over the railing. For a moment it fluttered like a captured butterfly in his hand, then he opened his fingers and it flew away, snatched out of his grasp by the wind and blown far out to sea.

There was no use in staying. 'Well,' said Aidan, edging away again, 'it was nice knowing you.'

Then he found his wrist caught in a vice-like grip – that superhuman strength he remembered from the night before. Just as then, he found himself staring into the watch-eye, with those ink-black hands telling the lie that it was 4.45, and the maker's mark written across the face. One again he smelled the sour tobacco breath, and felt the warm rain of spittle on his face.

'No, no, no,' tutted Arthur John Priest. 'Don't you remember? You're my ticket off this ship. I haven't forgotten that little stunt you pulled at the lifeboats, giving me away like that. So we won't be trying that again.' He pulled Aidan even closer. 'I know you've got some sort of time machine stowed away somewhere, and I'll give you fair warning – I'm booking myself a seat on it. Yes,' he said, 'you and me are going to stick together now like peas in a pod. I'm not letting you out of my sight.'

Aidan struggled to free himself, but, strong as he was, he couldn't get his wrist away from the more muscular, taller man. Desperately, with his free hand, Aidan poked him in his good eye as hard as he could, feeling the jelly squish under his finger. Arthur John Priest cried out, dropped the wrist and Aidan ran.

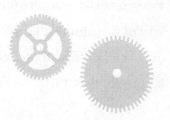

14 APRIL 1912
9.50 p.m.

A s Aidan escaped, his mind was racing as fast as feet. He'd failed in his Butterfly Mission, and his fellow time-thieves had failed too. Now what?

He ran back down and down into the bowels of the ship, past the poky stoke-holes belching out the heat of hellfires, through the vast turbine halls echoing with the din of the ship's heartbeat. All the time, he was jinking like a rabbit, changing direction, ignoring shouts meant to stop him and hands meant to stay him. He ran past the bulkheads, the watertight compartments Arthur John Priest had showed him: the *Titanic*'s great secret, meant to render her unsinkable. They had failed too.

Then he skidded to a stop.

Compartments.

He remembered what he'd told Luna about the bottle in the water. When it was full of water it sank. When it was full of air it floated.

Last time they'd lived through the 14th of April – yesterday, he supposed – the watertight compartments had been closed, but an ice spur had punched holes in the starboard compartments and they had filled with water. The compartments on the port side of the ship had not been breached, so they had been full of air. The ship had tipped and sunk.

His engineer's brain told him what must be done. If he could somehow keep the port side compartments *open*, they would fill with water too. He had to make the compartments do the *opposite* of what they were designed for. And although this sounded quite, quite mad, it was very logical – if the ship was balanced it would not tip. Even if the *Titanic* still sank then it would do so more slowly, giving everyone time to get into the lifeboats and be ferried to a rescue ship.

Aidan changed direction and ran through the maze of metal passageways to the port side of the ship, his hobnail boots clanging on the iron walkways. Using the blueprint in his head as a map, Aidan located the bulwarks and soon stood in one of the vast chambers – the mirror image of the one he'd stood in yesterday with Arthur John Priest.

There was no one about and he walked around it on silent feet – it was important that he wasn't seen.

Aidan knew what he was looking for. A compartment that could close like this, to achieve a watertight state, would use the same mechanism as a sluice gate, and sluice gates were something he knew about very well, having worked on canal systems with his father. He knew there would be a rack and pinion pulley for the vast iron door, a sliding closure lock and some sort of manual lever to engage the system. If he could somehow jam this lever, the compartment would remain open and would flood with water when the iceberg hit, and if he could do the same to the next four chambers all along the port side, the ship would be balanced and would not tip.

He looked round the huge room and then to the head of the vast iron door. Using the iron joists in the wall, he climbed like a monkey to the top of the room. Sluice gates were operated from the top, but this didn't really seem practical. He dropped to the floor with a clang and searched inside and outside of the door.

There was nothing. No lever, no crank, no switch.

Then he walked all the way to the other side of the great iron room and got to his knees, running his hand along the bottom of the metal wall.

'Looking for this?'

Aidan spun around, knowing what he would see. And sure enough, Arthur John Priest stood in the doorway. He'd opened a concealed panel in the wall and had his hand on a red lever.

'Listen to me,' said Aidan, both hands before him as if warding off a blow. 'I don't know what your business is on this ship. But the portside bulwarks *have* to be kept open. You know what will happen later. Then they will fill with water, and balance the boat. Maybe that way we can save the ship.'

'It's funny,' said Arthur John Priest, in a voice without humour, 'I said earlier today that we were similar. Now you have shown me how different we are. What makes you think I *want* the *Titanic* to stay afloat?' He looked up at the iron ceiling and Aidan felt as if he was in a cell and Arthur John Priest was his jailer. 'You know,' said the stoker in a pleasant, conversational way. 'You could probably survive in here for – what? Four or five hours. Eventually the air would run out. But of course, by then, you'd be on the bottom of the ocean.' All the time he was toying with the red handle. 'Anyway. Let's find out.' And with that he turned the handle sharply with a vicious twist, and the iron door, with a clink of the pinion and a shriek of metal, began to descend.

Aidan ran across the room, his footsteps booming. He made for the door but Arthur John Priest pushed him back and sent him sprawling. Again and again Aidan came at him and was repelled by the much stronger, older man, and unstoppably, the door descended. Desperate, Aidan clawed at his opponent, terrified by the thought of suffocating in an airtight compartment. The stoker had spoken the truth – he would be pulled down to a watery grave by his metal coffin, the floating city that was the *Titanic* turned to a necropolis on the sea bed.

The door had descended to head height, so Aidan couldn't be entirely sure of what happened next, but it seemed that another figure grabbed the stoker from behind, wrestling him away from the door.

The door was now just a foot from the ground, so Aidan rolled as fast as he could underneath it before it clanged shut for ever with an echoing boom. Arthur John Priest and the other figure were still struggling together in the gangway. The stranger shouted, 'Run, boy!' and Aidan did as he was told and didn't stop until he got to the Time Train.

As he ran, the only impression that remained of the stranger who had saved him was a glimpse of auburn hair, just like Luna's.

14 APRIL 1912
11.15 p.m.

When Aidan arrived back at the Time Train, panting and weak with relief, both of his friends were waiting. By the eerie light of the crystal columns, they looked thoroughly downcast. Konstantin seemed paler than usual, as pale as when he'd first met him, and Aidan feared for his clockwork heart. Luna, too, looked wan and glum, and there was no smiling tonight.

Aidan scrambled into the driver's seat and closed the tarpaulin. 'How did you get on?'

'Not well,' said Konstantin. 'I tried to get the captain to take the ice warning seriously. But that didn't exactly work, as Luna saw.' He explained to Aidan about the nasty little scene at the Captain's Table. 'And then I picked the lock, to get the binoculars from the cabinet, but they'd already been taken.'

'Yes,' said Aidan. 'By Arthur John Priest.'

'I *thought* it must have been him,' said Konstantin. 'The lads from the Watch said there was a fellow up there with one eye.'

'And my day went no better,' said Luna. 'I tried to make the captain heed the ice warning too, and got no further than you did, Konstantin. Then I made Mr Marconi take me to the radio room, and there was another ice warning there, from another ship, just come in. I tried to get it sent to the Bridge, but a man took it first.' She looked at them both in turn. 'A man with one eye.'

'Yes,' said Aidan, looking at his grimy hands. 'He chucked it in the sea, along with the binoculars. And then he tried to trap me in one of the watertight compartments. I had to escape to get back here – and if it wasn't for the help of a stranger then I would be there still. And there's another thing.' He looked up. 'Arthur John Priest *knew* me.'

'How do you mean?' asked Konstantin.

'He knew me from yesterday.'

'How is that *possible*?' said Luna. 'He hadn't met you yet.'

'I can't explain it,' said Aidan, 'but he definitely knew me. And this I remember: when I said we were the same, he said we were opposites. He told me I wanted the *Titanic* to stay afloat, whereas he…'

'He what?' prompted Konstantin.

'Well, he didn't finish, but tell you the truth, I got the impression that… well…'

'Well?'

Aidan felt bad saying something so terrible about anyone, let alone a working man. 'That he wanted it to sink. Why else would he throw the binoculars and the Marconigram into the sea? And he shut the compartments, so the ship could not be righted. Think of it,' he said, 'the three small changes we meant to make were all foiled by one man. It's almost as if… he's working against us.'

'Well,' said Luna dully. 'We were warned.'

'Warned?' asked Aidan.

'*Watch out for the Watch.* Papa didn't mean the Watch in the crow's nest. He meant the watch in the eye. He meant Arthur John Priest.'

Aidan sat up very straight as a thought occurred. 'Luna. Does your father have auburn hair like yours?'

'Yes,' she said, 'just the same. Why?'

'Because I think he just saved my skin.' Aidan explained about the auburn-haired stranger who had pulled Arthur John Priest away from the doorway of the bulwark.

'That does sound like him,' said Luna, sounding much more her old self, her cheeks flushing a little with pride. 'So he *is* still on the ship. I wonder if *he* can save it.'

'I hope he does a better job than us,' sighed Konstantin. 'We've failed to make any difference at all to the fate of the *Titanic*.'

They sat quietly and gloomily for a while, each one depressed by their own failures.

Aidan broke the silence. 'So. What happens now?'

'We wait,' said Luna. 'We struck the berg at eleven-forty yesterday. I noted the time.'

'Eleven-twenty now,' said Konstantin soberly, looking at the clock on the train's console. 'We can practically count it down.'

In the dim crystal light, they listened to the hum of the engines, so soon to be stilled. 'To think we were here in this spot, last night, talking about your book, *The Wreck of the Titan*,' said Luna, 'before we even knew what was going to happen.'

'Yes,' said Konstantin, drawing it out from his inside pocket and riffling through the pages. 'The very thing that happened to the *Titanic* straight afterward. And is about to happen again.'

Now Luna sat up too. As if in a dream, she took the

book from Konstantin's hands. The cover had a picture of a great liner sinking at a horrible angle, just as they'd seen the *Titanic* do last night.

'Konstantin,' she said, heart quickening. 'Where did you get this book?'

'My father gave it to me. He would give me books all the time when I was sick in bed, to keep me amused.'

Luna opened the book and leafed through the first few pages. As in all books, before the proper story starts there were all the pages in the front about where and when it was published and by whom. There was also a date. And those four numbers made Luna's jaw drop. She looked up. 'This was published in 1898,' she said. 'Four years *after* we left Greenwich.'

Aidan gave a long, slow whistle.

Konstantin grabbed the book from her. 'Let me see.'

Luna tried to put her thoughts into words. 'When your father gave this book to you,' she said slowly, 'it didn't exist.'

Now Konstantin looked up. 'What are you saying?'

'I'm saying,' said Luna haltingly, 'that your father has been forward in time too. He brought that book back with him. I'm saying,' she said, feeling her way, 'that he went a *long* way forward in time. I think he found someone to fix your heart. I think sometime far in the future someone has worked out how to put a tiny machine in someone's chest, to help their heart keep pace. I think he broke the rules, but he did it for the best of reasons.' She put a gentle hand on Konstantin's shoulder. 'He did it to save the life of his beloved youngest son. The clockwork heart wasn't a joke. It's real. You've got the future within you, keeping you alive.'

Konstantin laid his hand over his chest. The jacket over the scar over the clockwork heart. For a moment all three of them listened to it tick faintly. At last he said, 'Are you saying my father is a time-thief?'

'Why not?' said Luna. 'Mine is. I think that's why he's here, on the *Titanic*.' And she went on, 'I think Arthur John Priest is too. That's how he still knows Aidan. I think the rules are different for time travellers.'

'You're right,' said Aidan. 'He even admitted as much – that he and I were the same in some ways.'

'Look,' Luna said. 'We've accepted that time travel is possible. We have to. We're doing it now. Certain people, like my father, like yours, are doing it too. The author of this book,' she looked at the cover, 'Mr Morgan Robertson, must be a traveller, otherwise how could he write about a wreck that wouldn't happen for another fourteen years?

People are obviously hopping about the centuries all the time. My aunt told me as much. They've been stealing inventions from the future for some time. That's how they fund the society.' She thought carefully, trying to articulate what she wanted to say. 'They want us to save the radio from the ship. And that's fine. But it's not enough.'

'What do you mean?' asked Aidan.

'They set a lot of store by machines, inventions and discoveries. And they are all important things, no doubt. But *people* are important too.' She took a deep breath. 'If this ship goes down again we can save the radio, no doubt. But I want to save its inventor too.' She raised her chin, as she always did when she had her mind set on something. 'I want to save Signor Marconi.'

'How do we do that if the ship goes down?' asked Konstantin reasonably. 'Get him into a lifeboat?'

'He won't do that,' said Luna. 'He told me as much. So I was thinking – what if we take him with us?'

'You mean in the Time Train?'

'Yes.'

'I don't know if that's possible,' said Aidan doubtfully.

'I know who would know,' said Konstantin. 'The professor. Professor Edward Norton Lorenz, inventor of the Butterfly Effect.'

14 APRIL 1912
11.30 p.m.

Konstantin leant over to the dashboard of the train and turned the hands of the clock to 4.45. Chronos popped out with a *cuckoo!* and bounced gently, waiting, on his spring. Konstantin rotated Chronos on his spring so that he was peeping out of the driver's window, and wound the brass key, this time clockwise – forward in time – cranking it to its furthest extent. The little beak opened and a beam of light streamed out, as tall as a lamppost. The beam of light resolved itself into arms and legs and a head, and the professor appeared in the middle of the hold. He had the same blue-and-white transparent appearance as before – Luna could see the crates and cargo nets of the hold through his ghostly flesh. There was the pleasant smiling face, the suit of clothes in a loud check, and the thin, striped cravat tied in a neat knot and hanging down flat.

'Professor? Can you hear us?'

'Yes, son, and I can see you just fine too. When are you?'

Luna thought this was a funny thing to ask someone, instead of the more usual 'Where are you?' but of course it made all kinds of sense. 'We're in 1912 and we're on the RMS *Titanic*.'

'You're on the *Titanic*?' he exclaimed. 'Jiminy cricket! Then I recommend you get off it again as soon as possible. Why, it was the biggest maritime disaster in history. I'm sure I told those folks at the Butterfly Club any White Star ship *except* the *Titanic*.'

Now, of course, the children realised what the professor had been trying to say back in the Greenwich Observatory when the clockwork cuckoo had stuttered to a stop.

'I think you tried, sir. But Chronos runs down after about two minutes.'

'Of course – you're still on clockwork there. That's what comes of mixing temporal technologies. Tarnation! So we better hurry up.' He checked the little watch face, which, Luna suddenly remembered, he wore strapped to his wrist. 'You should get the hell off of that ship.'

'We'll go as soon as we can,' Luna assured him. 'But, Professor, there's someone we particularly want to save. Someone you sent us to meet.'

'Marconi, right? He died on the *Titanic*. Such a tragedy – he was really going somewhere with that radio of his. That's why I told you guys 1912. After that, he was gone.'

'That's just it,' said Luna. 'Can we save him?'

'How would you do that, honey?'

'Take him in the Time Train.'

The apparition shook its white head sadly. 'No, I'm sorry. Luna, isn't it?'

She nodded.

'You see, there isn't a Luna still walking around in 1894, while you're walking around in 1912. But there is a Guglielmo Marconi living in 1912, and you can't take the older Marconi back to a time when the younger Marconi still exists. For the two of them to be on the same plane would be a temporal impossibility, and the consequences could be disastrous. You can't meet yourself, honey.'

'So are you saying,' said Aidan slowly, 'that only time travellers can use the Time Train?'

'Exactly that, son. So unless there are other time travellers on board…'

Konstantin said, looking sideways at the others, 'There are. Two, we think.'

'Well, *they* can go back, sport, because they don't exist in the past. But no one else. Anything else before we run out of time?'

'Yes,' said Luna suddenly. 'Professor, Signor Marconi told me science is a race.'

'And he would be right. It's like Ancient Greece – Athens and Sparta had a terrific beef with each other for centuries.'

'Then, Professor, from the perspective of *your* time, can you think of anyone who would *want* the *Titanic* to sink? Someone who might be paying someone to make sure it never makes it to New York?'

'Well, honey, if the *Titanic* is Athens, you just have to figure out who is Sparta.'

Luna didn't even have to think. 'Cunard. They are the rivals to the White Star Line. And they have a ship, the *Lusitania*, in direct competition with the *Titanic*.'

'Well then they sound like a pretty good candidate.' The professor checked his wrist again. 'Just before we go, it's worth telling you something else. Something you might not want to hear.'

They waited, all feeling a little pit of dread inside.

'The other thing to consider, considering the period you're in, is a foreign belligerent.'

'A what?'

'He means a military enemy,' said Konstantin, the soldier.

'That's right, sport. You don't realise that in 1912 you're standing on the very *brink* of war.'

Konstantin tried to think of the conflicts of 1894. 'Do you mean with Spain? They've been giving us some trouble of late.'

'My dear fellow, no. I know why you'd say that, because of the era you come from. But no. I mean Germany.'

'Germany? That's part of Prussia.'

Luna and Aidan both looked at Konstantin, silent and sorry.

'But… but…' he said. 'That's *my* country.'

'Then, son, you have no *idea* what's coming down the track. You should really make sure that—'

At that point the professor's image flickered, froze, and then disappeared. Chronos's ruby eyes dimmed – the mechanism had run down.

'Clockwork be damned!' exclaimed Konstantin.

'No matter,' said Aidan, looking at the Time Train's clock. 'We can't worry about that far in the future. We've got troubles of our own. It's eleven thirty-nine and fifty-seven seconds. Three, two, one...'

Right on time, there was that tearing, rending sound, and the shriek of metal that they'd heard at exactly this time the night before. On this occasion, of course, they knew what it was.

The *Titanic* had hit the iceberg.

14 APRIL 1912
11.40 p.m.

'All right, troops,' said Konstantin. 'We head to the boat deck. We try to get *Herr* Marconi on a boat. Agreed? If that's now our Butterfly Mission, then so be it.'

'Agreed,' said Aidan, who looked at Luna.

'Agreed,' said Luna, but she had her doubts. Going on what he'd said last night, Signor Marconi would not get on a lifeboat and take the place of a lady, even if he lived for a million years. But she had to try and save her kind and gentle friend from the fate that the professor had so calmly recounted.

This time on the boat deck all three friends experienced together the eerie majesty of the iceberg, almost as big as the *Titanic* – shining out of the night and then retreating into the dark, like a passing ship in the night. Already the deck was beginning to fill with passengers, wondering what was amiss, their voices rising to a shrill level of panic. Konstantin pulled up his collar against the cold, and ushered the other two into the shadow of one of the massive funnels. 'Stay out of the way, Luna – you're a girl and they'll put you in a boat again. And Aidan – stay with her, and keep hidden. We can't risk Arthur John Priest getting hold of you. I'll be back directly.'

He centred his hat on his head, so that the white star was in the middle of his brows. Luna thought how grown-up he looked. 'Where are you going?'

'I'm going to find Herr Marconi. Where did you meet him last time?'

'He came looking for me here, directly after I'd spoken to my father. He'll be walking along the portside any second... *now*.'

And, just like clockwork, Signor Marconi appeared on deck, striding with purpose amid the chaos of the launch of the lifeboats, looking from left to right as if he was seeking something.

Konstantin marched over. 'Herr Marconi?'

The little man looked taken aback. '*Sì?*'

'Message from Miss Goodhart, sir. She has found a place in a lifeboat and begs you to do the same.'

Luna and Aidan, listening from behind the funnel, exchanged admiring glances at Konstantin's cleverness.

Signor Marconi narrowed his brown eyes. 'You are *sure*?'

'I handed her in myself, sir. This way. Captain's orders.'

Konstantin had overplayed his hand. Marconi stopped short. 'The captain? But I just left him. He was in the Marconi Room and he dismissed the operators, but he said nothing of this.'

Konstantin thought fast. 'The captain has instructed me to make sure his honoured guests get to safety.' They were so nearly at Lifeboat 14. Through the gathering crowd he could see the top of Harold's hat as the young officer directed the ladies into the vessel. He took Mr Marconi's arm.

'Unhand me!' said the Italian at once. 'As if my life was worth one lira more than anyone else's!'

Konstantin took his hands away and held both of them up in the air. 'I'm just doing my duty.'

'You're right,' said Marconi. 'Please accept my apologies. You are doing your duty. And now, I must do mine.' And he turned away.

'Where are you going?' asked Konstantin in a panic.

Marconi turned back. 'Miss Goodhart is safe?'

Konstantin nodded.

'You give me your word?'

Konstantin constructed his answer carefully. 'I give you my word of honour, that Miss Goodhart has a seat in a safe conveyance to take her off this ship.'

The little man breathed a sigh of relief. 'Then I think I will take myself off to the First Class smoking room, have a last cigar and a glass of Pignoletto. That's a wine from the hills outside Bologna, my home town and the most beautiful city in the world.' His face took on a dreamy look, as if he was transported somewhere else. 'There's a picture that hangs in there which I particularly like, of Plymouth Harbour. I will gaze upon that painting, drink my wine, and await my fate.' He clapped a hand on Konstantin's shoulder. 'Don't let me keep you, son. Good luck to you.'

Konstantin felt the least soldiery thing he could possibly feel. He felt like crying. He had just discovered another type of hero. A quiet one, who would take himself off into a smoking room, out of everyone's way, so as not to hamper the rescue of others, to calmly smoke a cigar and look at a painting while drinking the last glass of wine they would ever savour.

'Oh, and Officer?'

Now Konstantin turned.

'Save someone else, won't you?' Marconi said with his sad half-smile.

Konstantin nodded once, and hurried away.

15 APRIL 1912
12.20 a.m.

Save someone else, won't you?

The words echoed in Konstantin's head, their quiet power somehow louder than the panicked screams and cries around him. Those words stopped him in his tracks as he returned to his friends, turned him around and sent him back to the lifeboats.

Luna cared about Marconi, and that was all well and good, but he wasn't the only sympathetic soul on the boat. Konstantin couldn't leave Harold Lowe to drown. Harold, who had befriended him, had taken him to luncheon, had tried to save him by putting him in a lifeboat. It was time to return the favour.

He shoved his way through the crowd to the edge of the deck, where Lifeboat 14 was ready for launch. Then, just

As he knew he would, Harold Lowe called him over. 'Stan! Stan! Over here. I need you to pilot this lifeboat. You have the experience.' He tapped the gold stripe on Konstantin's arm. 'Quick, man.'

Konstantin grabbed Harold's wrist and looked him dead in the eyes. He lowered his voice. 'Look here. I'm a stowaway.'

Harold's eyes widened.

'That's right. A stowaway.'

'You're not an officer?'

'No,' said Konstantin savagely. 'I've never done anything. I've been in bed all my life, and lived everything second-hand. I've never fought a war, I've never been an officer and I'll never be a hero.' His voice cracked a little. 'And I've never piloted a boat. If I captain this boat they'll all die. You have to do it. You told me you'd tested the lifeboat for the Board of Trade – sailed it around Southampton harbour.' He remembered Harold's instruction from the day before. 'Just keep them afloat until a rescue ship comes.'

Harold looked to the waiting passengers and back at Konstantin. Too low for anyone else to hear he said, 'If you stay, you'll drown. You do know that, don't you? You might be new to this, but I've been on enough ships to know when they are going down.'

Konstantin gave a quick smile. 'I'll be all right somehow.'

'You'll need to keep the men back. They're behaving like savages. If they overrun the boat we'll all drown.' With that, Harold scrambled into the boat, which was by now heaving with women and children, the ropes that held it creaking and complaining of the weight.

'Stan?' shouted Harold. 'There's room for just one more.'

Konstantin could see a bent figure with a shawl about its head – hobbling like some old lady who needed rescue. But he wasn't about to be fooled again.

He pointed his forefinger at the shrouded head and said, 'Don't even think about it.'

Of course, the surrounding passengers were shocked that this young officer would be so rude to an innocent old lady – until Konstantin tore the shawl away.

The old lady had blunt features, a broken nose, a White Star uniform, and a watch for an eye.

'Stand clear there,' shouted Konstantin. He felt no sympathy for the man, knowing that he had tried to imprison Aidan in an iron coffin.

With a filthy parting look for all, Arthur John Priest disappeared into the crowd.

The valiant little band on deck began to play a tune that Konstantin recognised from the night before. The lifeboat was already winching downwards along the side of the ship, when a strident voice called, 'Stop! *I* will take the last place.'

The boat halted with a sickening jerk.

A figure strode through the crowd, most inappropriately dressed for a shipwreck in a black tailcoat and white collars, and a black tie in the shape of a bow. 'I am Mr Bruce Ismay,' said that gentleman, 'owner of the White Star Line. Stand aside, man.'

Konstantin stood his ground for a moment, unmoving. In the drama of getting Harold on to the lifeboat he had forgotten that there was destined to be another man on that boat, one who certainly didn't deserve his place.

'Boy,' said Mr Ismay, getting very close to Konstantin's face, 'I am the owner of this ship, and many others. Stand aside or I'll have you discharged.'

Konstantin felt disgusted by the behaviour of Mr Ismay. He said, 'If it is true that you are the owner of this ship, then you should act as a general does in combat. A general is the first in attack and last in retreat. You should show an example to all these good people, not run away. You should be first to board your ship and the last to leave it.'

Mr Ismay's eyes flickered, but he stood toe to toe with Konstantin, neither one giving way.

'Let him go, Stan,' called Harold, his voice dripping with contempt. 'We have no time.'

Lowering his eyes, Konstantin stood out of the way, and Mr Ismay struggled into the craft. At that moment, just as before, a huge distress flare, like the biggest firework in the world, burst high in the sky over his head in a fiery flower of rose and gold. A further sign, if it were needed, that his ship was in terrible trouble.

Konstantin banged his hand twice on the hull of the lifeboat. 'Anchors away, then,' he commanded. His last impression was of Harold, his face a picture of loss. As the boat lurched downwards on its winches, he shouted, 'Stan!'

Konstantin went right to the rail and leant over so he could hear.

'I don't know who you are, but you'll always be an officer to me.'

And Fifth Officer Harold Lowe saluted, rigidly holding his fingers to his forehead until he was out of sight.

15 APRIL 1912
12.25 a.m.

Luna and Aidan crouched by the funnel, the cold iron at their back, their arms warm where they touched. It was the first time they had been alone together since Luna found out that Aidan had been born Nadia and she felt suddenly shy of him. It made no sense. She'd always thought him by turns charming and infuriating and she couldn't unthink it now she knew he had been born a girl. And why should she? Why did it matter? Konstantin was taking an awfully long time, so even in the midst of the drama in which she found herself, Luna had a moment to be confused by these two boys who were now her friends. Konstantin acted tough and Aidan *was* tough. Konstantin was pretending and Aidan, somehow, wasn't.

She broke the interesting silence. 'I wonder how

Konstantin's getting on with Signor Marconi. He's been simply ages.'

Aidan blew his long black fringe out of his eyes. 'Give it a heartbeat and I'll go and see.'

'No,' she said, laying a hand on his forearm. 'I'll go.'

'But if Marconi sees you, he'll put you in a boat.'

'If Arthur John Priest sees you, he'll kill you.'

Aidan flashed his handsome and annoying grin and sat back against the funnel. 'All right, Luna. You win.'

As she got to her feet she hesitated. 'You don't call me Duch any more.'

'No.'

'Why?'

He shifted a little where he sat. 'Because someone gave *me* a nickname. I didn't like it. But he kept using it anyway.'

'Was it Arthur John Priest?'

'Yes. Then I began to think about how I would feel if someone called me Nadia.'

She could tell he found the word hard even to utter.

'It's not my real name.'

She shook out her skirts. 'Just so you know, Aidan, I didn't mind you calling me Duch.'

'Really?'

She tucked some stray strands of hair into her bun,

just for something to do with her hands. 'Yes. It's like Konstantin calling me *Fräulein*. You were the only one in the world who called me Duch.' She tried to explain. 'It was, sort of, our *thing*.'

Shyly she turned to go, but he caught her hand.

'Duch,' he said. 'Be careful.'

As she walked around the funnel, a snatch of a tune she knew well floated towards her on the icy air.

Yesterday.

'Papa?'

Suddenly he was there, and she was in his tight embrace again, his lashes fluttering against her cheek in a butterfly kiss.

'My Luna,' he crooned, concern in his voice. 'Why did you come back?'

'I wanted to save the ship.'

'You came in the Time Train?'

'So you know about that?'

'Oh, I know all about the Time Train.'

Luna mentally kicked herself. Of course he did. 'Listen, Papa. The professor says *you* can come in the Time Train with us.'

'Luna,' he said, holding her by the shoulders as he'd done before. 'I can't come home with you. I have something to deal with first. Or rather, some*one*.'

'Do you mean Arthur John Priest?'

'Oh,' he said, looking as if he'd tasted something nasty. 'You've met the gentleman?'

'Yes. It was him you meant, wasn't it, when you said *Watch out for the Watch*?'

'Yes. Yes, it was. I didn't want to scare you, if you were not destined to meet. But I wanted to warn you – and now I can be more explicit. Make no mistake, Luna, he's very dangerous.'

She nodded. 'He tried to kill my friend.'

'I know.'

'So it *was* you who saved Aidan!' she exclaimed. 'I *knew* it would be.'

'I did what I could,' said Papa. 'Sadly I was not strong enough to lock that fiend in the bulwarks in Aidan's stead.'

It was shocking to hear her gentle bear of a father speak so viciously, but he explained. 'You see, Luna, there are two types of time traveller. Time-thieves who want to harvest things from the future for the good of mankind. And time-anarchists who use their time travel to disrupt and destroy, to be agents of chaos. You are the former.

Arthur John Priest… well, he is the latter.'

'So he *is* trying to sink the ship.'

'Yes.'

'But… but… why?' She remembered talking to Marconi about Darwin and Wallace, and to the professor about Athens and Sparta. '*Is* he working for the Cunard Line?'

'That I don't know. I only know that I'm going to do all I can to stop him. That's why I stayed here, in the future.'

She considered. 'Have you been to the future before?'

'Yes,' he said. 'That's where I was, all those times, on "business".'

Luna had a thought. 'Has Konstantin's father been forward in time too?'

'Tanius Kass? Yes. Him too. He's a good man, the best. Look,' he said. 'There isn't much time. I need to find *you know who*.'

She nodded. 'But if you *do* manage to complete your business in time, will you come home with us?'

'If I can. I'll send you a message just as before. The letter, remember?' He smiled to himself as if at a secret joke. 'You must never underestimate the importance of letters. The Postal Service is one of the wonders of our modern age.'

It seemed an odd time for this observation, but Luna nodded again.

'And remember, when you go back to your own time *don't* be at the Greenwich Observatory at four forty-five p.m. on the 15th of February 1894. *Promise* me.'

Again, Luna thought what an odd instruction this was. It seemed so far away from the crisis they were living through now. But she said, 'I promise.'

'Good girl.' Papa kissed the top of her head. 'I'll see you again.'

'I know, I know,' she said. 'Yesterday.'

He held her cheek for a moment, smiled and was gone.

15 APRIL 1912
12.30 a.m.

There was no time to be lost.

The deck was increasingly crowded and the mood increasingly panicked. Luna was pushed and pulled as she fought her way through to where she'd boarded Lifeboat 14, but the boat had gone. There was no sign of Konstantin, or the other officer he'd befriended. But nor did she see Mr Marconi. She hoped against hope he was safe.

She made her way back to the funnel, now swimming against the tide of passengers flooding to the lifeboats.

When she got back, Konstantin was already there, talking to Aidan, low-voiced. When she went up to them they jumped, almost guiltily.

'*Fräulein* Luna, thank God. Quick. Marconi's all right. He's gone to the lifeboat.' Konstantin did not quite meet her eyes. 'I handed him in myself.'

'How did you get him to do it?'

'Told him it was captain's orders,' said Konstantin briefly. Luna was surprised but relieved. Marconi had seemed so definite yesterday that he wouldn't go.

'We should take the radio and get home,' said Aidan hastily.

'Agreed,' said Konstantin.

Luna hesitated. 'It feels wrong. It's stealing.'

'Look, Duch,' said Aidan. 'Marconi's lifeboat may get rescued, and I'm sure I hope it does. But if it doesn't, then the least we can do is save his invention for the future. Surely that will benefit mankind?'

Luna thought of what her father had said. *Time-thieves harvest things from the future for the good of mankind.* 'Very well,' she said. 'It's this way.'

Luna led Aidan and Konstantin to the little room, no bigger than a broom cupboard, hidden between the Bridge and the First Class lounge.

'Good,' said Aidan, as he opened the door. 'There's no one about. Let's be quick.'

'It's this bit here,' said Luna.

Aidan swiftly disconnected the four wires and yanked

the mahogany box from its moorings. Luna glanced at the clocks on the wall. The Southampton clock said 12.40 – and the New York one said 7.40. It was now the 15th of April. It took less than a minute to free the radio. It was quick and brutal, and Luna felt a moment of misgiving – such a beautiful machine, the result of so much of Marconi's brainpower, snatched away. But Aidan, who loved machines, seemed to have no such misgivings, so it must be all right.

'Done,' he said. 'Let's go.'

The three of them piled out of the room, jamming against each other in the doorway. But just then, they heard voices.

'In here. Hurry!' hissed Luna urgently.

She pulled the boys into the silent room. The lights were off, but somewhere in the dark she knew the transmitter crouched; silent now, its work done. She left the door ajar, because of course she remembered that the room was totally soundproof, and wanted to hear when the danger had passed.

'There's someone in the bunk room,' she breathed.

'What's that?' whispered Konstantin.

'It's where the wireless operators rest. Shh. They're coming out.'

First they heard a young voice, bright but anxious. 'But the captain dismissed us. He said the ship was going down. He said every man for himself.'

'I know,' said a deeper voice, older, more assured. 'But there's a chance we can contact other ships. To come and help us. Our place is by the radio. Let's keep going, Harry. Let's just keep going.'

'I don't know, Jack,' said the younger voice.

'We missed a lot of ice warnings today,' said the older voice. 'A *lot*. We were playing catch-up because the transmitter went down. We were too busy relaying birthday messages and stocks and shares to give the warnings the notice they deserved. And I for one don't know how sound I'll sleep if we get off this ship knowing we could have done more.' There was a silence. 'We need to stay here until the last spark has gone.'

'All right.' The younger voice again, suddenly resolute. 'What was that new distress call again?'

'S.O.S.,' said the elder. 'It might be our first and last chance to use it.'

Save Our Souls, thought Luna. She knew now that the two men were Mr Phillips and Mr Bride, the Marconi operators she had met earlier in the day. Swiftly and noiselessly, she pulled the door shut and the three of them froze while Phillips and Bride passed the doorway and went into the Marconi Room.

'Quick,' said Konstantin. 'Before they realise the radio's gone.'

'But…' Luna was torn. She felt desperate to explain to the two men what had happened and why their precious radio had gone. But she was overruled.

'Konstantin's right,' said Aidan. 'We need to get back before the Time Train floods. Because if it does, we might be stuck. We never tested it in water. Let's *go*.'

Of course, that decided it. They rushed along the freezing deck, which was already beginning to tip at a scary angle. Shards of ice slid across their path from port to starboard, and there was a rising chorus of panicked cries from the direction of the lifeboats.

The three of them ran to the funnel door and Luna reached for the handle. Then she stopped and drew back her hand.

There was paper tied there just as before.

'A letter from Papa!' she exclaimed, suddenly warm with the knowledge that he had written as promised. 'This is where he left the message yesterday.' Their special place where he had known she would find it.

'What does it say?' urged Konstantin.

Luna unfolded the letter and there was half of the inkblot, just as before, like a single butterfly wing, and below it, a scrawl of black ink. She read the message aloud by the icy light of the moon.

Dearest daughter,
Please write below the whereabouts of the Time Machine.
I will come home with you after all.
Best, Father.

Luna's heart leapt. 'He's changed his mind,' she said, hugging the letter to her. 'He's coming with us.' But when she held the letter to her bodice, the other half of the letter, the one she'd been sent yesterday, crackled in reply.

Yesterday.

She took it out and smoothed it on the iron of the funnel. Then she held the two halves together.

The Rorschach blot did not match – the two wings of the butterfly were entirely different.

She felt a chill at her back. It was the chill of disappointment, and more than that, fear. 'It's not from Papa. It's from someone else.'

'How do y'know?' asked Aidan.

She held both the halves together again. 'Papa asked me to check this blot – the butterfly shape, see? He said if they didn't match, it wasn't from him. And look, there's more.' Now she'd noticed the mismatched butterfly, she looked closely and noticed everything else that was wrong with the letter. 'Look. He put *Dearest daughter* instead of calling me Luna. He's written *Time Machine* but when he was talking to me he used the term "Time Train". And he's signed himself *Father*, not Papa, and has left off the little cross, which means he's sending me a kiss.'

'So who else could it be?' asked Konstantin.

'We know who it is,' said Aidan grimly.

Luna looked at him. 'Arthur John Priest?'

'Has to be, doesn't it? He must have overheard you talking to your father. He must be following him.'

Then Luna stopped being afraid and felt angry. To be followed and spied on by such a man was too much. 'Does anyone have a pencil?'

Both the boys did. Luna licked the lead of the pencil to make it blacker. Konstantin took *The Wreck of the Titan* from his pocket for her to rest on, and in answer to the request *Please write below the whereabouts of the Time Machine* she wrote:

Why don't you watch out for it?

'That'll fix him,' she said with satisfaction. 'Now we can go.'

'No.' Aidan put his hand over hers on the handle. 'He's probably watching, to collect the letter. Let's go back a different way and hope we lose him.'

The three time-thieves ran through the crowds of panicking passengers, past one, two, three funnels, and clattered down another set of galley stairs. Sloshing down to the hold, they could see that the water was once again threatening the wheels of the Time Train. They dived under the tarpaulin and Aidan set the dials for Greenwich. He forced the lever forward with a jerk, before a grimy hand could grab the brass rails or a blunted face gaze under the tarpaulin and find them out.

With a sickening lurch the hold of the *Titanic* disappeared, the stars somersaulted and they plunged into the howling darkness of time.

THE ROYAL OBSERVATORY GREENWICH LONDON

15 JANUARY 1894

15 JANUARY 1894
12.50 a.m.

'Why is it dark?'

They were back in the Butterfly Room at the Greenwich Observatory but it was dark as pitch outside, and the same full moon that had shone on the deck of the *Titanic* shone on them now.

It was eerie being in the twelve-sided room with all the butterflies, who were all back on the walls, immobile in the moonlight, their vivid, iridescent colours bleached by night to varying shades of grey – wings of gleaming pewter, bright silver, dull lead.

'Ah,' said Aidan. 'I forgot to set the time on the dials. Bit of a hurry and all that. So of course we fetched up at the same time at night – twelve-fifty a.m.'

They all looked around for the wireless radio, frightened

that it might somehow have disappeared in the whirl of the years. But no – there it sat neatly on the red velvet seat, like a fourth passenger.

Carefully, as if he was lifting a child, Aidan picked up the device and carried it out of the Time Train. He placed it neatly on the brass meridian line, wide as a handspan, that ran along the floor. It seemed to root the thing firmly in their own time. They all sat around it, exhausted, and then, as one, lay back on the cold wood floor to stare at the ceiling.

'Well,' said Aidan, in a strangely flat voice. 'We did it. We got the Marconi wireless radio.'

Konstantin said hollowly, 'I thought it would feel better than this.'

'I wonder if Signor Marconi made it off the *Titanic*,' said Luna.

Konstantin was silent. He knew the truth. Despite what he'd told Luna, he knew that the scientist hadn't even tried to board a lifeboat. He'd gone back to the First Class lounge, to have his red wine, smoke a cigar, and gaze at some picture he liked while the ship went down.

Luna sat up suddenly. 'I have to know. I have to know if he survived.'

Aidan, still prone, turned his head to look at her. 'How

could we possibly find out?'

'We ask the professor,' she said. 'Chronos should be charged by now.'

She scrambled into the Time Train and set the hands of the dashboard clock to 4.45. Out popped Chronos with his trademark *Cuckoo!* He did not seem any the worse for the journey, and she turned his brass key clockwise to call the professor from the future.

The apparition was even more luminous in the dark, glowing in the middle of the dim room. The professor looked somewhat different this time though – he was sitting down, in front of some sort of shiny box. The time-thieves sat about him, as if it was story time.

'Hello, kids. When are you?'

'Back in 1894,' said Konstantin. 'Where are you, Professor?'

'I'm in a library. I spend a lot of time in here, doing research.'

'Where are the books?' asked Konstantin, the reader.

Professor Lorenz laughed. 'Oh, there are plenty of books here, don't worry.'

'What's that in front of you?' asked Aidan, who, of course, was always interested in machines.

'This is a microfiche terminal. It's a machine which

stores photographs of lots of newspapers, going back hundreds of years. Think of it as a sort of magic lantern, full of photograms.'

Luna had a sudden thought. 'Professor, can you look something up for me? We think we made a small change, but we don't know if it worked. Can you find out somewhere if Guglielmo Marconi now survived the sinking of the *Titanic*?'

'Let me see.' They could see the professor touching the box in front of him, spinning a knob in his fingers. '1912, 1912, let's see. Ah. Here we are… "At two-forty in the morning on the 15th of April, the ocean liner RMS *Titanic* sank with all hands."'

'All hands,' said Luna, scarcely above a whisper. 'What does that mean?' But she knew what it meant.

'Everybody on board,' said the professor soberly.

'But… but… the lifeboats,' stuttered Konstantin.

'Lifeboats were deployed but no survivors were found alive, because no nearby ships came to the passengers' aid. Those who escaped the ship drifted until they froze or starved. *Titanic* sent no radio signals after twelve-forty a.m. on the 15th of April, despite there being a number of ships in the area. The *London Times* says, "This radio silence cannot be explained since the ship took two hours to sink, in which time distress calls could have been sent, but no nearby ships heard a single word." It goes on to say notable losses included Mr Bruce Ismay, owner of the White Star Line, and Captain Edward J. Smith and all his crew. Also the journalist Mrs Edith Rosenbaum Russell and – I'm sorry, honey – radio pioneer Guglielmo Marconi. It looks as if—'

And then, as always seemed to happen at the crucial moment, the image disappeared leaving them to the moonlight. Chronos's ruby eyes dimmed – he had run down.

'No radio signals after twelve-forty a.m. on the 15th,' breathed Luna. 'That was when we took the radio.' The three of them looked at each other, stunned and appalled. 'We changed one small thing and altered history all right. We carried out our Butterfly Mission. But not for the better – for the worse. We took the radio and anyone who could have been saved by it died.'

Luna looked at the precious radio sitting on the brass meridian line, squat and strangely powerful. She thought about Aunt Grace, about Konstantin's father, about hers. She thought about the Butterfly Club, about Queen Victoria, the Gabriel Medal and the prize money. 'The thing is,' she said soberly, 'we were so interested in stealing the radio that we never asked ourselves if it was right. This...' She touched the cool, smooth mahogany. 'This is someone else's idea. It is someone else's brainchild. This is Signor Marconi's property, may he rest in peace.'

The boys were silent, looking on.

'The Butterfly Club are in this mad contest with other countries,' she went on, 'just to make the Empire greater and richer. Not only that, they are in competition with their own country. I'm pretty sure my aunt's motives are as much to do with the Royal Society losing as much as the Butterfly Club winning. It's Athens and Sparta all over again.'

Aidan said, 'So what do we do now?'

Luna got to her feet. 'We have to put the radio back.'

Konstantin got up too and stood by her. 'She's right. It's the honourable thing to do.'

Aidan stayed seated on the floor, unsure. Luna went over to him. 'Aidan, you were right. Why were all those people on the *Titanic*, the 709 people in Third Class leaving Britain for a better life, if life was so good here? Britannia rules the waves all right. But the way it rules its people, well, that's another question.' She spoke aloud the thought that she'd had at the Captain's Table. 'Maybe Britannia *shouldn't* rule the waves. Or the airwaves. Or anything else.'

Now Aidan got to his feet, taller than either of them. He nodded his black head once. 'All right,' he said. 'Let's go.'

Konstantin and Luna scrambled into the back seat of the Time Train and Aidan lifted the radio carefully and placed it between them on the red velvet seat.

'No need to live the whole day again,' said Aidan. 'What time shall we go for?'

'Well,' said Luna, 'it would have to be a time *after* we'd stolen the radio. So after twelve-forty. And that means the fifteenth, not the fourteenth.'

'Good point,' said Aidan, setting the dials.

They braced themselves for the sickening whirl through space and time, and landed with a jolt in the hold of the RMS *Titanic*.

RMS *TITANIC*

15 APRIL 1912

15 APRIL 1912
12.50 a.m.

Things were different this time.

The ship had already started to take on water. 'Hurry,' said Luna.

They tumbled out of the Time Train and Aidan picked up the radio. They hurried up the galley stairs, their footsteps clanging on the metal, and out of the funnel door.

By now, the deck was crowded with panicking passengers and no one heeded them – they were able to run directly to the Marconi Room and put the radio back in its place. Expertly, speedily, Aidan reconnected the four wires. The clock on the wall told them that the radio had been disconnected for a mere ten minutes.

The instant they replaced the radio, voices could be heard from outside the room.

First they heard the young voice, bright but anxious. 'But the captain dismissed us. He said the ship was going down. He said every man for himself.'

'I know,' said the deeper voice, older, more assured. 'But there's a chance we can contact other ships. To come and help us. Our place is by the radio. Let's keep going, Harry. Let's just keep going.'

'I don't know, Jack,' said the younger voice.

'We missed a lot of ice warnings today,' said the older voice. 'A *lot*. We were playing catch-up because the transmitter went down. We were too busy relaying birthday messages and stocks and shares to give the warnings the notice they deserved. And I for one don't know how sound I'll sleep if we get off this ship knowing we could have done more.' There was a silence. 'We need to stay here until the last spark has gone.'

'All right.' The younger voice again, suddenly resolute. 'What was that new distress call again?'

'S.O.S.,' said the elder. 'It might be our first and last chance to use it.'

The time-thieves heard the two radio operators go into the silent room to restart the transmitter.

'Quick,' said Aidan. 'There's nothing else we can do here.' They slipped out of the Marconi Room, just as the noisy transmitter began to clatter and whirr and spark into life. They were safely on deck before the two men took up their places in front of the radio. Luna went to the door of the Marconi Room and peeped through the round window in the door. Both radio operators were bent over their transmitters, hard at work, tapping out those three pleading letters again and again. *S.O.S., S.O.S., S.O.S.*

There was an agonising silence.

Then, oh so faintly, Luna heard the tiny staccato voice of the Morse code, transmitting back, from somewhere out in the ether.

'Anything?' said Mr Bride, the younger.

'Yes!' said the elder, Mr Phillips, in triumph. He was transcribing the message on his notepad, his pencil a blur. 'I've raised the SS *Carpathia*. She's not far away. She's on her way.'

Luna did not go in – she didn't wish to interrupt the vital work of those brave men for the second time in a day. But she pressed her lips to the cool glass of the window in a kiss. 'Thank you,' she whispered.

15 APRIL 1912
1 a.m.

No one heeded the three time-thieves as they sped along the icy deck, as everyone was busy saving their own souls. But as they ran past the ornate windows of the First Class lounge, Luna saw a familiar figure inside.

This person, alone among all the passengers, wasn't running or screaming, but was instead totally still. Luna's footsteps stuttered and stopped. She turned and pressed her nose to the window, as she'd done many times at the sweet shops in Piccadilly to gaze at the lollipops and sugar plums. But this time, she was looking at a man. He was standing, a cigar in his mouth, a glass of wine in his hand, looking at a painting, just as if he was in his parlour at home.

She gasped. 'It's Signor Marconi!'

The boys looked uncomfortably at each other. 'Come on,' said Aidan, pulling at her sleeve.

She shrugged the hand away. 'He's just standing there. Why isn't he in the lifeboat?'

'Duch...' began Aidan.

'No, not you,' she interrupted. 'It was *you*, Konstantin, who told me he got into a lifeboat.' She pointed an accusing finger at his face. 'He didn't get to a lifeboat, did he?'

Konstantin looked at the deck.

'I *knew* he wouldn't go,' cried Luna. 'We have to get him.'

'And do what, Luna?' blazed Konstantin, for the first time forgetting his careful manners. 'We can't take him with us in the Time Train – the professor said we couldn't. And he won't get in a lifeboat. Believe me, I tried.' He pointed inside the lounge. 'That's how he's *chosen* to go. He's *chosen* to let the water claim him. Not to panic. Not to try to escape, not to take the place of someone else in a lifeboat, but to die with peace and honour.'

Luna stared at the figure. 'It's no good. I have to talk to him. I have to try to persuade him.'

'No,' said Aidan, wrapping his strong arms about her, holding her still.

She fought like a wildcat. 'Take your hands off me!

How dare you?'

Aidan spoke into her hair. 'Listen, Duch, if he sees you, he'll put you on a boat, we'll have to get you off again, and he'll end up in exactly the same place, looking at this picture, drinking his wine.' He held her until she stopped struggling.

Then softly, he said, 'We have to go.'

Luna, her heart breaking, let herself be pulled away, along the deck, turning her head to look at the man in the lounge for as long as she could.

Next, they passed the Bridge, with the lights now flickering off and on, illuminating the bright brass instruments and the great, glossy ship's wheel, now useless. But once again there was a solitary man inside, his hands on the wheel, a man in a white dress uniform, his chest covered in medals.

This time it was Konstantin who stopped. 'It's the captain,' he said.

Luna, her heart full of Marconi, would hardly have recognised him.

'Wait a moment,' said Konstantin. 'I have to talk to him.'

'Jesus, Mary and Joseph,' groaned Aidan. 'Not you as well. We're kind of in a hurry here.'

'I have to,' insisted Konstantin, his jaw set in a determined line.

'He's doing precisely the same as Marconi. What happened to "That's how he's chosen to go"?' said Luna, the unfairness of it choking her voice. 'What happened to "Let the water claim him"?'

'I'm not going to try and stop him,' said Konstantin. 'But there's something I want him to know first.'

'For God's *sake*,' began Aidan, but Konstantin opened the door and stepped on to the bridge. For a couple of his clockwork heartbeats he watched the captain, steering as if he were on a calm and balmy sea, for all the world as if the ship was not breaking up and crashing around his ears. The far-seeing sea-blue eyes stared dead ahead, seeming not to notice Konstantin.

'Captain,' Konstantin said gently. 'Where are you steering to?'

The captain did not look at him, but kept his blue gaze ahead. 'I'm steering a steady course, until another vessel comes to our aid.'

'Someone *is* coming,' said Konstantin. 'The Marconi boys are signalling. Someone will come.'

The captain gave the ghost of a smile. 'Perhaps. And they might be in time for the people in the lifeboats, but the ship herself won't not last long. No matter. My place is here, and here I'll stay. It's time to Be British.'

Konstantin didn't know what this meant. It seemed to him that courage, or the lack of it, was nothing to do with which country you came from. But it wasn't the moment to argue.

'Sir,' Konstantin spoke as if to a child, 'won't you come away now, and find a place in a lifeboat? They would not deny you – you are the captain.'

Konstantin tried to prise the old hands away from the ship's wheel. The fingers were cold, and strong, and immovable.

'I wouldn't take such a place if I was offered it,' he said, echoing what Signor Marconi had said. 'I am the general of this army, and a general should be the first in attack and the last in retreat. It would shame me to take the place of anyone else.'

Konstantin took his hands off the captain's and shrank back. This was so exactly like what Konstantin himself had said to Mr Bruce Ismay the day before that he could not argue. 'It does you great credit to say that.'

The captain turned his head very slowly and looked at Konstantin properly for the first time.

'You are the young officer from luncheon, are you not?'

Konstantin admitted that he was.

The captain's granite face softened. 'I said some hard things to you, my boy. But I suppose you were right. Now I will be remembered for this – the captain that sank the *Titanic*.'

'I said some hard things to you too, sir,' said Konstantin. 'But I was wrong about you. You are a hero.'

And then he saluted.

He'd thought that nothing short of a chisel would lift the captain's hand from that wheel – he was wrong. The captain, in a reflex ingrained in him from all his years at sea, raised his right hand and saluted back.

15 APRIL 1912
1.10 a.m.

Konstantin joined the others outside on the freezing deck, which was now tilting dangerously. 'Come on,' he said, 'I'm ready now.'

Back at the galley door Luna looked instinctively for a note tied to the handle, but there was nothing. Had she lost Papa too?

Straining, she heard a snatch of song over the roaring of waters. She wrenched the door open to let the boys through. 'Go. I'll be right behind you.'

'Good Jesus,' exclaimed Aidan, 'not *another* delay. Duch, there's no *time*! The Time Train's probably under water by now!'

'I'll be a minute,' she promised, 'no more. You wouldn't let me see Signor Marconi, but I *have* to see Papa. Just *go*!'

She rounded the vast funnel and there was Papa, just as he'd been before. Luna caught his hand. 'Come with us this time. You're allowed. The professor said.'

'I'll be all right,' cried her father above the chaos. 'I've survived this ship before, I can do it again. Remember to look out for the post.' He raised the hand that held his to his lips and kissed Luna's fingers.

Then he pulled his own hand away, but before he could do so fully so she turned his wrist and pulled back the sleeve of the greatcoat. The patch of skin between cuff and glove was luminous white and quite, quite blank.

She looked up and green Goodhart eyes met green Goodhart eyes. 'You don't have the butterfly tattoo.'

He gave her half a smile. 'No. I'm not one of them.'

She had so many questions. If he was not part of the Butterfly Club, why not? Had he travelled in time *without* their permission? Was he working *against* Aunt Grace, his own sister? But there was no time for all that. She knew she had to go.

'I'll see you yesterday, Papa.'

'Yes, Luna, you will.' And then he was gone.

Despite the rush she was in, she looked after him for a moment. And then, far away on the horizon, she saw an answering flare, like a distant firework, burst high in the sky.

Another ship.

Someone was coming to *Titanic*'s aid.

Back in the hold, the boys saw Luna approach with obvious relief. This time they both held out their hands to haul her into the Time Train.

'Right,' said Aidan, setting the dials before she'd even sat down. 'Greenwich Observatory, 15th of January 1894.' He looked up briefly. 'What time? Shall we say noon, in time for the Butterfly Club meeting?'

'No,' said Luna, suddenly inspired. 'The same time of night that we arrived before. We need to catch the professor in the library – when he's at that magic lantern that can read all the newspapers.'

The boys looked at her.

'We need to see if this all worked.'

Aidan shrugged. 'If you say so, Duch.' And he grasped the ivory knob of the brass lever and threw it forward, plunging them into the past.

THE ROYAL OBSERVATORY OBSERVATORY GREENWICH LONDON

15 JANUARY 1894

15 JANUARY 1894
12.50 a.m.

Back in the Butterfly Room of the Greenwich Observatory, the time-thieves wound up Chronos and called upon Professor Lorenz once more.

He took their request seriously and scrolled through his magic-lantern machine to find the same newspaper from 1912.

'Well, I'll be damned,' he exclaimed.

'What is it?' asked Luna, clasping her hands tightly together as if in prayer.

'"Mr Jack Phillips and Mr Harry Bride, Marconi operators, despite being stood down from duty by their captain, remained at their posts by the wireless radio, relentlessly sending out the distress call. Due to their selfless bravery, several ships came to the *Titanic*'s aid.

First to arrive was the SS *Carpathia*, a liner of the Cunard company."'

'*Carpathia* was a *Cunard* ship,' said Luna, in wonder. 'A Cunard ship came to *Titanic*'s aid. The White Star Line's great rival, but in an emergency, none of that mattered.'

'How about Harold Lowe, Professor?' asked Konstantin.

The professor scrolled some more. 'Sounds like Fifth Officer Harold Lowe was one of the heroes of the hour,' he said. 'He took Lifeboat 14 back to the wreckage, searched for hours for passengers on the water, and saved more than a dozen lives.'

Konstantin was delighted Harold Lowe had survived, and not only that, he had saved many others by going back for them and rescuing them from frozen waters.

'Mr Bruce Ismay, the owner of the White Star Line, also survived.'

'I'll bet he did,' said Aidan darkly. 'He made sure he was one of the lucky ones.'

'Oh, I don't know,' said Luna. She imagined that, for his remaining days, people would look at Mr Bruce Ismay from the side of their eyes, and talk about him from the side of their mouths, and condemn him for what he did. 'Maybe not so lucky,' she murmured.

Konstantin said, 'What of the captain?'

'It says that he died as he lived,' said the professor sombrely, 'at the wheel of his ship.'

'And Mr Marconi?' Luna asked, hoping against hope that something they'd changed had somehow saved him from his fate.

'Gone too, I'm afraid, dear.'

She'd half-known, but it was still a shock. She thought of him, drinking his wine and looking at that picture until the water closed over him. Her mouth twitched downwards, and her eyes felt hot.

'Are you okay, honey?' asked the kindly professor.

'Yes,' she said, her voice breaking a little. 'I will be. It's just...' She thought about Signor Marconi, inviting her to lunch, defending her from the captain, teaching her about the stenograph, about Darwin and Wallace. About science. 'I just liked it better yesterday,' she said.

The professor nodded sympathetically. 'When all your troubles seemed so far away, huh?'

Luna started. 'What did you say?'

'Sorry honey, just a reflex. I sure didn't mean no disrespect.'

'No, I know – but why did you say that?'

'Honey, that song was top of the hit parade, even in the States.'

'What's the hit parade?'

'The charts. A list of the bestselling songs of the week. It's by a band called The Beatles, written by two English fellas called John Lennon and Paul McCartney. The question is, how do *you* know it?'

'My father sings it all the time.'

'Then, honey, I have to tell you that your dear old dad has been as far into the future as 1965.'

No sooner had he said this than his image stuttered and Chronos, reliable as clockwork, ran down and was silent.

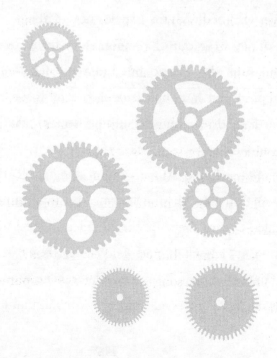

15 JANUARY 1894
1 a.m.

Once the professor had gone, and they were alone with the moonlight, they all lay down again, overwhelmed with the hopelessness of all.

They were out of danger, away from the water that had sunk the *Titanic*, but Luna still felt the water was seeping into her soul, leaking out of her eyes and into her hair, threatening to sink her too. Her father, if he'd even survived the wreck, was still far away on another plane, perhaps as far as the unimaginable 1965. Their own Butterfly Mission had been a total failure. They'd failed to save the ship, they'd failed to steal the radio for the Butterfly Club, and she was terrified of facing those eminent ladies and gentlemen later that day and admitting as much. Worst of all, Signor Marconi, that lovely, lovely man bursting with intelligence and ideas and love for his family, had been taken by the waves.

'Such a waste,' she said, almost to herself. 'Who knows what Marconi would have gone on to do if he'd lived?'

Konstantin, too, was down in the mouth. 'I feel dreadful for the captain too,' he said to the ceiling.

Aidan, the most practical of the three, was only glad to be home. He couldn't help thinking that 'feelings' of this sort were a luxury of the upper classes. He had made no connections aboard the ship that he would miss even for one second, and could only hope that the *Titanic* had taken the wretched Arthur John Priest down with her. He was just happy that he would never have to see that fiend with a watch for an eye again. But Luna and Konstantin were his friends and he felt that he must at least try to give them some comfort. 'We did what we could – look at all the people that the *Carpathia* picked up. We saved hundreds of lives by putting the radio back.' He put his hands behind his head, his usual sleeping attitude. 'To be sure, I'm sorry for Marconi,' he went on. 'But it's not such a bad end for a captain. To go down with your ship at the end of a long career, on your last voyage.'

'I think he'd have preferred a happy retirement,' said Konstantin gloomily. 'If only he hadn't swapped ships from the *Olympic*. Then he'd…' He sat up suddenly. 'That's it!'

'What's it?' asked Luna, with little interest.

'David Blair,' said Konstantin.

'Who's David Blair?' asked Aidan.

'He's the unluckiest blighter in the Empire,' answered Konstantin. 'Or, he *was*.'

'Explain,' demanded Aidan, lost.

'When I was trying to find the binoculars on the *Titanic*,' began Konstantin excitedly, 'Chief Officer Wilde told me that the key to the cabinet was still with Officer David Blair in Southampton. He'd forgotten to pass it on, you see, when Wilde replaced him as Chief Officer on the *Titanic*. Wilde called him "the unluckiest blighter in the Empire". Actually, it turned out that he was the *luckiest* blighter in the Empire because he *missed the Titanic.*'

'So what's your idea?' said Aidan sleepily. 'That we find David Blair and get the key to the cabinet?'

'No. I don't think that would work – Arthur John Priest would just steal the binoculars again, in another loop of time. I don't think, with the best will in the world, we'll be able to save the whole ship,' admitted Konstantin. 'Only *small* changes, the professor said.'

'So – what, then?' asked Aidan.

'We don't go back to the 14th of April again. We've

been back twice. It's futile. We go back *further*.' Konstantin looked from Luna to Aidan. 'We have to make *Guglielmo Marconi* the luckiest blighter in the Empire. *We have to make him miss the boat.*'

Aidan sat up too, suddenly fired up. 'We'd have to somehow persuade him not to get on.'

Luna shook her head, which wasn't easy as she was lying down and her bun made a sort of cushion. 'That won't work. He was trying to get to New York as fast as possible to file a patent before Mr Nikola Tesla, his rival, could—' She stopped.

'What is it?' the boys chorused.

Now she sat up too. 'It's Athens and Sparta. The professor said it himself. Or Mr Darwin and Mr Wallace. The *Lusitania* is the answer. Don't you see?'

'*No*,' they chorused.

'The *Lusitania* was *Titanic*'s great rival.'

'You are not making sense,' said Konstantin.

'The RMS *Lusitania*, Cunard's pride and joy, left Southampton *three days before* the *Titanic*,' said Luna, her tears drying. 'We just have to get him on that.'

SOUTHAMPTON HARBOUR SOUTHAMPTON ENGLAND

7 APRIL 1912

7 APRIL 1912
10 a.m.

Southampton harbour was bustling, the ships' masts rising like a forest.

The deep dock was crowded with every type of boat, from the tiniest tug to a huge shining ocean liner, dwarfing the city itself and gleaming expensively in the sun.

The RMS *Lusitania*.

Even from the clifftop the time-thieves could see the hive of activity, people crowded on to the dock and the deck, swarming over the ship, tiny as ants on an anthill. They could tell this was a ship that was almost ready to sail. There was not much time.

They left the Time Train where it had landed, in the graveyard of a little clifftop church, well hidden under some chestnut trees, and fortunately only attracting the attention of some interested pigeons. It took the three friends only a short time to find the little white cottage by the church. Signor Marconi had described it well. And if the yellow roses around the door weren't enough of a clue, there was a little girl playing outside. A girl in a dress the rusty scarlet of a Red Admiral butterfly. She was playing with an odd little figure, not a doll, exactly, but a little manikin made entirely of cogs and springs and pistons. This, Luna knew, was the work of a fond father. She went up to the child. 'Are you Degna?'

The little girl looked up, squinting against the sun. '*Sì.*'

Luna imagined how they must look – a young lady in a brown suit, a young gentleman in a smart uniform bright with buttons and bands, and another young gentleman in grubby work clothes, face and hands grimy with soot.

'Is your father at home?'

'Inside,' said the little girl, with a strong Italian accent, 'with Mamma and Giulio.'

Mamma and Giulio. Marconi's wife and son.

'Could you take us to him?' asked Luna politely.

'No,' said the little girl bluntly. '"Degna, if you are allowed to play outside you must not talk to strangers. And on no account must you let anyone into the house. There are too many people who want to bother Guglielmo

Marconi with their crackpot ideas." That's *exactly* what my pappa said.'

Luna's lips curled into a smile. It was a fair imitation of Marconi. It seemed impossible to get past this little gatekeeper, as she sat determinedly on the steps, a chubby, formidable presence, playing with her clockwork manikin. Then Luna had an idea.

'Here,' she said, 'I'm actually acquainted with your father. Look, I have his kerchief.' And she drew out from her sleeve the silken handkerchief Marconi had given her, at that last luncheon on the doomed *Titanic*. 'Is this his?'

The little girl looked at the G and the M entwined, and frowned a little. Then she looked up at Luna. 'Yes. That's my mamma's sewing.'

'Would you at least allow me to return it to him?'

The little girl considered for a minute. Then suddenly she smiled. '*Sì.*' She sat her manikin down neatly on to the step, got to her feet, and brushed down her skirt. She gave a pudgy hand to Luna. Luna took it and Degna led them inside.

They walked in on a contented scene of family life. The Marconis had clearly just finished lunch. A maid fussed around, clearing away the debris, and the sun shone in through the big bay windows. Signor and Signora Marconi were lingering over their wine; each had a crystal glass before them, and the bottle stood between them. Signora Marconi had a baby boy on her lap, a chunky little chap in a sailor suit, playing happily with a locket around his mother's neck which was glinting in the afternoon sun.

Luna hated to break up the scene, but if she did not, the family would never share a moment like this again.

Marconi, on seeing them, got to his feet, as he was in the presence of a lady. But of course there was no recognition in his face as he had never met Luna before. Luna was discovering one of the cruelties of time travel. Although she knew him well, and had grown very fond of him, almost as a second father, he no more knew her than he would have known a tinker who had come to his door. But Luna gave herself a stern talking-to. It didn't matter if he knew her or not. He was alive!

Konstantin spoke first. Funnily enough, it was the wine on the table that provided his opening remark. From where he stood he could just about read the label. 'Is that Pignoletto, from the hills outside Bologna?'

It was the right thing to say. Marconi positively beamed. 'That's right!' he said. 'Do you know Bologna?'

'Someone once told me it was the most beautiful city in the world,' said Konstantin.

'It is, my boy.' The Italian chuckled. 'Indeed it is. Can I tempt you to a glass? Mary, can we have chairs for our guests?'

Now the atmosphere was much friendlier. When Luna and Konstantin were seated – the maid, having sized up Aidan's place in society from the state of his clothes, pointedly didn't give him a chair, so he was obliged to stand over by the wall – Signor Marconi smiled on them.

'Now, what can I do for you?'

He couldn't have made it easier, but now Luna was here she didn't know what to say to her former employer.

Her former employer.

She had been his stenographer. The notes for the patent of his new radio, notes she had made herself on the stenograph, were still stuffed into the pocket of her jacket, crackling reassuringly under her hand. It was those precious papers that gave her the idea.

'Signor Marconi,' she began. 'This is Fifth Officer... Stan... from the White Star Line. He has a message for you about your upcoming voyage on the *Titanic*.'

Konstantin stared at her, his grey eyes wide.

She ignored him. 'Unhappily, the White Star Line is unable to provide you with a stenographer for the voyage.' She trod heavily on Konstantin's foot.

'That's right!' he yelped. 'No stenographer.' He'd almost forgotten he was wearing his White Star uniform. 'I'm from the White Star Line and I'm afraid I have to tell you that we will be unable to accommodate your request.'

'No stenographer?' Marconi's dark brows drew together. 'But I specifically requested…'

'I know,' said Konstantin. 'But I'm afraid it is quite impossible.'

'Well,' said Marconi. 'There are still three days to go until we sail. I'm sure I can arrange someone in that time.'

Luna got up and brushed down her skirts, just as Degna had done. 'Well, if you're sure. We'll leave you in peace to finish your lunch. We apologise for the interruption. Gentlemen?'

Of course, Konstantin stood when she stood and Marconi did too. The maid was already showing them to the door when Luna turned back, as if she had just remembered something. 'Oh,' she said casually. 'We were going to suggest that you travel on the *Lusitania*, which is boarding today. The *Lusitania* is due to dock in New York three days before the *Titanic*. Jolly useful if you were trying to beat someone to New York. Someone like… Mr Nikola Tesla.'

'Tesla?' Signor Marconi's eyes narrowed suspiciously.

'What do you know of Tesla?'

'Oh, only that he is booked on the *Titanic* too,' said Luna airily, crossing her fingers against the lie. 'Officer Stan told me, didn't you, Stan?'

'That's right,' said Konstantin, catching on. 'Quite an honour to have such an eminent...'

'... *physicist*,' whispered Luna out of the side of her mouth.

'... physicist aboard.'

'Yes. Both of you arriving in New York at the same time will make it a close-run thing.' Then she remembered. 'I mean, after all, science is a race. Everyone's heard of Charles Darwin, haven't they? But no one's heard of Alfred Wallace.'

Signor Marconi looked at her intently. 'No more they have, *Signorina*,' he said wonderingly. 'No more they have.' He looked at Konstantin. 'Will there even be a spare berth on the *Lusitania* at such short notice?'

'Sir, the ship has a Marconi Room named after you. They will not deny you passage,' he said, hoping it was true.

Like most grown-ups, Signor Marconi was not immune to a bit of flattery.

'Very well, then.' Marconi put Degna down and stroked

her head fondly. 'I suppose this is farewell for now, my dears.'

Degna was not having that. 'Can we come and wave you off? *Please*, Pappa.'

It was clear that Marconi could not refuse the child anything. 'Very well, then.'

7 APRIL 1912
1.30 p.m.

The little procession made its way down to the docks. Marconi held the hands of his wife and daughter, the maid carried Giulio, and Aidan and Konstantin carried Marconi's trunk between them. And all the time, the *Lusitania* loomed larger and larger, until they were right next to her and waiting in her shadow with the other passengers.

There was a gangplank across the dock, for the First Class passengers to board the ship, and an officer in a Cunard Line uniform stood on the shore with a clipboard, marking the passengers off on a list. Konstantin stood up very straight. 'Allow me, *Signor*,' he said to Marconi, and went to talk to the man in uniform.

His new-found confidence led him straight to the front

of the queue, firmly but unapologetically excusing himself to all the expensive-looking passengers. He touched his cap to the young officer, who looked not much older than him, and spoke in his ear.

'I have Mr Guglielmo Marconi with me.'

'Marconi?' The officer looked up from his manifest. 'As in Marconi radio?'

'The very same. He was meant to sail on the *Titanic* in three days, but needs to get to New York earlier.' Konstantin looked about him as if he was about to share a secret. 'Between you and me, this will be a blow for the White Star Line, if Mr Marconi travels with Cunard instead.'

The Cunard officer puffed up with pride. 'We always keep the Royal Suite empty in case of such eventualities – for heads of state and persons of that nature. As we are so close to sailing and the suite is still free, we'd be honoured to accommodate Mr Marconi.'

At this point the gentleman himself appeared at Konstantin's elbow. 'And you have a stenographer on board? I need to file a patent the instant I land at New York.'

Konstantin held his breath.

'Certainly we do, sir,' said the officer respectfully. 'I'll have him sent to your suite directly.'

Konstantin felt relief fill him up like a flask.

Signor Marconi took affectionate leave of all his family, kissing his wife and daughter fondly and ballooning his cheeks to make the baby laugh.

Luna watched it all with a lump in her throat. Thanks to this small alteration, the exchange of one ship for another, Signor Marconi would see his little family grow, and have many more precious years for his inventions. As he crossed the gangplank, turned for one last wave and disappeared into the belly of a ship, she breathed a sigh of relief.

A crowd had gathered on the dock, much like the one that would gather in three days for the launch of the doomed *Titanic*. As the great ship pulled away from the dock and a cheer went up, Luna watched little Degna waving frantically. It was impossible to see her bowler-hatted father among the many bowler-hatted gentlemen crammed against the rail of the ship, but Luna knew he was there, waving back.

So that her father might see her, the little girl waved the handkerchief Luna had given her, the white silk windmilling above her head. As the *Lusitania* sailed away, Degna ran along the dock, a streak of red in her scarlet dress, just as Luna had first seen her from the deck of the *Titanic*.

The time-thieves linked arms and followed the Marconis along the dock until they were obliged to stop at the edge of the harbour. Still they watched, as the great ocean liner became a good-sized yacht, then a tug boat, then a speck, and finally disappeared. Only then did Degna turn to Luna and give her back the handkerchief.

Luna looked at the square of silk in her hand, lovingly embroidered with the letters **G M** for Guglielmo Marconi. Carefully, tenderly, she folded it and gave it back.

'Keep it,' said Luna, as Marconi had once said to her. 'Give it to your papa the next time you see him.'

THE ROYAL OBSERVATORY GREENWICH LONDON

15 JANUARY 1894

15 JANUARY 1894
12.50 a.m.

The time-thieves had chosen the same time as before to return home, hoping to find Professor Lorenz in the library, looking into his magic lantern box. And so it was. The professor's hologram was seated at the microfiche and Luna asked him the crucial question.

'Did Marconi survive the *Titanic*? He wasn't on it, honey. And he went on to be a giant in the field of radio telegraphy. Oh, and you'll like this,' said the professor, scrolling away. 'This is an article from the inquiry into the *Titanic*'s sinking.'

'What's an inquiry?' put in Luna.

'A big court case where they find out what actually happened and why it happened. Well, not only was Marconi there at the inquest, but he was actually commended by name. Listen: "On 18 June 1912, Marconi gave evidence to the Court of Inquiry into the loss of *Titanic* regarding the marine telegraphy's functions and the procedures for emergencies at sea. Britain's postmaster general summed up, referring to the *Titanic* disaster: 'Those who have been saved, have been saved through one man, Mr Marconi… and his marvellous invention.' Marconi was offered free passage on *Titanic* before she sank, but had taken the *Lusitania* three days earlier. As his daughter Degna later explained, he had paperwork to do and preferred the public stenographer aboard that vessel." There,' said the professor. 'The *Titanic* was a dreadful disaster, no question, but the hundreds who were saved because of Marconi's radio. It's here in black and white.'

Luna breathed a sigh of relief. He'd lived. Marconi had lived to see his daughter grow.

But of course that put her in mind of her own father, and once she'd thought of him, she had to ask. 'Is there anything about my papa?'

'What's his name, honey?'

'Daniel Goodhart.' Luna felt odd saying her father's full name like that, rather than calling him Papa.

This took a bit longer. 'Daniel Goodhart. Daniel Goodhart,' murmured the professor, scrolling left and right. 'No news of him directly that I can see. But that doesn't mean he didn't make it. He isn't listed among the dead, and there were some pretty incredible escapes. Some guy even posted himself off the ship in a mailbag.'

Then, suddenly, Luna remembered that last hectic exchange with her father on board the *Titanic*. *The Postal Service is one of the wonders of our modern age.* It was practically the last thing he'd said to her – a very odd farewell. She remembered, too, hearing at Queenstown that some enterprising man had posted himself off the ship in a postbag. At that point they'd all thought that nameless man a fool to miss such a great adventure. Now she knew he was no fool but in fact her father, Daniel Goodhart.

'What about a fellow called Arthur John Priest?' asked Aidan, and waited with a sense of foreboding as the professor sped through the newsprint.

'Survived,' said the professor, much more quickly than Aidan expected. 'It says so here.'

'Wait,' said Konstantin. Something didn't quite add up. 'The survival of a humble stoker made the newspapers?'

'Well, he was somewhat of a special case,' said the professor.

'What do you mean, sir?'

'Only that it wasn't the first time, or the last. He survived the shipwrecks of the *Olympic*, the *Titanic*, the *Alcantara*, the *Britannic* and the *Donegal*.' He sat back in his chair, and as the image began to stutter and fail, he could just be heard saying, 'I don't know how you know the gentleman, but he sure sounds like a time traveller to me.'

15 JANUARY 1894
9 a.m.

Even this combination of exciting and troubling news could not keep the time-thieves awake for long.

They hadn't properly slept in days, and although they talked for a little about who had survived the *Titanic* they were very soon fast asleep, right there on the wooden parquet floor of the Butterfly Room, splayed out on both sides of the meridian line, divided by time itself.

Luna was the first to wake. The morning light had restored colour to the butterflies, as if someone had been busily painting them since dawn. She looked about the room at the Dukes of Burgundy, the Red Admirals and the Dingy Skippers. At the Great Purple Emperors, the Cabbage Whites and the Agrias butterflies, vivid and still and caught in time. And there, in the midst of them, the clock.

She sat up.

The grandfather clock, with the double-sided casement which formed the secret door to the Butterfly Room, showed nine o'clock.

For a moment, she let the boys sleep, becoming increasingly anxious as the hands of the double-sided clock edged round. It was then, out of nowhere, that she remembered her father's dire warning.

If you love me, please ensure that you are nowhere near the Greenwich Observatory at the hour of 4.45 p.m. precisely on Thursday the 15th of February 1894.

A month's time. What would happen here in just four short weeks? Why must she stay away? But then she thought of a more pressing problem. At noon − in three short hours − the eminent members of the Butterfly Club would gather: Mr H.G. Wells, Mr Conan Doyle, Konstantin's father, Aunt Grace and all the other important figures of scientific, intellectual and artistic London. Just for now, she was more afraid of her aunt than her father's warning.

The time-thieves had saved Guglielmo Marconi's life but they had nothing, absolutely nothing else to show for their troubles. There was no radio, there would be no

Gabriel Medal, no royal approval from Queen Victoria, no prize money for the society. Luna dreaded the look in her aunt's green eyes.

Unable to wait any longer, she woke the others. 'What do you think they'll say when we tell them that we didn't fulfil our mission? That we didn't manage to steal the radio from the future?'

'We explain,' said Konstantin, blinking sleepily. 'That it would have cost lives.'

'And also, because we would have been stealing the radio from Marconi,' said Aidan, stretching like a cat. 'It was his idea, his property. It wouldn't have been fair.'

Luna looked around the room again, at the butterflies, at the clock. 'What if we *didn't* steal it from him?' she said slowly. She looked back at the boys. 'Remember when we asked the professor if we could bring him back, and he said we couldn't because his younger self already exists in our time?'

'Are you suggesting we go get him from Italy in 1894?'

'No need to go even that far,' said Luna. 'He was doing early telegraphic experiments in England in 1894.' The strangest realisation dawned on her. 'According to what he told me, he's here in London. *Right now.*'

'All right,' said Aidan, getting groggily to his feet. He

had learned by now that it was useless to contradict Luna when she had her mind set on something. 'Where to? I'll set the dials.'

'Actually,' said Luna, 'I had a more old-fashioned mode of travel in mind.'

15 JANUARY 1894
9.30 a.m.

'Tell me again,' said Aidan, 'why we are in a hansom cab when we have a perfectly good Time Train?'

As a lover of engineering he was naturally thrilled to be crossing the brand-new Tower Bridge, with its twin Gothic turrets and opening mechanism to let tall ships through, but he did rather wonder why they were doing it in a horse and carriage.

'With any luck we'll catch Signor Marconi doing the public display of the first radiographic message,' Luna replied.

'Where?' asked Konstantin, who was just as thrilled to see the Tower of London, a toybox of a castle stuffed with soldiers, as Aidan was to see the bridge.

'He did the demonstration at the Post Office headquarters in Carter Lane, near St Paul's. If we hurry, we can catch him after the event.'

Soon they arrived at the tall Post Office building at the corner of Carter Lane, right in the shadow of the magnificent dome of St Paul's Cathedral. They knew they were at the right place because they could see a crowd of smart-looking ladies and gentlemen spilling out of the entrance like bees from a hive.

As they got down from the cab, Konstantin instructed the cabbie to wait. They approached the grand doors to the tall building where a poster shouted:

Be Amazed

As You Are Admitted to the Greatest Discovery of the Age

WIRELESS TELEGRAPHY

The Invisible Art of Transmitting Through Space Without Wires

WITH THE INCREDIBLE INTELLECTUAL ITALIAN

SIGNOR GUGLIELMO MARCONI

Luna thought it looked for all the world like those posters for the magicians that packed the houses at the Palladium Theatre with promises of daring escapes or bullet catches.

But this was no magic show.

This was the newest and latest fashion.

This was science.

They hurried up the stairs and emerged on to the roof of the building, into the chilly open air. The gentlemen of the press were there, holding their magnesium bulbs high to take a photogram of the young scientist. There was an excited murmur of talk, as if something amazing had happened, an everyday, penny miracle.

Luckily they were not too late. The experiment was over, but a young man was carefully packing up his apparatus. A young man with mouse-coloured hair swept back from a noble forehead, and soulful brown eyes. He couldn't have been more than twenty, but Luna put her hand to her heart.

It was *him*.

'Signor Marconi?' said Luna eagerly.

'Yes?' He looked up and smiled shyly, no recognition in the brown eyes.

She felt a little crestfallen. He didn't remember her.

How could he?

'We have an invitation for you,' blurted Konstantin, who, as the one in the uniform, had already been voted as the one who would do the talking. 'How would you like to come to the Royal Observatory at Greenwich, this very afternoon, to join a club of the most eminent scientists, explorers and cultural figures of our age?'

Signor Marconi smiled a little and shook his head. 'I have heard of such societies of course, but I fear I am too small a figure for such an honour. I am merely an amateur in the field of radio. My work is only just beginning.'

'We have it on very good authority that you are destined for great things. You might almost say,' said Konstantin with a twinkle, remembering what Professor Lorenz had told them about Marconi's future, 'that you are set to become a giant of radiographic communication.'

Marconi considered. 'I *have* always wanted to see the Royal Observatory – the home of the Meridian.'

'No time like the present,' said Aidan, and then it struck him, as the words left his mouth, that he'd probably never spoken a truer word. 'Our masters are very anxious to meet you.'

'And who, pray, are your masters?' asked Marconi, somewhat nervously.

'Didn't we say?' The three time-thieves looked at each other and started to smile. 'They are known as the Butterfly Club.'

15 JANUARY 1894
12.30 p.m.

As the time-thieves led a wondering Marconi through the grandfather clock door into the Butterfly Room, they could see that the Butterfly Club were already gathered. They emerged behind the gentlemen in their dark tailcoats and top hats, the ladies in their bright butterfly-coloured dresses and bonnets.

Someone was speaking from the other side of the room, holding everyone's attention. It was Mr Arthur Conan Doyle, the famous writer with the impressive moustache.

'The trouble is,' he was saying in his soft Scottish accent, 'such an expedition will require considerable funding.'

Then Aunt Grace spoke. 'Egypt, you say?'

'That's right,' said Conan Doyle. 'Egypt. The Valley of the Kings.'

A new voice now. 'Regretfully, I think we must say no for now.' It was the halting Prussian accent of Dr Tanius Kass, Konstantin's father. 'If our young caterpillars return victorious, and we win the thousand gold sovereigns that come with the Gabriel Medal, then we will think again.' Konstantin didn't think his father seemed particularly concerned, considering they had been gone for days. Then Dr Kass said, 'But, of course, they have only been gone for thirty minutes. We must be patient and hope for good news.'

'That's our cue,' said Aidan. 'Might as well make an entrance.'

It was a terrifying room to walk into, and as the three time travellers and their bemused guest filed along the brass meridian line to the centre of the room, every eye turned towards them.

Aunt Grace, her hair glowing like garnets, opened her arms to Luna, but then kissed the air either side of her face. 'Luna,' she said. 'I am truly glad to see you again.'

As ever, Luna found her aunt very difficult to read. There was a catch in her voice which rang true – but Luna couldn't work out if Aunt Grace was more excited by her return or by the little man they had brought with them.

Konstantin's father walked up to Konstantin, stiff as a

pair of shears, and shook him by the hand. He smiled a crooked half-smile, so like Konstantin's. '*Lieber Sohn*,' he said, clapping him about the shoulders admiringly. 'You look so different.'

'Perhaps I had a change of *heart*,' Konstantin said pointedly, pressing his fingers to the thick felt greatcoat covering the scar at his chest. He saw his father's eyes flare a little in comprehension.

The only uncomplicated reunion was that between Aidan and his father. Michael O'Connell, dressed in his navvy's clothes embellished with the cogs and chains of his trade, clasped his son to his chest and ruffled his black hair, a gesture as affectionate as any kiss. 'My boy,' he said, with a sound that was half-chuckle, half-choke. 'My boy.'

'And who is this?' asked Aunt Grace, green eyes shining greedily.

'This,' Luna said, 'is Signor Guglielmo Marconi, inventor of the wireless radio.'

Aunt Grace, for once, looked quite out of countenance. 'I… well, that is to say, we are delighted. But… how?'

'It's a *very* long story,' said Konstantin. 'The short version is that the RMS *Titanic*, the ship we found ourselves on, hit an iceberg in the North Atlantic and sank. We did not manage to save the invention, but the inventor.'

'I'm afraid I have been conveyed here under a misapprehension,' put in the little man. 'I have no radio yet. It is true I hope to develop a wireless radio one day, but my work is still in its infancy.'

Aunt Grace's smile froze ever so slightly. 'Mr Marconi, I have not the pleasure of understanding you. Are you saying you have *not* yet developed a wireless radio that can speak across continents?'

There was an awkward silence.

'Yes!' broke in Luna. 'Yes, of course he has!' She reached into the pocket of her suit and pulled out the notes she'd taken for Signor Marconi himself, eighteen years in the future. An entire afternoon of transcribing his words: every element, every specification, every wire and circuit was minutely described, in detail as fine and interconnected as clockwork.

She handed the sheaf of papers to him and he leafed through them, page by page. He looked up, dazed. 'It's here. It's all here. My design for a continuous spark circuit, complete and entire.' He gazed at Luna. 'Where did you get these?'

'It will take some explanation,' said Luna. 'But the short answer is – from the older version of you.'

Bemused, the Italian looked back at the notes in his

hand. 'This could be built in a matter of days.'

'You are in the company of the finest scientists and engineers in the world,' said Aunt Grace. 'We will build it for you.'

At that, Marconi, Aunt Grace and Dr Kass went into a sort of huddle, and Mr Conan Doyle joined them too. Waiting at the sidelines, Konstantin became aware that a little man was nudging him in the ribs.

'Hey, fellas. And lady.' He nodded politely to Luna. 'Old Conan Doyle there ain't the only writer in here. Some of us are just startin' out, ya know – tryin' to make our way.' He spoke a little like Professor Lorenz, with a southern American accent. 'Wonder if you'd like to help a fella out?'

He extended a hand to them, a little card between his first and second finger, and all three of them saw the butterfly tattoo on his wrist. The card read:

MR MORGAN ROBERTSON
WRITER OF FICTION

'Fact is, I think your adventure would make one helluva book.'

Konstantin looked, aghast, from the card to the little

man, a chill gathering at the back of his neck. 'You wrote *The Wreck of the Titan.*'

'Not yet,' he said cheerfully, 'but I sure am fixin' to. And that's a catchy title. Mind if I use it?'

'Not at all,' said Konstantin faintly.

'If you fine people wouldn't mind furnishing me with a few of the details sometime?'

'Of course, of course,' said Luna politely, 'we'd be glad to.' But she was really trying to get Mr Robertson to go away so she could hear what Mr Marconi was saying.

Signor Marconi was bowing to Aunt Grace. 'Then, Madam, I think we have a bargain. If you will admit me to your society, and allow me to retain the patents of my designs, I think I may just win you your medal.'

Aunt Grace's face was transformed by her smile. 'Then I bid you welcome, as our very latest member of the Butterfly Club.'

As the applause subsided, Aunt Grace said, 'But I am afraid, Mr Marconi, that you will only retain that title for a matter of moments. You join us just as we are about to welcome another friend – it is quite the day for new members and no mistake.'

At that instant the door with the double clock opened.

For a moment the figure blocked the light beyond. It

was already tall but was considerably heightened by a glossy top hat, and already wide but its shoulders were broadened by a black opera cloak.

'Signor Marconi, children,' said Aunt Grace with a flourish, 'meet the newest member of the Butterfly Club.'

The figure walked down the meridian line, swinging a silver-topped cane. He inclined his head and lifted his top hat. Then, as if to see them all better, the gentleman lifted the patch over his left eye.

In the socket, in place of an eyeball, was a watch.

THE BEGINNING

A LITTLE BIT ABOUT THE PEOPLE
AND THINGS IN THIS BOOK

Captain Edward James Smith died at the wheel of the *Titanic*. His last words were reported to be 'Be British'.

Mr J. Bruce Ismay took a place in a lifeboat and survived the wreck. It is reported publicly that he was condemned as a coward for the rest of his life.

Fifth Officer Harold Lowe took Lifeboat 14 back to the wreckage and saved dozens of passengers from the freezing ocean. He was, and is, considered a hero.

***Titanic*'s coal stacks** in the hold were on fire long before the ship left Southampton and were burning throughout the voyage. The last photographs taken of the ship show a black scar on the starboard side where it was scorched by the fire. Some say that the fire weakened the hull and allowed it to cave in on impact with the iceberg.

A lucky gentleman did indeed post himself off the *Titanic* at Queenstown in a mailbag. It is thought that he just wanted a passage to Ireland and no further.

Mr Morgan Robertson, an American writer, wrote a book called *The Wreck of the Titan*. In it, the *Titan* collided with an iceberg in the North Atlantic, three days out of port. In the book, the lookout shouted, 'Iceberg dead ahead!' at impact. This wouldn't be remarkable at all, were it not for the fact that the book was written in 1898, fourteen years before the *Titanic* launched.

Frederick Fleet, lookout of the Watch, survived the wreck and was asked by the *Titanic* inquiry if a pair of binoculars would have prevented the ship from crashing into the iceberg. He said, 'They would have given us time to get out of the way'.

The key to the binoculars cabinet which could have saved the *Titanic* was sold at auction in 2007... for £90,000.

Jack Phillips and Harold Bride, the two Marconi operators, bravely stayed at their posts to tap out distress calls until the water flooded the Marconi Room. It is said that Phillips, the elder of the two, felt guilty for ignoring the ice warnings of the day and was determined to make amends. Bride survived the shipwreck. Phillips did not.

Signor Guglielmo Marconi was booked on the RMS *Titanic*, but changed his mind at the last moment and sailed instead on the SS *Lusitania*, three days earlier. He was present at the *Titanic* inquiry, which ruled that his 'marvellous invention', the wireless radio, had saved hundreds of passengers. He himself lived a long and prosperous life. When he died in 1937, all radios on the BBC network and all radios aboard ship fell silent for two minutes in his honour.

Despite multiple efforts to recover the *Titanic*'s **Marconi Radio**, it still lies at the bottom of the Atlantic.

Arthur John Priest, boiler-room stoker, survived not only the shipwreck of the *Titanic*, but also the wreck of the *Olympic*, the *Alcantara*, the *Britannic* and the *Donegal*.

Whether or not he is a time traveller has yet to be confirmed.

THE BUTTERFLY CLUB
WILL RETURN...

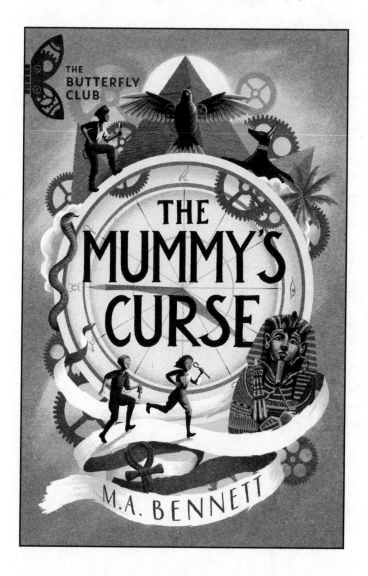

THE
BUTTERFLY
CLUB

THE
MUMMY'S
CURSE

M.A. BENNETT

TURN THE PAGE FOR A PREVIEW

25 JANUARY 1894
11.59 a.m.

Thursday found Luna Goodhart curled up in a window seat, staring out at the snowy London street.

She couldn't wait for the Hackney carriage to come to take them to the Butterfly Club, and this time she was ready well before her aunt. She'd chosen her dress carefully – it was the vivid indigo of the Purple Emperor Butterfly, a specimen of which was pinned to the hallway wall in the midst of all its brightly coloured brothers and sisters. She'd also put on a warm carriage cloak and a fur muff in readiness. It was important that she dressed in her best for that afternoon, she fervently hoped, she would be seeing her fellow time thieves again.

It was odd, after spending every waking minute with Konstantin and Aidan, to adjust to not seeing them at all.

Konstantin, so far as she knew, was living with his father in Whitehall, somewhere near Horse Guards' Parade, which seemed a fittingly military place for him to be. Aidan was living with his father in lodgings in Kilburn, nice and handy for working on the railway tracks for a brand new line at King's Cross. It had only been a week, but she missed them terribly. She missed Konstantin's broken Prussian accent, his old world courtesy and his tin soldier bravery. She missed Aidan's machine-mad passion and his crazy clothes cobbled together with cogs. She even missed his insolent grin. Being back in the tall skinny house in Kensington, with nothing but the butterflies on the wall for company, was a poor substitute for the two brothers she had found.

She had wondered too, in the past week, if she could expect the return of her father. So convinced was she that he'd been the enterprising fellow who'd managed to post himself off the Titanic in a mail bag, that she'd almost expected him to walk back into her life. At the very least she'd expected a letter, and she'd shaken out the pages of every boring book in the library, hoping to find a letter with a Rorschach blot, but there was nothing in them but long scientific words affixed firmly to the pages. Life seemed to pick up where she'd left it off, and however many times she thought she'd seen a lock of auburn hair in a crowd, peeping from a stovepipe hat or a bowler, it wasn't Papa.

The casement clock in the hall chimed noon, and Aunt Grace came to stand behind her, laying a pale hand on her purple shoulder. Aunt Grace had also dressed in her best – the acid orange of a Banded Orange Tiger Butterfly, a hue which clashed beautifully with her auburn hair. Aunt Grace had been an angel all week – much kinder than she'd ever been, so delighted was she with Luna's success aboard the Titanic. It had taken the Butterfly Club a matter of days to make Guglielmo Marconi's continuous spark wireless radio from the notes Luna had taken from the physicist's dictation, and now the secret society were on course to win the Gabriel Medal and the thousand gold sovereigns that were in the gift of Queen Victoria. So Aunt Grace had spent the week practically purring.

Taking advantage of this good mood, Luna felt she could be a little more forthright than she had been before. 'Hurry up, Aunt! The hansom cab will be here any moment.'

Aunt Grace smiled, the way she'd been smiling all week, like the cat who'd got the cream. 'Actually, my dear, you are going on a little expedition first. I will meet you at the Butterfly Club later.'

'On my own?' Luna, who had been to the future and back, still didn't relish the thought of a solo cab ride around London.

'No, no,' said her Aunt. 'You will have a very special chaperone.'

At that moment there was the clamour of horseshoes on the street. A very grand carriage, pulled by four black horses instead of the single nag which usually pulled a hansom cab, stopped in front of the house in a flurry of snow and a spark of hooves. The four were perfectly matched and stood tossing their heads, as if they knew how handsome they were. Their coats were so shiny they looked like they were made of patent leather. The black coach was just as shiny, and through the falling snow Luna could just make out the golden monogram on the carriage door. It read:

A C D

A gloved hand opened the door from the inside and a gentleman in a top hat leaned forward. Luna recognised the moustaches first. They belonged to Mr Arthur Conan Doyle.

ACKNOWLEDGEMENTS

I was always taught as a child that I must remember to say thank you, so that's what I'm doing here.

Thank you first of all to three wonderful women – Jane Harris who has championed my writing through two series now, Felicity Alexander who transformed the manuscript from a caterpillar into a butterfly, and Teresa Chris who is responsible for steering the good ship M.A. Bennett.

I'm grateful to Emma Roberts and Jane Hammett for their forensic copyediting and proofreading.

Thanks to Inclusive Minds for introducing us to their network of Inclusion Ambassadors.

A huge thank you to Charlie Castelletti for their thoughtful and thorough early read of the manuscript.

Two wonderful artists, designer Thy Bui and illustrator David Dean, really brought the book to life with their wonderful cover and part titles.

Thank you to the entire team at Welbeck Flame for helping The Butterfly Club series to fly, with such dedicated hard work and enthusiasm.

I'm grateful to historian and friend David Bownes for digging up information on Elizabeth Ann Holman, who was the inspiration for Aidan's character. Elizabeth Holman lived in Victorian times and was born a woman, but lived life as a man and worked on the railways as a 'navvy'.

I won't bore you with all the books and websites I read about the Titanic, but there are two that proved invaluable. *Titanic – A Journey Through Time* by John P. Eaton and Charles A. Haas includes wonderful photographs and reconstructions that really bring the doomed ship to life, and the *Encyclopaedia Titanica* is a wonderful website which has everything you want to know about the Titanic and its valiant crew.

I couldn't write without reading, so thank you to Evelyn Waugh for 'a long word of the heart' and to H.G. Wells for his time machine.

Thank you to Conrad and Ruby for knowing all the coolest butterfly names. My love of butterflies began in their company when they were little, in the caterpillar-shaped Butterfly House at London Zoo.

Thank you to Sacha for always remembering to wind up my clockwork heart.

And last but not least, a huge thank you to someone I won't name. A very brave someone who was the only boy at my daughter's all-girls school. He has shown more courage on his own voyage than I will ever know.